# DEMON LOST

## HIGH DEMON SERIES, BOOK ONE

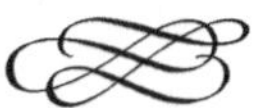

## CONNIE SUTTLE

Print Second Edition (2018)
Print ISBN: 1-63478-062-0
Print ISBN-13: 978-1-63478-062-9
eBook ISBN: 1-93975-904-8
eBook ISBN-13: 978-1-93975-904-7



Published by:
SubtleDemon Publishing, LLC
PO Box 95696
Oklahoma City, OK 73143

Cover art by Renee Barratt @ The Cover Counts

*To Walter, Joe, Larry, Lee, Dianne, Sarah and Mark.*
*Thank you.*

# ACKNOWLEDGMENTS

As always, this book is the result of collaboration. If it weren't for the support of my editor, my cover artist and my beta readers, it would be less than it is. All mistakes, as usual, are mine and no other's.

About the Author:
Connie Suttle lives in Oklahoma with her husband and a conglomerate of cats. They have finally banded together to make their demands, which has proven disconcerting to all humans involved.

You may find Connie in the following ways:
Facebook: Connie Suttle Author
Twitter: @subtledemon
Website and Blog: subtledemon.com

*Blood Destiny Series:*

Blood Wager

Blood Passage

Blood Sense

Blood Domination

Blood Royal

Blood Queen

Blood Rebellion

Blood War

Blood Redemption

Blood Reunion

Blood Destiny Series Boxed Set (Books 1-10)

Blood Recall

Blood Alliance*

*Legend of the Ir'Indicti Series:*

Bumble

Shadowed

Target

Vendetta

Destroyer

Legend of the Ir'Inditi Boxed Set

*High Demon Series:*
Demon Lost
Demon Revealed
Demon's King
Demon's Quest
Demon's Revenge
Demon's Dream

*God Wars Series:*
Blood Double
Blood Trouble
Blood Revolution
Blood Love
Blood Finale

*Saa Thalarr Series:*
Hope and Vengeance
Wyvern and Company
Observe and Protect*

*First Ordinance Series:*
Finder
Keeper
BlackWing
SpellBreaker
WhiteWing

~

*R-D Series:*

Cloud Dust

Cloud Invasion

Cloud Rebel

~

*Latter Day Demons Series:*

Hot Demon in the City

A Demon's Work is Never Done

A Demon's Due

~

*Seattle Elementals Series:*

Your Money's Worth

Worth Your While*

~

*BlackWing Pirates Series*

MindSighted

MindMage

MindRogue

MindMaster*

~

*Black Rose Sorceress Series*

The Rose Mark

Rose and Thorn

Black Rose Queen

Queen of Thorns and Roses

*Future Wars Series*

Buffer Zone

Black Zone*

*Other Titles from SubtleDemon Publishing:*

Malefactor

Transgressor

Underhanded*

by Joe Scholes

*Forthcoming

CHAPTER 1

"Jayd, we have to find Kifirin's tears."

"Glindarok, my love, what are you talking about?" Jaydevik Rath, King of the High Demons, looked up from a pile of reports sitting on his desk. Glinda stood before him, beautiful as always, the river of white-blonde hair she'd inherited from her grandmother cascading about her shoulders. Carefully, Jayd covered the top report with a hand.

"Jayd, don't bother trying to hide it," Glinda's blue eyes flashed a warning. "How many did we lose to Baetrah this time?"

"Sixty-three, most from Greth," Jayd sighed. "I should know better than to hide anything from you."

"The High Demons are dying," Glinda muttered regretfully and dropped onto a chair beside Jayd's desk. "I hoped Jhase and Jheri might conceive as soon as they were mated, but that wasn't the case. The High Demon houses are losing hope, Jaydevik. They see no new females coming to them and that spells doom for all of Kifirin. That's why we must find the jewels my father called Kifirin's tears. My father always said that Kifirin hid them in the palace somewhere, and that we'd find them when our salvation was at hand. I felt sure we'd find them after Lissa fought off the Ra'Ak, but they never turned up. What if it's just a myth, Jayd? What if there's nothing to save us, now? Le-Ath Veronis is the balance for all the worlds instead of Kifirin. What if there's nothing that can bring us back?" Glinda wiped away tears as she stared at her husband.

"Come here, my love," Jayd pulled Glinda into his lap. "Kifirin made a promise to me when the balance was moved from the High Demons to the vampires. He told me he would do whatever was necessary to keep our race alive. We have to trust him, I think."

"I hope he does something soon, then," Glinda buried her head against Jayd's shoulder. "We've lost so many already."

$\sim$

"Addah will be here tomorrow."

Those words from my brother Edan told me much. It was time for the annual conscription notices and one of us would be sent to the military. The notices were sent to the heads of households and Addah, our father, would come to tell us who would be sent. Edan was my second oldest brother and outside the age to be taken, but Wald, Ilvan and I were all eligible. I was barely eligible at nineteen turns, but still eligible, all the same.

"This is no excuse to let your minds wander," Edan snapped, bringing me back to reality and forcing me to mind my sauce. The four of us worked at our father's second restaurant in Shirves and many times we'd gotten better reviews than the first restaurant in the capital city of Targis, where my father worked as master cook.

I was third from last of my father's twenty-seven children from eight wives—and the only daughter. Addah often boasted that he knew how to breed sons. Sons were master cooks. Addah's only daughter—me—could only hope to be what I was—an assistant.

I'm sure it would mean nothing to Addah Desh that his only daughter had designed the recipes for most of the popular dishes served at number two. All the credit went to my brother Edan. I had no voice in the family since my mother had the misfortune to die in childbirth. I was her only child, farmed out for servants to raise until I reached the age of eight.

Edan's mother, Marzi, was first wife, though it irked her greatly that second wife Farla had produced the first son. First son Fes worked at Desh's number one with father and received much praise and credit. Edan was overcome with jealousy about Father's treatment of Fes until Desh's number two started getting better reviews. Now it was a contest between Edan and Fes, while the rest of us stood back and watched the rivalry. Desh's numbers three through five couldn't even compete.

"Reah, you will cook the yaris fish that father is so fond of tomorrow," Edan's mouth was next to my ear. I wasn't sure why he bothered to whisper—everybody in the kitchen knew who cooked that dish. "Do it well, or you'll be beaten," he added. Also something everybody in the kitchen knew. Edan was past thirty-eight turns and had been beating me since I'd been handed to him after my eighth birthday.

After a broken wrist and multiple cracked ribs, Edan learned to save the hard blows—those came when he felt he could get away with it and not be questioned by medical personnel at the nearby hospital. Edan always told father I was clumsy and accident-prone. I did my best to be neither. Sadly, Edan's contempt and abusive treatment left the door open for cruelties from Wald and some of the others. Some of the kitchen help taunted me at times, too, although they held back from any physical abuse. They never attempted to outguess Edan's polarities on the issue.

I added wine to the sauce while Wald mused on what he might do for the Alliance's army. "We might cook for the High General," Wald smiled over his sautéed onions. "That would certainly please father." Wald and Ilvan both lived for the day when father noticed them. Edan always received the attention. As for me—I was waiting for the day father married me off to someone. I hoped it would be someone who didn't think beating a small woman was sport—someone who lived in another city so Edan could no longer get his hands on me.

~

"Edan, the yaris fish was exceptional, as always," father beamed at Edan. Edan, Wald, Ilvan and I all stood inside the office behind the kitchen at Desh's number two. Father sat behind the desk as the ranking family member. I'm sure Edan didn't like it one bit—he'd taken money from the restaurant to decorate his office with a handmade desk, rich rugs and wall hangings. I had only vague memories of what father's office looked like in Desh's number one—I hadn't been there in eleven turns.

"Now, on to business," father was smiling and drawing a small comp-vid from his pocket. "As you know, the Alliance sends out the conscription notices every spring. This year, we have a family member selected." I looked sideways at Wald and Ilvan—both expected to be chosen. They may have wanted to get away from Edan as much as I did, although he never laid a hand on them.

I turned my eyes back to my father. I looked nothing like him. He had dark, thinning hair atop a wide face that turned pink with exertion when he worked in a hot kitchen. Father wasn't heavy and his dark-brown eyes would sometimes twinkle when he spoke with Edan or some of his regular customers. They never twinkled at me.

I'd had the temerity to be born with nearly white hair—the hair belonging to my mother. I also had her green eyes instead of father's brown. I'd never met any of my mother's family—didn't know if any still existed. When my mother died, the other wives had seen to it that every memory of her had been wiped away. Father was left with seven wives and twenty-seven children. Now, at age eighty-nine, he was in his prime since inhabitants of the Alliance world of Tulgalan lived to be nearly two hundred.

"I think you will all be pleased with the Alliance's choice, since it will not impact the family," father was still smiling and looking at my brothers. An icy finger began to crawl its way down my spine. Father turned to me. "They have chosen Reah, and they assure me that she can help in their kitchens, since she is not tall enough to carry weapons or repair machinery." A moment was all I had to stare at my father before I fell to the floor in a dead faint.

~

Whining to Edan was futility at its best, so I didn't try. He'd slapped a comp-vid down in front of me as I sat beside his desk two days later. "I don't care how many times you've written out the recipes, write them again," he demanded. "And include every bit of instruction on what to add when. Desh's two will not suffer merely because the Alliance chose to take you away for six years."

I didn't bother to look up at my second oldest brother, or sigh, even, which is what I wanted to do. The truth is I was terrified of my brother. He'd hurt me too many times. Broken too many bones, slammed me into too many walls. He looked like father, too, and that was a tremendous help as far as father was concerned. It helped not at all with the women he saw occasionally. The moment they found out what he was truly like, they deserted him as quickly as they could. I couldn't blame them—if Edan hadn't threatened to kill me several times, I would have run away long ago. Capturing my lower lip in my teeth to keep it from trembling, I began to tap recipes into Edan's comp-vid.

# CHAPTER 2

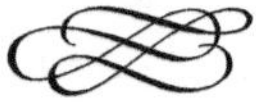

"Recruit Desh, your performance during preliminary training is exemplary, but you understand that your height and weight are against you." I stood before the post commander as he read my report on the handheld lying on his desk. My height and weight were indeed against me. I didn't come to the commander's shoulder and struggled to carry the heavy gear we bore on training exercises. "In most cases, we might have sent you home if you hadn't shown such determination," the commander went on.

He had silver in his red hair and someday it would all be a silvery white. I'd watched people during my short life—all kinds wandered into Desh's. The ones I watched the closest were the ones I envied the most—fathers and mothers with children who were loved. Not the ones who were coddled and spoiled, but the ones who received a smile and praise when it was deserved. The ones who received careful guidance otherwise. I'd never had that and often dreamed about it.

"I am proud to serve the Alliance," I lied to the commander, my head down. That was how I knew to talk to males. Edan had seen to that. Truthfully, I had no desire to go back to Edan and his mistreatment. The shouting and verbal abuse from my Alliance instructors was nothing compared to what Edan could dish out.

"I am aware of you background," the commander added. Of course he was. There probably wasn't a soul alive on Tulgalan who wasn't. Desh's was the place to take your wives or your promised. The upper middle class frequented Desh's for special occasions; the wealthy came to Desh's more often than that. End-days were always crowded, with tables covered in linen, snowy napkins and silver polished to its brightest shine.

"Therefore," and I heard the expected words from my commander as if I were listening through cotton wool, "we will be sending you to work in the kitchen that serves the Governor of the Realm." His last four words made my head jerk upward. A commander or lesser general I might have expected. Not the Governor of the Realm. What did they expect from me? Even father had pulled me into Edan's office before he left, warning me not to give away family recipes. He didn't think I knew any, but he wanted to be sure. His threats were nothing compared to those Edan handed out. Edan's promise to end my life if anything got out—including his abuse—was heartfelt and heeded.

"I thank you for the position," I stammered. Saluting the commander after he dismissed me, I walked out of his office and down the hall, feeling numb.

Two days later, my duffle of meager belongings slung over a shoulder, I shuffled aboard a transport bound for the capital city. Desh's number one was there and Targis teemed with people. More than ten millions in the city and surrounding areas. Only dim memories of the city itself remained with me, however. I hadn't seen it in person since I was eight and shoved onto ground transportation, traveling to the nearby city of Shirves and my brother Edan. The trip from the training base to the capital city wasn't very long; even so, I was tired when I arrived and found the hoverbus scheduled to deliver me to the Governor's complex. Ushered into the Governor's kitchen by an Alliance officer who'd met me at the gate, I was introduced to the master cook and his two assistants.

"Master cook Vyn, this is Reah Desh," the officer gave my full name, causing me to blush to the roots of my hair. Any hope of remaining anonymous was lost with that introduction. The two assistants, Leetha and Morane, saved their glares until the officer left us. Of course, master cook Vyn didn't hold back, either.

"If you expect to come here and flaunt your name in front of us, then you are sadly mistaken," Vyn snapped immediately. "You will do as I tell you and nothing more. Is that clear?"

"Yes, Master Vyn." My head was down, just as it had been for Edan all those years. Any aspirations I might have held regarding experimentation and designing new recipes flew away. I was foolish to hope. It had never brought me anything but pain. I would likely be set to peeling root vegetables or cleaning the kitchen. My hands were clasped tightly together to stop their trembling. I hoped that Master Vyn didn't hand out slaps or blows with his instructions.

Peeling and slicing vegetables was exactly what I did for Master Vyn. Leetha and Morane provided nasty little digs the entire time while they sat at a small table against a wall and drank tea while watching me work. I was exhausted by the time I finished cleaning the kitchen late that first evening.

If verbal barbs had been all that Leetha and Morane were capable of handing out, then my life might have been manageable. The fifth day I worked in the Governor's kitchen, I cleaned it after all the dishes and cooking utensils had been washed and put away. Master cook Vyn was waiting for me and shouting the moment I walked into the kitchen the following morning.

Flour, sugar and salt had been scattered over every surface of the kitchen. I stood in the doorway, my shock and dismay evident as I surveyed the sabotage. There was no doubt in my mind as to who'd actually done this. I was going to take the blame, however, if Master Vyn had anything to say about it. Truly, I wanted to ask him to send me elsewhere. Almost anywhere would do. He and his two assistants were almost as unbearable as Edan.

Wordlessly I went to the pantry to find the mopvac. Why would he think that I would do this, when it only made more work for me? Perhaps he was a part of it—how was I to know? I cleaned while Master Vyn shouted. Breakfast for the Governor would be late if Master Vyn didn't stop soon. When he didn't, I went to get the eggs out of the keeper myself and set about putting something together for the Governor and his family.

Master Vyn continued to shout the entire time I shaved ham and carefully laid it over the roundbread I'd made. Gently cooked eggs and my own sauce recipe followed, with sides of sliced, fresh fruit. By that time, the servant had come for the tray, which I gladly handed to him. He wanted to get out of hearing distance just as much as I did. Then I set about cleaning up what I'd used to prepare breakfast, hoping that Master Vyn would run down soon. Eventually, he did.

Leetha and Morane had come in by that time—Vyn never said anything to them when they showed up late. Vyn also didn't suspect that I knew they were all sleeping together. I would have treated it as no concern of mine if it hadn't meant worse treatment for me. I supposed that after their late night of destroying my clean kitchen, they needed the extra rest.

Vyn stood with his arms folded, glaring at me while I prepared the midday meal and then fish for dinner. The streamfish was crusted with herbs and spices then delicately fried before the drizzle of browned butter sauce was applied. Sautéed snap beans and other vegetables, accompanied by fresh, crusty butter rolls were sent to the Governor's table. I cleaned up the kitchen afterward while Leetha and Morane sat at their usual table drinking tea and gossiping. Vyn had left the kitchen the moment the trays were sent out.

"I hope you don't have to clean up another mess tomorrow," Leetha's voice was as falsely sweet as artificial sugar as she and Morane walked out of the kitchen while I mopped the floor.

"I won't, tomorrow is my off-day," I retorted before thinking. I recognized the look she gave me before she disappeared through the door. It held the promise of revenge for imaginary slights.

I didn't go inside Desh's number one as I walked the streets of Targis on off-day. Instead, I walked past the restaurant—twice. I held no expectations of a father happy to see his only daughter, or of an offered meal to a member of the family. It was an end-day and reservations would be required. I wouldn't even get a corner of the kitchen and a meal.

Sad, I know, that I had a family such as this. A bookstore lay across the street, with flashing images of the latest in both fiction and nonfiction. Sitting down at one of the free news kiosks inside the store, I did a search on all the news-vids concerning the family restaurants since I'd left for the military three months before. Since then the annual reviews had come out, so I settled in to read them.

"Surprisingly, Desh's restaurant in Shirves did not achieve its usual excellent rating," the food critic wrote. "Desh's Capital City restaurant has regained the crown for the finest eatery on Tulgalan. Edan Desh was not available for comment but Addah Desh was quite happy with the results. *My second son has had the honors for the past three years; it is time that he gave his father a break, yes?* Addah told me." I ended the reading with a sigh, wondering if Edan missed his whipping girl as much as he missed my cooking.

The streets of Targis had changed so much in eleven years. Of course, things would appear different to an eight-year-old child. I wandered through parts of it that seemed familiar to me before catching the pub-trans back to the Governor's complex. As expected, I entered through the rear entrance so as not to disturb or embarrass the Governor or his family. Master Vyn waited impatiently outside the door of my tiny room as I made my way down the narrow, dimly lit hallway to my quarters.

"I expect you to prepare meals and I expect you to hand the credit to me, Leetha and Morane or I will make your life unlivable," he began. Setting my single purchase of a book on comp-vid down carefully on my bed I turned to face Vyn.

"Whatever you say, Master Vyn," I said tiredly. Briefly, I entertained thoughts of Master Vyn being beaten by Edan, but quickly squashed that idea. No sense or satisfaction might come from seeking revenge—even the imaginary kind.

At first Vyn expected me to clean up after I'd cooked all day but soon realized that it was exhausting me. Of course, it took the second time of my fainting after extremely long days to convince him. Leetha and Morane didn't take kindly to having to clean after that and they complained and moaned the entire time. I still chopped and prepared all the vegetables when they should have had to pitch in. Vyn didn't push it with either—he was afraid that sex would be withheld.

I was almost enjoying myself—even with the long hours and exhausting work. New recipes came of my efforts and the Governor's favorite was an ox-roast carefully folded around a paste of mushrooms and herbs, with more of the paste laid across a pastry that wrapped the folded roast. The pastry would bake to a flaky crispness with the mushroom concoction inside, which blended perfectly with the meat juices, creating a wonderful meal when served with fresh greens sprinkled with a light dressing. Even Vyn would hope that some of the ox-roast would come back from the Governor's table—he enjoyed it, too. He never said that he liked it or offered any compliments; he merely ate as much as he could with a glass of good, red wine.

~

"There is an escape pod drill tomorrow afternoon," Vyn informed me haughtily before leaving the kitchen after the trays went out one evening. "Be sure you know which pod is designated for you and go directly there. The exercise will be timed and the Governor will not be pleased if we do not all perform to expectations." I stared up at Vyn —he wasn't particularly tall but still he was taller than I.

"Yes, Master Vyn," I lowered my head. He'd been basking in the Governor's praise over the meals that were produced in his kitchen. I didn't point out the obvious to Vyn—that many of these dishes hadn't come from his kitchen before I'd joined the staff. Surely, the Governor of the Realm hadn't obtained his position by being so stupid.

Before going to bed that evening, I made my way down the long hall to the chamber where the escape pods were stored. Each pod had a separate navigation system, preprogrammed to deliver anyone inside to a safe place on a nearby moon. Enough oxygen was stored inside to keep an occupant alive for days if necessary. I found the pod assigned to me—it bore my name on the outside tag. All seemed in order, so I turned away. My bed was calling and I yawned as I made my way toward it.

~

Purposely not preparing anything important that I might be pulled away from the following day, I was putting a vegetable dish together for the evening meal when the warning bells went off. Leetha and Morane, both giggling merrily, ran out the door ahead of me. I trotted more sedately behind them.

Vyn hadn't bothered to show up all day, making me wonder what was going on. Perhaps Leetha and Morane had given him all he could take in bed the night before and he was resting afterward. Doors were already being slammed on pods when I entered the hall so I made my way to the designated pod, closed the door, strapped myself in as was required, waited for the exercise to end and the all clear to sound.

As I waited, my pod began to shake. I heard the couplings holding it in place snap away outside. Perhaps I screamed, I don't remember, when my pod detached completely and shot through the opening slot in the roof as if fired from a blast cannon.

Ripping the communication device off the pod wall while I still had gravity, I pushed the button to call technicians on the other end. The device was completely dead—someone had disabled it. As practical jokes went, this one was perhaps the worst I'd ever experienced. Still, I expected the pod to be recalled—all of them were programmed for that in case of a misfire. Nothing happened—no recall came, the pod picked up speed and I knew the moment I traveled past the atmosphere of Tulgalan; the communicator floated out of my hand and bounced into one of the rounded walls. I know I screamed then—even I knew the moon was on the other side of Tulgalan and I was headed toward the emptiness of space with nothing left to stop me.

# CHAPTER 3

Hardel Zim, Governor of the Realm of Tulgalan stared across his desk at his kitchen staff. What remained of his kitchen staff, anyway. One of his employees was floating aimlessly in space at the moment. A ship had been dispatched to pick up the wandering orb, but the three in front of him were guilty of conspiracy.

"I have the vids—did you think we wouldn't bother to check them?" The Governor slapped the comp-vid on his desk, making Vyn and his two assistants jump. "The images are there, Master Vyn. Now, I'm sure you think you knew what you were doing, reprogramming the pod, but if any harm comes to that girl, you will be charged with murder. And what was this over, I ask you? Jealousy? Is that it? Knowledge that she was better than you? She could have come to me at any time and let me know what was happening, yet she did not. Can you explain that to me?"

"I have no excuse, sir." It was Vyn's turn to hang his head. Leetha and Morane had been afraid to look at the Governor from the beginning.

"Do you want to be the one to explain to Addah Desh that his daughter is floating in space because you sabotaged her escape pod?

Do you?" The Governor flung out a hand in a helpless gesture. "Because I can assure you that I don't want to be the one to tell him."

"We never knew he had a daughter," Vyn muttered. "I thought she was a niece or cousin."

"That is clearly not the case," the Governor said in disbelief. "Do you have anything to say for yourselves before I send you to the holding cells?"

"We made a mistake, sir." Vyn still wasn't looking at the Governor.

"Well, Ilvan, what have you to say?" Addah Desh watched Ilvan carefully. Three days had passed since word had come from the Governor, reporting that Reah's escape pod had been tampered with, sending her flying away from Tulgalan at light speed or better toward some unknown destination. The one who'd reprogrammed the pod hadn't known much about the workings of the newer pods and had badly miscalculated the programming. The ship sent to find Reah had yet to catch up to her.

"I always thought Edan would kill her," Ilvan admitted with a sigh. He stared at his tailored trousers and toyed with the edge of the matching tunic. The sons had all gotten the finest when it came to clothing. Reah had used what little Edan gave her to buy at used clothing stores.

"Edan?" Addah crossed his arms over his chest.

"Father, Edan beat her. All those broken bones and bruises over the years? She wasn't clumsy. Edan did that to her. The only reason we didn't take the prize this year is because Reah wasn't there to cook. Those recipes were hers and not Edan's. He threatened her. We all knew it. We knew, too, that Edan would threaten us if we didn't ignore it. She's likely dead, now. I know you don't care and Edan cares less. I'm done, father. I have a little money. I'm moving away from the family. Perhaps I'll start a business of my own, doing something that has nothing to do with cooking. Good-bye, father." Ilvan rose and walked out of Addah's office.

Addah waited until he was sure that Ilvan was away from the building before screaming for his assistant.

"Master Desh?" Barun appeared in Addah's doorway so swiftly, it was as if he'd been summoned by magic.

"Barun, get Edan on the vidcom," Addah demanded.

"Right away, Master Desh."

The newer pods were equipped with foodpaks and a waste receptacle. Without either of those, I would have panicked more than I did. I was hysterical most of the time. I wept. I vomited and wept more until I was completely numb. I lost track of time—the date/time lights had been deactivated, as was the tracking signal.

Sure that someone had meant to do this to me, I resigned myself to a slow and agonizing death. I'd be floating aimlessly through the universe until the energy ran out, leaving me in a frigid cold from which I wouldn't wake. There were no windows on the pod and the vidscreen failed to activate. I couldn't even see the stars I traveled through on my way to oblivion.

What did work was the gauge for the oxygen levels. It reached a quarter and then an eighth. My time was coming to a close and I knew it. Nobody was left behind to say farewell to—no family to think fondly of. Many times over the years, I figured that Marzi, Edan's mother, had encouraged Edan to do what he did to me. I'm sure she didn't have to do much in that respect—he took pleasure in causing my pain. He and some of the others would often muffle laughter, watching me move stiffly about the day after a beating. Perhaps I should have attempted to think happier thoughts, there in my last bit of time. I didn't.

"Edan, do you know why I asked you here?" Addah now looked over his desk at his second-born.

"I assume it is to tell me which of the family you are sending to replace Ilvan and Reah."

"I will be sending replacements, but that is not why I asked you to come."

Edan watched his father. A request from Addah Desh was a demand from anyone else. Addah presented a much better demeanor to the public than he ever did in private. "You are disappointed, then, that we did not perform to expectations during the last review," Edan offered. "Ilvan was partly to blame."

"Ilvan had nothing to do with it," Addah turned his head and stared out the large window inside his office. He'd had a garden planted outside long ago, hiring a Refizani gardener to tend it for him. The Refizani knew medicine and they knew gardening. "I called you here to tell you why I sent Reah to you at such a young age," Addah said, turning back to his son.

"I often wondered why you did that," Edan muttered.

"You remember her mother, don't you, Edan? Little Raedah? She was beautiful, wasn't she? That river of white-blonde hair, and the green eyes that flashed when she was excited or amused. Not very strong emotionally, though. Reah is much like her, don't you think?"

"Father, you know that was long ago. Nearly twenty turns."

"Yes. She was barely twenty-two when Reah was born. You were eighteen, as I recall." Addah watched his son closely.

"Yes, you sent me to Shirves and brought Fes back to Capital City shortly after the birth of Reah."

"Yes. And after Raedah's death as well. You recall that, don't you?"

"Of course, father."

"Do you still have no idea why I sent Reah to you?" Addah frowned at Edan.

"None, father. Please tell me, as she is most likely dead, just as her mother is."

"Reah was not my child. I had the DNA tests run, Edan. Reah is yours. Whether by rape or by consent I do not know, but that child was yours. I was hoping you would take responsibility for her, yet you did not. And only recently have I discovered that you abused her while she was in your care. Most likely with Marzi's blessings, she has always been heavy-handed any child except her own. I have learned, too, that all the recipes getting the top awards were Reah's. You hid her from me. I could have had her here and both restaurants would have benefitted." Edan knew his father was furious. He forced himself not to squirm in his chair.

"You have damaged our business, Edan," Addah continued. "I find that intolerable. If you'd let me know, I wouldn't have used my influence to have Reah conscripted instead of Wald. His name was chosen, not Reah's. You're harming my reputation, now, and for what, I ask? I am ashamed to call you my son. Does your mother know she was condoning the abuse of her granddaughter? Did you ever tell her that you and Raedah were together? Did you?" Addah's face turned pink as if from exertion.

"Father, that must be a lie. Resubmit the tests—that cannot be true. I have fathered no children," Edan insisted, standing up stiffly, as if the action would drive home his point.

"Do you think I did not have them run repeatedly? The results were the same every time. Reah is your daughter. Perhaps was your daughter, as things stand. I had an exceptional master cook within the family and I missed it. The Governor of the Realm, thinking to pay me compliments, raved over the food he was getting from his kitchen while she was there. None of it any of the recipes we use. She did not betray us in that way, developing new things that we can never lay claim to, now that she is lost. You have attempted to recreate what she developed in Shirves and have failed. Would you have continued to lie to me, Edan? What do you think I should do with you?"

"It is no use, mother—he has had the legal papers changed. Nothing comes to me if he dies. I can only enjoy what I have while he lives. After that, everything goes to Fes and the others. He claims that Reah was my child. Mine. You told me to go to Raedah, mother. You wanted to discredit her—get her out of the family. You said she didn't belong. Yes, I followed your instructions. She wasn't willing, so I took Raedah by force. Reah was born as a result. Father showed me the papers, mother. The tests were run eight times with the same results." Edan paced in front of his mother.

"But what will he do if Reah is recovered? Will he bring her back—install her as a master cook when her Alliance service is over?"

"He almost said as much," Edan muttered.

"Then it is your duty to see that she is brought back as the daughter that she is. This is your way to get your part when the time comes—through your daughter. She is enough under your thumb, I think, that she cannot say no to you." Edan glanced up at his mother. Marzi was still beautiful, with dark hair carefully styled and clear, gray eyes that tempted many. She'd turned Addah's head from the moment she'd walked into his restaurant all those years ago, intent on wiggling her way into the life and fortunes of the man who'd managed to entice an entire city with his cooking.

"But what if she won't have anything to do with us? The military changes people, mother. She may refuse us."

"Then court her. Tell her you didn't know she was yours. That you were in love with her mother and resented her because you weren't her father. Now, you have evidence to the contrary. She will have the father she never had before, Edan. As my son, surely you know how to lie convincingly."

"Mother, everything I know I learned from you."

"Yes, my son. You certainly have."

The temperature regulator was failing and the air becoming stale. The dead communicator still floated around me as I prepared myself for what was to come. Should I close my eyes? Attempt to sleep so I wouldn't know—gasping for my few final breaths in terror and pain? What should one contemplate, during one's final moments?

Tulgalan no longer put criminals to death, as much as I might like to see the one who'd done this to me suffer. Tulgalan's worst were now shipped to a planet filled with criminals—Evensun it was called. I hoped it waited for the one who'd implemented my death. Evensun was watched closely by the ASD—Alliance Security Detail. No technology or space travel was available to those sent there, and it was survival of the largest and strongest. A sentence to Evensun may as well be a death sentence. Rumor had it that anyone sent there died quickly. I comforted myself as much as I could with those morbid thoughts.

That was the sort of thing running through my mind when the small communicator suddenly dropped, hitting me in the temple before bouncing away and clattering against the side of the pod. Jerking in my seat, I stared stupidly at the communicator. Its fall was impossible—it should still be floating while we sailed along through space. At least that's what my addled brain told me. I admit, my mind wasn't very clear at the moment and when the pod began to bounce along as if it were hitting bumps in a road, I was at a loss to explain it. Later I reasoned it out—we—the pod and I, were skipping on the atmosphere of a planet.

Without a vidscreen or anything else to tell me where I was, I couldn't figure it out at the time. The bouncing became more violent and if I hadn't been strapped in, I might have died of the blows taken from slamming into the sides of the pod. The seat and the restraining straps did their job, though, and when the bouncing stopped, something snapped loose on the outside of the pod and we were jerked upward.

It was the canopy deployment, but I was dazed enough as it was and could only wait for what happened next. Even with the canopy lowering us gently to whatever world we were about to land upon, the pod still experienced a jarring jolt upon landing, bouncing a time or two before coming to a stop. That's when the pod burst open, just as it was supposed to, and I saw daylight for the first time in days. I don't remember anything past that for a while.

"We can't retrieve her."

Addah Desh stared at the ASD operative. He'd identified himself as Lendill Schaff. Addah was bewildered—when had the ASD gotten involved? He thought the military had been sent after her. It was their mistake, after all. "What do you mean?" Addah blustered.

"It means," Lendill sighed patiently, "that the pod found its way to a non-Alliance world. We have a treaty with that world at the moment. We can't invade their space, they can't invade ours. I'm afraid your daughter is lost."

"Do they even know to look for her?"

"We sent the communication. They know a pod misfired. That's what they think, anyway. They also know they can do whatever they please with her when they find her. If she's still alive; the pod was on the last of its life support—if it had any left that is—when it entered Mandil's airspace."

"So we may never know if Reah lives or dies." Addah grumbled, his eyes darting over Lendill's face.

"True. My condolences to you and your family, Master Desh. I'm sure the Governor will send his apologies and condolences soon. You are also welcome to come to the trials of the three who betrayed her."

"Why did they do that to her?" Addah asked.

"Rumor is the master cook was jealous."

"Then I expect to be compensated for my daughter's death. That was a master cook in the making," Addah stood, his voice a near-shout. "Do you know how much she would have brought to my business? Do you? Tell the Governor I will entertain an offer."

"Master Desh," Lendill gripped Addah's collar and drew him forward, his nose almost meeting the cook's, "When a conscript signs with the Regular Alliance Army, they sign all their rights to the Alliance. If a conscript dies, you get condolences and funeral expenses. That's it. Your daughter's body won't be returned to us, so you won't qualify for funeral expenses, either. I know you placed a bribe with an official to have her taken instead of one of your sons. Now, shall I bring charges against you for that, or shall we call it even?"

~

"They won't know if we bury the evidence."

Chlind stared at Seval for a moment or two. "You mean bury the pod?"

"Yes. We need another girl to make up for Dela running back to her mother. This one will know to keep quiet. She'll stay alive that way." Seval grinned.

"She really isn't tall enough," Chlind stroked his short beard in contemplation.

"Who cares? She'll be put to cleaning or washing dishes." Both men stared at the unconscious girl still strapped inside the escape pod. They'd gotten word, just as the other travelers did, of the pod that had misfired on Tulgalan. Mandil's Royal Family would most likely put her to death anyway if they found her.

"Get the shovels," Chlind muttered. Seval ran back to the transport to retrieve the required tools.

~

Dizziness swept over me the moment I woke and I felt ill.

"Get to the hole if you're going to be sick," were the words that greeted me. A face blurred over mine and didn't come into focus for a while.

"Who are you?" I mumbled, trying to keep my stomach from heaving. I couldn't remember if there was anything in it to heave up.

"Chlind. On our way to the main desert outpost to deliver girls," Chlind grinned. I should have asked where I was. Perhaps that question would have made more sense.

"You're on Mandil," Chlind kept smiling. The moan that came from me didn't sound familiar. Mandil. A non-Alliance world. Word had it that they sold women as slaves. Was that what I was?

"We know what you are," Chlind went on. "So it's in your best interest to be silent. The Royal Family will likely want you dead if they find you. Public executions are still done here, you know."

I stared in horror at Chlind. He was gleefully informing me of my fate, should I be discovered. When I failed to respond, he continued. "We needed another girl to fill our contract for the outpost. You're that girl. Do as you're told and you'll keep your life. The hole is over there." Chlind pointed to his right. Heaving my body off the hard seat I'd been dumped on, I stared out the window. All I could see was clicks and clicks of windswept sand.

"It'll turn greener in a few clicks," Chlind was reading my mind. "Bear in mind that escape is out of the question unless you do want to die. They'll leave your bones in the desert for the scavengers if you do that."

Staggering into the aisle, I refused to look at Chlind as I made my way to the hole. I heaved up almost nothing before I stopped, and then relieved myself as best I could. The amount of water the sink might dispense at one time was limited, so I washed as much as I could before returning to my seat. I had no clothing, no money, no bearings and nowhere to go except where Chlind was sending me. Yes, I often thought about asking him to leave me in the desert to die, but I didn't. Who knows whether that was a good or bad thing?

The papers handed to the ranking officer were forged—in my case anyway. He looked me over carefully, evaluating what Chlind had brought him with a critical eye. "What's this one good for?" The officer handed Chlind a skeptical frown.

"Cleaning or kitchen work, your choice," Seval, Chlind's partner offered the soldier a grin. "It says in the contract that two out of the twenty can be designated drudges."

"It doesn't say that they can be minuscule," the soldier laughed.

"But she's not difficult to look at," Chlind chimed in.

"No, but she's delicate business. This is the high desert. Don't you have any sense at all?"

"Must have left it in my other clothes," Seval agreed amiably.

I wanted to tell them I was right there, but then I was a slave.

Granted none of the other girls on the transport were chained or restrained in any way, but they'd probably gotten the desert speech, just as I did.

"Know your way around a kitchen?" The soldier turned to me then.

"Yes," I nodded. I could find my way around most any kitchen. I found myself more than grateful that everyone spoke Alliance common, even if it was accented and Mandil wasn't an Alliance world.

"Then we'll put you in the kitchen unless somebody gets interested. Doesn't matter how pretty you are, they'll want their women a little tougher and with more meat on their bones."

That sounded fine with me. I wondered what kind of men these were. The soldier was wide across the shoulders with a tanned, weathered face and hair that might have been a light brown, once. The intense light and heat of the desert had bleached it like muslin until it was nearly the same color as mine.

He and the other soldiers I saw moving about were all dressed in sand-colored uniforms. They matched the desert they stood upon and all had close-cropped hair. Seval had given me a leather string so I could braid my long hair and tie it to keep it off my neck. "The desert is hot and unforgiving," he'd told me while I tied the end of my braid.

"Clothing may be a problem, too," the soldier mused as I stood before him. "Never mind, we'll find something and somebody who can take it up. Next." I was led to the side with the other girls who'd been checked in, while the one behind me took my place.

"This is the kitchen," I was led inside an expansive space later by one of the oldest soldiers I'd seen at the post. The kitchen was equipped with a huge, solar-powered stove, a bank of cold-keepers, a pantry that could provide housing for a rather large family and three soldiers, all of whom were peeling root vegetables.

"How many here at the post?" I asked.

"Around three hundred, including the twenty of you that just arrived. But you won't cook for everybody—just the girls who came in with you," the old soldier replied. "Troops have their own cooks and kitchens, on the other side of the post. They have the big job. Now these here," he nodded toward the three men, "they're doing punishment time. So if you want anything edible, you'd best cook it yourself." The old soldier left me there, laughing as he walked away from me.

"When are the mealtimes?" I asked the youngest of the three. Yes, I was intimidated, but I wanted the girls at the post to have the best meals I could make for them since they'd been sold just as I had.

"Late meal is served in two clicks," the youngest one replied. "We were told to peel roots so we're peeling roots."

"Then you may have done your job well enough already," I muttered. A mound of peeled, unwashed roots were piled on the steel table before them.

"Good. We'll take a break," the oldest one said. He and the other two walked out of the kitchen, leaving me alone. I don't know why I expected them to come back; they never did. I prepared the meal myself. Some sort of fowl was in the keeper, with other types of frozen meats in the freezers. I made meat pies quickly, giving myself plenty of time for them to bake. Frozen vegetables were mixed and cooked in water and broth with butter and sauce—at least the supplies seemed sufficient if plain. I didn't have time to do a dessert—perhaps that could come one or two days per eight-day—maybe on off-days. If Mandil had off-days. I was too afraid to ask.

"Commander, more have been sighted." Aris' Rangers had returned from scouting the desert west of the outpost.

"You didn't approach any of them, did you?" Aris looked up from his paperwork—Ranger Bel had caught him at his desk.

"No, Commander. We found one deserted village—about forty lived there if our estimates are correct. All missing, now."

"How many were children, do you think?" Aris knew the children wouldn't be a threat—the demons didn't turn children. They were eaten for sustenance. Only the adults would be turned, unless there weren't enough younglings to satisfy the demons. Then the smaller adults, preferably the females, would also serve as a food source.

"Perhaps ten or so—we didn't find evidence of more than that."

"Then thirty more, maybe, out there to do damage." Aris sighed.

"Any word from the palace?" Bel wanted to sigh as well.

"They'll send more before the next moon-turn, but we only have so many Rangers and Ranos rifles. Those are the only weapons effective against these things."

"I know. Perhaps if we negotiate with the Alliance—tell them what we're dealing with?" Bel suggested quietly.

"Bel, you and I know that the Prince Royal will not even consider it. I'm not sure he fully understands the gravity of the situation."

"Yet he sees fit to send twenty women, worrying about our other needs."

"Yes. And those women will be the first targets if the demons come this way. Are any vehicles in need of repairs? We need everything we have in good repair in case a quick move is necessary."

"They're working on them now, Commander Aris."

"Why don't you and the others join me for dinner later? We'll discuss what we know. How did the villagers take the evacuation orders?"

"Like we thought they might—they aren't considering the threat—they think they are not in danger."

"Fools," Aris grumbled. "If those creatures get hungry, the village will fall, just as the others did."

My three helpers never came back, which meant I cleaned everything by myself before going to find a bath and bed. At least there was warm water—when night fell, it got much colder than I thought it might. I also had a small room with a tiny bed right off the kitchen that I didn't have to share.

I woke to the sound of someone blowing a raucous tune on a bugle. On Tulgalan, there were three loud tones to wake the troops. Thinking about tossing rocks at the bugler from behind walls or bushes, I climbed awkwardly out of bed. Since I wasn't fully recovered from my ordeal inside the pod, I hauled myself (with a bit of difficulty) toward the kitchen to prepare breakfast. My three helpers were still missing. I wondered if it were my duty to report them to anyone.

Several women from the day before came to haul the wheeled cart with the trays away. Their quarters were down a long, narrow hallway, in a wing separated from the kitchen. I was grateful for that separation. It kept me from dwelling on what was happening, there. Two of the five who came to pick up the food were already talking about this soldier or that. I wasn't sure I wanted to hear any of it, no matter how much they liked the men. One of the women winked at me before she left. Unsure what to do about that either, I set about putting yeast bread together for the evening meal.

"Did you miss us?" The three missing men arrived in time for their midday meal, looking as if they'd awakened minutes earlier. They smelled of beer and sweat. I didn't ask them where they'd been. Sitting down at one of the tables in the kitchen, they arrogantly waited for their meal to be placed in front of them. They ate while I put the other plates together and handed those meals to a different set of five women.

"We just wanted to tell you that dinner last night was excellent," one of the women told me. "I don't think I've ever eaten this well, before."

"It was the best I could do with the supplies I had," I replied. "We'll have shaved ox-roast for dinner tonight. I hope you like it."

"Shaved ox-roast? That sounds naughty," one of my three helpers snickered.

"It could be, if you're speaking in the traditional sense," I muttered, kneading dough. The three men stuffed their faces without another word, left their plates sitting on the counter and took off again.

~

"Do you have enough for six extra plates? We're entertaining," the third set of five women showed up to get the dinner trays.

"Yes," I nodded. I had enough for eight additional plates but no more than that. Hastily I prepared an extra six meals and my visitors went away with plates of shaved ox-roast in brown sauce with tiny vegetables, fruit and fresh rolls. There was wine in the pantry and I sent something that would go well with the meat dish. That was the night I met two of the Rangers who worked at the outpost. They came with the five women to return the trays.

"May I ask your name?" The first Ranger stood across the counter from me as I wiped down surfaces. He stood at six blocks tall with short, dark hair and a neatly trimmed beard.

"I am Reah," I said, not meeting his eyes. I felt safer that way.

"Reah, that was the best meal I've gotten at this gods-forsaken hole," he said. "I am Bel, and this is my fellow Ranger, Delvin." The other Ranger was grinning as I looked up at him briefly. He also had dark hair but his eyes were brown, whereas Bel's were a green-gold. Delvin was slightly shorter than Bel, too.

"Most pleased to meet you," I nodded in a noncommittal fashion. I had no desire for them to find that I wasn't on Mandil legally, or to be hauled off to the Prince Royal for sentencing as a result.

"You can come and have dinner with us again," one of the women traced a finger down Delvin's cheek in a suggestive manner. I turned away so I wouldn't have to watch.

Yes, I knew about sex—my dayschool classes had included instruction on reproduction while I was learning. I'd also seen men bring their wives, lovers and companions—male and female—the whole time I'd worked in the kitchens at Desh's. Edan had made me afraid of almost every male. Anyone who'd attempted to approach me saw me shying away from them. Even a few recruits during my basic military training had approached. I had backed away quickly, too frightened to allow them a chance. Perhaps love and sex were meant for others. I truly had no desire to be treated as Edan had treated his female companions.

Busying myself with putting away pots and pans, my visitors were gone when next I looked up. Breathing a relieved sigh, I made my way to the small bathing room just outside my bedroom, cleaned up and fell into bed, exhausted.

That became my life for the next two eight-days. Rising early to prepare meals—not finishing until late at night. Guards patrolled the entire post while I slept; I knew that. I couldn't say whether it made me feel safer or not, I just knew that it was. The women had started asking regularly for extra plates of food for the evening meals until it reached twelve in number. I automatically prepared an extra twelve meals, now. My three helpers only showed up for meals, disappearing immediately after and never bothering to take their plates and glasses to the sink for washing. I came to think of them as pigs and figured I knew why they were being punished.

My third eight-day began and I had yet to receive time off. It made me wonder if slaves weren't entitled. Breakfast was over for the morning and I was starting on the midday meal when the back door into the kitchen opened with a thump and Bel walked in, followed by three others. Not my three—I saw that right away. What excited me was what they carried—wooden boxes loaded with redfruits and other vegetables.

"Think you can do something with this?" Bel was grinning as I stared at the fresh bounty with astonishment.

"Yes—yes, of course," I did my best to keep the bubbling excitement from my voice as I wiped my hands on a towel. "I can certainly do something with this." The boxes were set on the stone tile floors of my kitchen. The three who had hauled in the fresh produce were all dressed similarly in white tunics and trousers. They also wore close-fitting white caps on their heads. I'd never seen such dress before, but it made sense for the desert, I think.

"Are there enough redfruits to make something for the entire outpost?" Bel looked hopeful as the three men hauled in another load. Nearly three hundred troops manned the outpost. I eyed the fruit with a critical eye.

"Perhaps," I said. "If I stretch it as much as possible. When did you want this?"

"Is dinner tonight too early?" Bel kept his hopeful expression.

"If I begin working now," I said. One of the three men hauling in the produce covered his mouth with his sleeve as he coughed. One of the others said something to him in a language I didn't understand very well. It was a dialect of the common speech, but heavily accented.

"Where are those three louts that work with you?" Bel asked, waving at the three men who took off out the door.

"They only show up for meals," I said, pulling crates of redfruit toward the sink for washing.

"You've been doing all this yourself?" Bel cursed creatively when I nodded. I was used to hearing words of that nature—Edan could curse with the best soldiers I'd ever met.

"Yes, Ranger Bel. I didn't know whether to report them or to whom," I answered truthfully, piling fruit into a wire basket and turning on the water taps. I would have to peel and slice the fruit quickly, then roll out pastry dough and add spices and sugar if I were to have a dessert ready with the evening meal.

"Reah, how old are you?" Bel had his hands behind his back. That frightened me. Edan often hid a heavy wooden spoon or a metal ladle behind him before striking me in the past. I swallowed nervously as I did my best to meet Bel's eyes.

"Nineteen turns," I admitted, lowering my eyes and my head. If he were going to beat me, I didn't want to see his hands coming.

Bel cursed again, only this time he was calling Chlind and Seval names I hadn't heard before.

"Little Reah, the only reason we allowed you to stay after Delvin and I got a good look at you was the way you cook. We reasoned that no child could cook like this. No female below the age of twenty-five is allowed at any outpost. I will have to talk to Commander Aris about this." Bel whirled and strode through the back door so fast it rippled the leafy vegetation in the crates.

I wanted to cry. Just sit in the floor right there and then and let go. I'd held it back since weeping my eyes out inside the pod. If these people turned me out, I had no place to go. Nobody to go to. That would let me live, anyway. What was I going to do? Instead of weeping, I began to peel redfruit.

I didn't see Bel again until the kitchen was nearly clean after dinner. "Come with me," he ordered and I followed him as he strode down a lengthy hall of thick, whitewashed stone into a wing of the post I hadn't explored before. Truthfully, I'd been so busy in the kitchen I hadn't had time to wander. I was too frightened now to pay much attention to my surroundings. I kept my eyes focused on Bel's broad back and tried to fight off my fear.

"Reah, this is Commander Aris." Bel moved aside once we were inside the spacious office, and I received my first look at the outpost Commander. He stared at me for moments as I stood before him. I was so frightened I was afraid I'd burst into tears. He was a lion of a man with thick, shoulder-length dark-gold hair, swept back from his forehead. He didn't stand as his rank dictated, otherwise I think he would have dwarfed Bel, whom I thought was quite tall. The Commander's shoulders were broader, too and I imagined that he'd gained his rank by working for it.

"Reah, how did those two miscreants bring you here when you were underage?" Commander Aris asked me after moments of silence. He sounded as if he'd just gotten his voice back.

"They found me and told me I should come with them," I hung my head. I nearly jumped when I imagined that I heard a voice inside my head. I'm sure it was my fear—giving me hallucinations when there was nothing there. *Hush, no harm will come,* the voice said. I drew a shaky breath and managed to put it out of my mind. The voice didn't come again.

"Do you have someplace to go?" Commander Aris' voice sounded almost harsh against the gentleness of the voice inside my head.

"No, Commander. I have no family here." That was the truth, sad as it was. I didn't really have family on Tulgalan, either. None that wanted me, anyway. I had to steer myself away from those thoughts. The tears might come despite my efforts.

"Bel, what do you think?" Commander Aris turned to the Ranger.

"I think those redfruit pastries we had tonight were the best I've ever tasted," Bel said. "Sir."

"Then let's keep this between us," Commander Aris said. "I'll make sure our little cook is off limits to the troops, and you, Bel, will hunt down those three and make it clear to them that they are to work off their punishment, not laze about and receive better meals than the others. Reah, you have been feeding the highest-ranking officers here the past two eight-days. Did you know that? This is what the extra twelve meals were for. I am sorry I did not think to check on this sooner. I was enjoying my food without realizing where it was coming from."

"I don't think she's had any time off, Commander." Bel offered.

"I know this. Have meals sent to the women on last-day from the other kitchen. Reah, that day will be yours to do for yourself. I will arrange for extra clothing as well." That statement made me blush—I had three outfits and they hung off me. I'd managed to stain them, too, with this or that while I was cooking. I had no aprons to wear over my clothing to prevent it.

"You have permission to approach me if you have problems or questions," Commander Aris added. I was shaking by that time and clenching my hands to keep it from showing. "Bel, take our cook back to her kitchen before you go in search of her unwilling help."

Bel nodded to the Commander and herded me from his office. I wasn't sure how I'd come out of that meeting alive. Not only intact but with an open invitation to come to them with problems. My cooking skills were finally being recognized, and for now they were keeping me alive on an alien world.

# CHAPTER 4

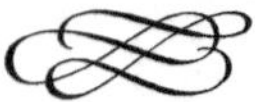

My three helpers showed up clean and on time the following morning to prepare breakfast. I learned quickly that they didn't have much in the way of cooking skills. I set them to cracking and beating eggs with dry milk for the egg dish I was preparing. The cooked egg would be folded around chopped meat and vegetables. It was a good, healthy breakfast, made better with the bit of sauce I ladled over it at the last moment before sending it off to be eaten. I worked on the bread dough while my three cleaned up the dishes and countertops after breakfast. I let them eat first and they liked what they received very much. They weren't talking much—I'd curtailed their small vacation, somehow. That didn't keep them from eating, though.

"Where did you learn to cook?" The youngest of the three ventured to ask over the evening meal that we shared, sitting around a tall counter on stools.

"I learned from my family. They're all gone now." That much was true, in a certain sense. They were gone from me—most likely forever. Mandil was non-Alliance and didn't look to join during my lifetime. They always held themselves separate and what little I knew about them said they condoned slavery, had wizards with real power among the population and many other, unusual facts. Information from non-Alliance worlds tended to be spotty at best, so I had no idea whether any part of what I remembered from my classes could be counted as truth. I didn't want to tip my hand either by asking about any of it. I had to keep my eyes and ears open, just so I could learn as much as I could.

What made me most curious was why the outpost was needed. I didn't get the idea that any of the surrounding desert villages were staging uprisings. There had to be some reason the troops were stationed here. And the Rangers? They went out to scout the local areas—Bel had come and gone several times during my stay—I'd overheard the women discussing it. They liked Bel and Delvin quite well, it seems. What were the Rangers scouting?

"Reah, what do you have in the way of extra food?" The old soldier who'd shown me the kitchen came through the back door as we were finishing up.

"I can put something together—how much do you need?" I asked.

"Enough for these three." The older man, whose name was Galdi, told me, leading in three children. The oldest couldn't have been more than nine turns.

"I can certainly find something for them." I slid off my stool and pulled two more stools over. Galdi helped get the children settled on the stools as soon as we'd helped them wash small hands. I pulled leftover food from one of the keepers—it hadn't had time to chill completely—and served roast fowl with a gravy and baked potatoes. A bit of fresh juice was provided, too—I used the last of the citrus fruit brought in with the redfruits. The children ate hungrily, eventually chatting with Galdi and my three helpers.

"Their parents handed them to us—their headman wouldn't let the adults leave but they were frightened for their children," Bel came in moments later. He'd been speaking with Commander Aris, I learned. Bel had sent the children off with Galdi to be fed before sitting down with Aris.

"What will you do with them?" I whispered urgently. Why were they in danger? Was there something in the desert that I should worry about?

"They'll be taken back to Crown City," Bel replied. "We have fresh troops coming tomorrow, so the transports will take the children and a few of ours back with them. They'll be cared for." Bel patted my shoulder lightly. I stiffened when he did that. Bel noticed and dropped his hand quickly.

"I don't know what she was more afraid of—what's hiding in the desert or my touching her," Bel paced before Aris' desk later.

"Just be careful around her, I think she's afraid of any male. It isn't you," Aris attempted to calm his Ranger.

"What caused that? Do you have a guess?" Bel turned his gaze to the Commander. Aris did have a guess but it wasn't something he wanted to discuss, even with his second-in-command.

"I don't wish to speculate," Aris replied instead. "Don't worry; I'll find a reason for this, eventually."

The children ended up spending the night in the women's quarters down the hall. They were taken right in by several, hugged, kissed and put to bed. It made me sigh. That had never been my due, growing up in a large family that should have known better. I crawled into bed after cleaning the kitchen a second time. I'd wanted to ask Bel about the danger in the desert, but that would have revealed my ignorance. Most likely the others knew all about it; they just hadn't discussed it within my hearing. Sleep wouldn't come right away as it normally did and I tossed for hours before the voice visited me again in my exhaustion. *Sleep, little love*, the voice whispered. I slept.

I felt off the following day but decided it was due to a late night and lack of sleep. I had difficulty rising the day after that. Feverish best described the third day and I ached all over. The youngest of my three helpers, Stef, asked me if something was wrong after a while. I stared at him stupidly before dropping to the floor as blackness enveloped me.

"One of those three that brought the vegetables and fruit had the fever —Galdi remarked on it," Bel said later. Reah had been brought to the outpost physician who'd placed her in his tiny hospital. She was his only patient at the moment.

"I didn't even think to ask if she'd been inoculated—all the others were," Bel added.

"Chlind and Seval," Aris growled angrily. Bel worried whenever Aris growled. That low, threatening sound was a sign that Aris was extremely angry.

"I'll be happy to knock their heads together if we see them again," Bel agreed.

"I'll knock their heads together." Aris stood outside the door to Reah's hospital room. The physician was administering fluids through an IV. Poor Reah hadn't wakened since fainting in the floor.

"Do you think she'll be all right?"

"Bel, we will make sure she's all right," Aris muttered, stalking away. Bel stared after his commander, wondering how it was that he could be so sure about something that had killed many villagers already.

"The IV is fine, we'll leave that," a voice sounded beside me. At least that's where I thought it was. I felt awful and my headache was an agony. Perhaps it was more hallucination—more voices inside my head. I was ill—I knew that much.

"Hold still," the voice came again. It was one I didn't recognize. Cool hands were placed on my heated forehead. Pain lessened immediately. "It will not last much longer. The healing will come quickly now." The hands were removed. I felt their absence when they were taken away. I might have moaned, I don't know. Other hands were on me, then, gathering me up. I was helpless to resist. *My little love shouldn't suffer so*, the voice came inside my head. More fingers stroked my cheek. I slept as soon as the kiss was laid against my forehead.

~

I knew I'd been hallucinating—the post physician informed me that my fever had gone quite high and he'd been worried that I might not survive. "You're still with us," he smiled at me when I opened my eyes to look up at him. "If we'd known you hadn't had the inoculation, I would have given it to you the moment you arrived. Next season, don't forget to have it done, hear?"

My head still felt as if it were stuffed with cotton so I nodded, not trusting my voice. A sore throat came with this illness; it was a terrible chore to swallow the painkill the physician gave me. I wasn't up to solid food either so I received broth, water and juice for three more days. Something else happened during that time; my kitchen was combined with that of the regular troops and I was put in charge of the menu and asked to show the four head cooks how to prepare some of the dishes. This turned out to be a very good idea—my three miscreants were outranked by everyone else in our combined kitchen and they weren't able to shirk their duties again. They were getting used to me, too and often looked to me to see how I wanted something done. That made me feel good.

I wasn't allowed to work for more than three clicks at a stretch before taking a rest break. The physician said no more long days for me and that was that. Breakfast was something we portioned out among the cooks. That meant that I only had to rise early two days out of the eight in every eight-day. Sleeping in was a luxury I hadn't had since I was small. Of course, the late risers did the dinner menu and supervised the late cleanup, but it was a good trade-off.

More vegetables had come in from one of the villages and Widnal, the oldest cook and I were in the yard outside the large kitchens, inspecting what had been brought. Bel, who'd come out to speak with the villagers walked over, grabbed my arm and pulled me inside the kitchen.

"Stay inside," he hissed at me and took off at a run down the corridor toward the Commander's office. In very little time, the Commander was rushing through the kitchen with Bel at his heels. I watched them through the open doorway as the Commander began speaking with one of the men who'd brought the food. Time slowed for me as I watched the Commander pull the blade he wore at his side and swing it faster than I could see, beheading a man who stood nearby. What was even more shocking than that was came immediately; the headless man exploded. Not as bits of flesh and blood, though—it looked to be black sand or small pieces of rock. I'd seen vids of sandstorms in my classes, and this was what one looked and sounded like, only on a smaller scale. The Commander, Bel and Widnal knew to duck and shield their eyes. The villagers didn't and they bore the full brunt of that exploding force.

Failing to understand the villagers afterward and still recovering from the extreme shock of the incident, I listened while they all gabbled at once. Bel and the Commander herded them toward the post physician's hospital so their eyes and skin could be examined and treated.

"Little cook, that is one of the things we guard against," Widnal spoke quietly at my side. "Many of the troops have never seen it. Try not to let it frighten you—the Commander is quite adept at recognizing these things."

Slowly turning to blink at Widnal's kind countenance, I almost wasn't able to form the words to ask my question. "What are those— those things called?"

"We call them demons. Commander Aris calls them spawn. If one of those creatures bites any of us, that is what we become. We no longer have control over our actions; at least that is what I hear. That one could have bitten any one of us while we stood there and the Commander would have had to kill us as well."

That thought made me shiver. "Bel—he recognized it too," I muttered.

"Yes—all the Rangers are good at that. That is why they go out often. All our Rangers have wizard abilities and that's why they are sent on scouting trips. The other troops would be searching blindly."

"I've never seen a wizard before," I admitted without thinking.

"Most likely you have, young one, you just weren't aware." Widnal nodded to me and together we hauled in the vegetables and began cooking.

~

"You saw a dusting?" Stef sounded awed and jealous at the same time. He was working with me, drizzling a sweet glaze on the fruit and pastry dessert for dinner.

"Stef, it was awful," I mumbled, working faster to keep the image out of my mind. That poor man—or demon—being beheaded so swiftly. The explosion and the black particles slamming into the side of the stucco walls outside the kitchens would likely remain in my mind forever.

"We always hear about it but we never see it," he grumbled. "Somebody else always gets to shoot the ranos rifles."

"The ones who have the marksman's pay," Widnal slapped the back of Stef's head to return him to his task. "Keep getting into trouble and you'll never have the opportunity."

"Don't remind me," Stef whispered and went back to drizzling glaze.

~

My night to supervise the late cleanup had ended and I was ready to find my bed on the other end of the post. The last of the kitchen help had already left to get some sleep. Bel found me alone in the kitchen.

"Commander Aris wants to see you," he beckoned with a hand. I settled the kitchen towel over the edge of the sink and worried my lip while I stared at Bel. Bel was a wizard. I hadn't expected that. Was it his voice I heard in my head at times, or was that just a hallucination as I'd thought before? It didn't sound like his voice, but then it didn't sound like anyone I knew or had met since bouncing onto the surface of Mandil. I nodded at Bel after searching his face briefly with my eyes. Following him down the now-familiar corridor, we eventually reached the Commander's office. Bel knocked once, then opened Aris' door and led me inside. Aris was sitting at his desk as he usually was when I came there.

"Please sit," he nodded to me and signed another paper that lay under his hand. It amazed me that Mandil still used paper instead of the comp-vids and other electronic devices common across the Alliance. I had to remind myself that Mandil wasn't Alliance.

"I know you saw that today," Aris finally looked up at me. I sat directly in front of him in a chair carved of dark wood. Something else the Alliance used little of nowadays—wood was extremely expensive and there was a huge tax for cutting trees—they had become a scarcity in some sections of the Alliance. I could only nod at the Commander. The image of the dusting still appeared in my mind, unbidden and horrible.

"We have guards posted and there are wards set around the post at night. We just never expected spawn to walk up in daylight," Commander Aris sighed. I watched his eyes—they were a golden brown, lending to the lion-like appearance he had.

"The ones he was with didn't think to question why the demon wasn't speaking," Bel snorted at my side.

"That is one of the ways to tell spawn from humans in their early stages," the Commander continued. "In the first two eight-days, they appear as the humans they once were before being bitten. Once they are bitten, however, they lose their ability to speak. They may nod or shake their head, but that's all. They do not regain speech unless they manage to live a full five turns or more. By that time, there are other ways to determine what they are."

"What about the others with him?" I asked my question timidly, not expecting an answer. This sounded like privileged information—information to which no mere cook was entitled.

"They received a brief lesson on recognizing the enemy before they left the post today," Bel answered my question. "They are still refusing to leave their homes, even after they saw this. I fail to understand it." Bel shook his head.

"They still believe they can protect themselves with what power they have. It will not help them if they are attacked by more than three at a time," Commander Aris growled. That growl would have made any jungle cat proud. I swallowed nervously at the thought.

"Little cook, we brought you in to tell you not to worry overmuch about this," Commander Aris said, his voice back to normal. "We will be placing wards day and night now, so no more might slip in as easily as this one did today. It is my hope that you will not witness another dusting."

I could only nod at his words—witnessing another dusting wasn't particularly high on my list of things to do at the moment, although Stef was crazy to see it for himself.

"Will you be all right or would you like the physician to give you something to help you sleep?" Bel asked.

"I really don't want anything," I looked down at my hands; they were clasped tightly together in my lap.

"Are you sure?" Bel knelt beside my chair.

"I'm sure," my voice was barely above a whisper. My military instructors would be ashamed of me—they'd worked hard to prepare me and my fellow recruits for the possibility that we'd see death firsthand. I'd seen it today, though it had been something evil. It had once been humanoid and that's what bothered me.

"If you change your mind, just knock on the physician's door. He'll have something waiting," Bel patted my hands before standing and moving away. I nodded, not looking at him. Commander Aris said I could go so I stood and walked out of his office, closing the door carefully behind me. I heard the rumble of Bel's voice after I left. I didn't try to decipher what he said as I made my way toward my tiny bedroom.

~

"The shields will hold against one or two, but what if we're attacked by an entire village that has been turned?" Bel turned his gaze on Aris after Reah's footsteps disappeared down the corridor.

"No idea. Tell the men to look sharp, and make sure one of the Rangers is on duty with the night guards." Aris shook his head before cursing spawn in general, and then cursing the one who'd made them.

~

The news was all over the post by the next day and even the five women who came to pick up breakfast for the pink wing (that's what Stef and the others called it) asked Widnal and me about the dusting. Widnal answered their questions; I busied myself with kneading dough for fresh loaves of bread. Stef was still bemoaning the fact that he didn't get to see—he'd had the day off. Widnal eventually sent the women on their way; he and I were working the breakfast shift so we'd get off earlier.

An early night was welcome; I wanted to explore the hot baths the post had. Anyone was welcome to go and make use of the large, heated pools. I'd only heard of them and hadn't yet gone exploring. Widnal promised to show me where the pools were on his way back to the common barracks.

The post was quite large and might have taken at least half a click to walk from one end to the other. I saw the transports that had arrived earlier in the day—more troops had come in, bringing our numbers to five hundreds. Two additional cooks had been sent and would begin their shifts in the morning. Widnal and I were scheduled early again, so we would be giving them instructions. I squared my shoulders as I walked beside Widnal. He smiled down at me, a hidden dimple showing in his cheek.

"Don't fret, if any of the new ones gives you trouble, Bel will have their heads," Widnal's smile widened. I had begun a tally in my head, one column *for* Bel being the voice in my head, one column *against*. Widnal had just added another check in the *for* column.

Tall, tropical trees stood here and there on the sand-covered grounds of the post. There wasn't much green growing anywhere except around an old well on the grounds. A few plants and a fence of steel pickets stood around it, "to keep the troops from falling in on dark nights," Widnal teased as we walked past it. The main building on the outpost held two stories, with the barracks separate and much larger than the building that held the officers' quarters, the kitchens and the pink wing.

"They sent another fifteen girls," Widnal's voice was quieter as he gave me that information. "Commander worries that they'll be targets if the demons get organized."

That information sent a shiver through me. Commander Aris had told me only last night that they were placing wards around the property at all times, not just at night. Could those things actually break through, though? I was afraid to ask Widnal, as I was too terrified to hear what his answer might be.

"Here we be," Widnal said, stopping at a single-story building between the main building and barracks. He made a shooing gesture with his hands—he wasn't coming inside with me. Honestly, I didn't know if I wanted to go in either. If there were people inside enjoying the bath, I might be too embarrassed to climb into the hot water naked. That was the rule—no clothing of any kind allowed in the water. Other things weren't allowed either, but some of those rules were blatantly ignored if you believed some of the troops. Taking a deep breath, I reached out and grasped the metal door handle with my hand.

Steam wisped off the surface of the large, hot pool as I walked inside. The water was heated with solar power, just as the outpost was powered in that way. I hadn't seen any clouds since coming to this portion of Mandil, so there was plenty of power to be had here. I was grateful that it was too early for anyone else to be there—except for the perimeter guards, they were all at dinner. We'd sent the trays out just before Widnal and I had left the kitchens.

Towels were stacked on a carved wood table off to the side and a low bench with hooks and pegs above it lined the walls beside the table. Clothing would be hung there—dressing and undressing occurred on the bench or flagstone floor surrounding the rectangular pool. No other rooms occupied the building—the pool took up most of the space. Undressed hurriedly anyway, I hung up my clothing and slipped into the hot water with a grateful sigh of pleasure.

"Little cook, I haven't seen you here before," Delvin's hop into the water woke me from a light doze. I'd fallen asleep while sitting on the stone bench built along the side of the pool.

"And you shouldn't come in alone if there's a chance you might fall asleep," he warned with a grin. I knew the dangers of that—I just hadn't realized how tired I was. Deliberately not looking down into the clear water as Delvin sat two armlengths away, I nervously agreed with his statement.

"Don't worry, nobody is going to bother you here, just enjoy the bath," Delvin looked away. I remembered that he was probably a wizard, just as Bel was. I had only seen the other Rangers in passing and didn't know any names. I barely knew most of the kitchen staff now—I'd always been terrible with names. Perhaps it was self-protection. If I didn't know them, they couldn't hurt me as badly. I hadn't gotten close to anyone during my military training or as cook for the Governor of the Realm—my last official assignment for the Alliance had certainly turned out badly.

"I heard you saw the dusting the other day," Delvin went on.

"I did," I lifted my hands from the water—my fingers were quite wrinkled. How long had I dozed off?

"I've only seen it a time or two in daylight," Delvin admitted. "Not much fun if you're close enough to get hit with the particles."

"I was inside the kitchen," I admitted. "Close enough to see but the walls kept me from getting hit."

"I didn't sleep much after I saw it the first time," Delvin said.

"I kept wondering about the man he'd been before," I muttered.

"I agree. Demons don't turn anything else, you know," Delvin told me conversationally. "If they're hungry and there's no humanoid available, they'll eat animals. Otherwise, they leave them alone. They prefer tender flesh—women and children—when they feed. They generally choose to turn the males and devour the others."

That was information I had no desire to hear. No wonder Commander Aris worried about the women at the outpost. "Are there other posts nearby?" I should have kept that question to myself—my curiosity could reveal my ignorance and give my alien status away. Delvin didn't seem surprised at the question, causing me to relax a little.

"Two more—twenty trids in both directions," he pointed to the east and west. Trids were old measurements—one could walk a trid in half a click. That meant a ten-click trek in either direction, unless one had transport. A full click might get you there in that fashion.

"Look who's here," Bel walked in with the Commander and one of the other Rangers. It made sense—they were served before the troops. I'd most likely invaded their time in the baths.

"I'll go," I said, blushing. I was about to get out with four sets of male eyes on me.

"No, stay a while," Delvin grinned. My chin came to the top of the water, whereas his shoulders were above the surface of the steaming pool. I stayed—Delvin didn't seem to think it was a bad thing that I was there.

"Get out of the kitchens early?" Bel dropped into the water on my other side. I was looking straight ahead so as not to embarrass myself. None of the others were embarrassed in the slightest. Commander Aris slipped in beside Bel, with the Ranger I didn't know next to him. I turned to look into Bel's eyes.

"Widnal and I had the breakfast schedule so we could work with the two new cooks," I replied honestly.

"When can we get more of the toasted roundbread with bacon, egg and sauce?" The last Ranger leaned forward to ask. "I'm Hish, by the way."

Hish had blue eyes and straight, close-cropped brown hair. His face was weathered, just as the other Rangers' were. "I need yellow citrus to make the sauce and we didn't get any in the last delivery," I said. "The sauce is made from eggs, and we don't get many of those, either. I can only serve it once in a while, as a treat."

"Then we'll ask for more yellow citrus and extra eggs," the Commander chuckled. He brushed back dark-gold hair with wet hands, dampening the length. It still looked like a lion's mane to me. They talked of other things then, as if I weren't there. They spoke of the new troops and how they were fitting in; some of whom were considered troublemakers already. The discussion turned to the cooler season which was still moon-turns away and other topics. More Rangers came to join us as they talked, as did several officers. I was the only female present, and thinking more and more that I should have climbed out of the water when Delvin first showed up.

The topic of discussion had turned to the additional bedding needed in the barracks for cooler weather, when an alarm began to sound. I hadn't heard the alarm before. With practiced precision, Bel hauled me from the water one-handed, grabbed a towel for me and lifted his clothing off a hook. I wanted to shriek but knew it wouldn't help the situation—all the others were flinging on clothing and rushing toward the walls surrounding the post.

Bel hauled me along under his arm, tossed me inside the nearest door to the main building, slammed it almost in my face after shouting at me to stay inside, pulled his trousers on and ran after the others. I was shaking and pulling my towel tighter around me. Were we under attack? That's what it looked like to me. Not knowing what to do otherwise, I trotted toward the kitchens.

The entire population from the pink wing were there ahead of me, all talking in hushed voices and doing their best to peer out the windows. "What are you doing?" I shouted. "Have they not told you to stay away from the windows?" My point was verified moments later when bullets ripped through the thick glass. Shards sprayed across kitchen counters, slivers littered prep tables and splinters—both wood and glass—slapped against cabinets. "Get down!" I shouted at the women. With all of them shrieking at once, I had to shout a second time before they dropped to the floor.

Still wrapped in only a towel, I crawled toward a cabinet that held my largest skillets. Grabbing the heaviest one I could wield comfortably, I pulled it out and crawled back, stationing myself between the door and the broken windows. The enemy could come in by either means. The women would have been safer if they'd stayed in the pink wing. It had more walls around it.

Two women were huddled in a corner, bleeding and crying. I thought to go to them, but that thought was interrupted by a fire bottle hefted through the broken window. It crashed onto the stone flooring and flames now spread and pooled across the slate-gray flagstones. Ripping off my towel, I dunked it in the sink, getting it wet before wringing it out and throwing it over the blaze on the floor. Several more wet towels later, the blaze was contained.

Still naked, I ran low until I could lift my skillet and take up my post again. When the first man burst through the door, I knew he wasn't ours—he was dressed in desert garb. I hit him with my pan and he fell, his head cracked. Was he humanoid or one of the demons? I grabbed a large chopping knife from a nearby block. His head was coming off if he rose. He didn't.

Another burst in. He fell when I hit him hard across the face, but he didn't lose consciousness. This could be a demon. I'd received exemplary performance certificates during my military training because I'd been faster than the others. Much faster. I had no idea how that was, but my instructors were happy with me because of it. Moving as swiftly as I could, I slicing the demon's throat. It took two swift passes and he was clawing at me when I removed his head. He dusted, just as the other had that Commander Aris killed, spraying me with hard, stinging particles.

I kicked what was left of the door shut, waiting for more to come. They didn't. Someone was now shouting outside that it was safe. I didn't trust that until I saw Bel and Delvin coming through the door. Bel was still dressed only in trousers; therefore, Delvin removed his shirt and wrapped me in it. Four of the women were cut by flying glass when the windows blew inward, so they were taken to the physician. Thankfully, he now had help—two more physicians had come with the last troop arrivals.

"What happened here?" Bel asked when the injured had been taken away. My voice shook as I explained what had taken place.

"You killed it?" Now Delvin was looking at me in shock.

"What was I supposed to do? Stand there and let it eat the others?" I had my arms wrapped as tightly across my middle as I could get them. Truthfully, I was now feeling nauseous. Soldiers came and removed the unconscious man. I wasn't sure he was going to wake— I'd hit him as hard as I could with a cast-iron skillet. I was glad Delvin's shirt came to my knees, too; I was shivering now. I'd killed a demon and possibly a man as well. It didn't matter that they'd been trying to kill us—this was a first for me and I found it unsettling.

"Aris may want to ask questions about the attack, but that will come later," Bel steered me toward the bathroom next to the kitchen. "Girl, if you're going to be sick, I'll stay with you if you want," he said softly as he led me to one of the flushseats inside.

"I'll be embarrassed if you stay," I muttered, gagging.

"Then call out if you need anything," Bel pulled a chunk of glass from my hair before leaving me alone. I heaved until my stomach was dry. And then heaved past that. I was weak and feeling horrible afterward but I washed my face and hands, rinsed out my mouth and made it into the kitchen. A handful of troops were already putting squares of wood into empty windows and sweeping up the glass and other debris. My towels had been removed already but the burn marks remained on the flagstones.

"Let's get you to your bedroom," Bel was still there, waiting on me.

"Why did you wait?" I asked. "You look exhausted." He did—I was only telling the truth.

"I think the Commander would have my head if I didn't see his best cook safely to the other wing," Bel grinned tiredly. He walked me the entire way, got me inside my tiny bedroom and closed the door behind him. I listened for his footsteps as they walked away from me.

# CHAPTER 5

"Bel, I expect you to keep that thought to yourself." Bel nodded—he and the Commander both had their suspicions about Reah. Bel had been the one to take it farther, making the guess that she'd had military training of some sort. "She's no spy—they would have sent someone else," the Commander stood and stretched. He and Bel had gotten an early morning after a late night. Remains of their breakfast trays still lay on Aris' desk. "Besides, there's no information to be had here—unless the Alliance wants to know about spawn attacks." Aris covered a yawn. "I'm inclined to think it was just as reported—a misfired pod they couldn't catch before it landed here. So, unless you want to get our little cook beheaded in Crown City, keep this to yourself."

"I don't want anything to happen to her," Bel muttered. "I just wanted to let you know what I was thinking. I'm hoping I'm the only one thinking it, too. We could be in real trouble if this is discovered and they learn we knew already."

"Right now they're all thinking about the attack last night. Let's leave it at that, all right? Send Reah in after the midday meal. I want to talk to her." Bel nodded and left Aris' office.

"Little Reah," Aris muttered as he sat down at his desk. "Don't bring attention to yourself again."

~

Bel sent me to the Commander alone. It was the first time he hadn't come with me, and that made me worry. Hoping that all Commander Aris wanted was a report on the attack as far as the kitchens were concerned, I pushed my fears to the back of my mind and knocked on his door as firmly as I could.

"Come." He was expecting me. I closed the door softly behind me and came to stand before his desk. He looked tired. He also looked as if he didn't want that pointed out. I stayed quiet. This was a military outpost, after all. Troops didn't tell their commanding officer he looked tired. I followed standard protocol.

"Sit, Reah." I sat in the same chair I'd taken the last time. "Now, tell me what happened in the kitchens last night," Commander Aris said, running a hand through his thick mane of hair.

"Bel tossed me inside the main building—the west door—and ordered me to stay inside. I ran toward the kitchens; I have no idea why—and found all the women from the pink wing there, looking out the windows. I shouted at them to get down just as the bullets shattered the glass. That's when the four got wounded, Commander."

"I understand that," he nodded at me. "What happened next?"

"Someone threw a fire bottle through one of the broken windows. I took the towel I was wearing and got it wet in the sink, then threw it over the burning fuel in the floor. I had to wet other towels to cover it completely. I grabbed the heaviest skillet I could handle and waited between the door and the windows in case the enemy made it past our troops."

"And did any come in?" An eyebrow lifted as those golden-brown eyes watched me closely. Would this result in my arrest? Would I be handed to the Prince Royal for beheading? And all because I'd saved the women they seemed so worried about?

"Yes, Commander, two came in." I was too tired to lie—I'd been up to help with breakfast—one of the new cooks had gotten injured in the fighting so I'd taken his place.

"You hit the first one, I understand—hard enough to crack his skull?"

"I guess. He was unconscious. I was afraid he was one of those things."

"What about the second one?" Commander Aris steepled his fingers on this question.

"I got a knife, just in case the first one got up. When the second one came in, I hit him just as hard in the head. He fell, but didn't lose consciousness. I used the knife on him—two strokes to remove his head. He dusted, I believe is the term."

"Were you frightened?"

That question I didn't understand. "Of course. I was scared witless," I admitted. "And fighting that thing with no clothes on. What do you think? That I was happy to be involved in hand-to-hand combat with a creature I've never heard of while completely naked so he wouldn't eat the women screaming inside my kitchen?" My fear and stress must have made me say what I did—I never had outbursts like that. Of course, I'd never come that close to dying before, except for the pod and Edan's beatings, anyway.

Commander Aris' response to my outburst was also completely unexpected. He laughed. Just threw back his head and boomed with laughter. Maybe it was the mental image of a skillet-wielding, naked nymph fighting off attackers that did it—how was I to know? I waited until he stopped chuckling.

"Reah, you performed above expectations. I've never seen one of those things killed with only a skillet and a knife before. If you were one of my troops, I'd give you a promotion and commendation. As it is, I'm upping your pay."

"Pay?" That came as a shock to me. What pay? I wasn't getting paid. My question made the Commander frown immediately.

"You didn't receive your weekly bags? What happened to them?" He was standing quickly and shouting for Bel. Bel burst through the door as if some emergency required his attention. He stopped short at finding me sitting in my chair and the Commander standing behind his desk. "Reah hasn't gotten her money. What happened to it?" Bel stared at the Commander for a moment, puzzled by his question.

"I'll be right back," Bel promised and left almost as quickly as he'd come in. Ten ticks may have passed before Bel was back with another officer and the oldest of my three miscreants. His name, if I remembered correctly, was Ralst.

"I had to place the truth spell," Bel shoved Ralst to his knees in front of the Commander's desk. He was so close he almost touched my knee. I drew back to avoid contact. "Paymaster Dex here says that Ralst has been collecting Reah's bags. Tell the Commander what you did with her money, Ralst." Some sort of power permeated Bel's command—the air was thick with it.

"I gambled with it," Ralst whined. He didn't want to tell the truth any more than I wanted to hear it right then.

"Do you have any of it left?" The Commander crossed arms over his chest.

"No."

"Just as I thought," Commander Aris huffed. "Dex, sell all of Ralst's belongings and compensate Reah as best you can. Bel, send Ralst to lockup and make sure he's on the next transport back to Crown City."

"Right away, Commander," Bel and Dex hauled Ralst out of Aris' office.

"Reah, you are not a slave. All women come here willingly. It is a way for them to earn money and nothing more," Aris gazed kindly at me across his desk. I nodded—I was beginning to learn about Mandil. Much of the information the Alliance had on this world was wrong. "I don't know what Chlind and Seval did to you, and right now I don't care. You're here with us now and we'll protect you as best we can. Just follow the rules and we'll get along. You're dismissed." Aris' eyes were on the papers covering his desk as I walked out of his office. He knew and he wasn't going to do anything about it. I just had to remain inconspicuous, stay silent and not call attention to myself from now on.

~

Later, I learned from Widnal that six of our troops died in the fighting the night before. He hinted that Wizardry had been used to destroy the enemy but didn't elaborate and I didn't ask. Stef and Nedis, the two remaining miscreants, seemed sullen while they worked, but that was none of my doing. Ralst was charged with theft—I learned that much. He was to be tried by a military tribunal in Crown City. Which brought me to another question—if I were being paid, where was I supposed to spend the money? There wasn't anything at the post—no little shops or such. My clothing, such as it was, was supplied by the post itself. The other women had come with bags and trunks; I'd arrived with nothing. It was a question I couldn't ask, so I resolved not to fret about it. Either I'd find out or I wouldn't.

As it turns out, I found out sooner than I thought I might. A note had been slipped under my door when I went to bed three nights later. I'd considered going to the baths again, remembered what happened the first time and took a warm shower instead. The note was in a plain paper envelope. I pulled the folded paper out, thinking that I'd never received anything other than comp-vid messages before and read the short letter.

*Reah,* it began, *in three days, the first twenty women are being given liberty to visit Crown City on a two-day pass when the next transports leave the post. You are one of that twenty and it would provide a break for you if you choose to go.* It was signed *Commander Aris.* Sighing, I set the note on my tiny, bedside table. I did and didn't want to go. What was I supposed to do? I had money now—Paymaster Dex had delivered the small bag of coins himself—it was all he could get out of Ralst's things. I'd also gotten one eight-day's full pay since then, and it was more than the amount Ralst's belongings had gotten for me.

"So, are you going?" Bel and Delvin came into the kitchen as I was supervising cleanup the following evening. They'd been out on patrol and had come begging for a late dinner. I reheated ox-roast for them and added vegetables, fruit and a glass of good wine. They looked as if they could use it.

"Going?" It didn't come to me immediately.

"To Crown City. We're due for a break so we're going as well. The transports can haul sixty, so most of the Rangers and some of the officers are going. Reah, this is wonderful." Bel finished off his portion of ox-roast and washed it down with the last of a bottle of wine.

"Want more?" I asked.

"No, I'll never get out of bed in the morning and Aris wants a report first thing," Bel grinned. "Come to Crown City, Reah. You'll like it."

"I'll think about it," I said. The trip was in two days so I'd have to decide quickly.

"I have an extra bag for your clothes," Delvin offered. "I'll bring it by tomorrow. Just in case." He was grinning, too.

Two days later, I was sitting beside Delvin on a transport bound for Crown City. Bel sat near the front as the others loaded onto the transport. The last one to arrive, shockingly enough, was Commander Aris. Delvin must have noted the surprise on my face as Aris sat next to Bel, right behind the driver. The door closed and we drove away from the outpost.

"He gets time off, too," Delvin nudged me while nodding toward Aris.

"Who gets the honor of herding the others around?" I asked breathlessly.

"One of the two captains from our last reinforcements. I think Aris had him in his office for two clicks yesterday, and a lot of 'do nots' came out of his mouth, I think," Delvin grinned. "Stop worrying about it; we'll be there in less than four clicks," Delvin leaned back in his seat and settled in to nap.

My first impression of Crown City reminded me of the vid images I'd seen of Serendaan, an Alliance world. Onion-shaped domes atop tall, rounded buildings abounded with smaller, more squat and square buildings built of stucco sprinkled between. Color was everywhere and to the uninitiated it was nearly blinding at first. Even the shops had colorful rugs, clothing and scarves hanging outside in the open air, advertising what was sold inside. I tried not to gawk but couldn't help myself after a while.

"You can stay with us at the military station or find a room for yourself," Delvin hefted my bag after pulling his from the compartment over our heads. "Barracks are free; a room will cost you," he added, smiling. I shrugged my acceptance and trotted after him.

We'd been dropped off near the entrance of the military station. I saw some of the women heading toward Crown City, while others walked inside the gate to the station. An entire building was devoted to housing for post visitors, I learned, with small, neat, serviceable rooms for each of us. How my room came to be sandwiched between Delvin's and Bel's I had no idea.

"Come along, we'll find something to eat," Bel pulled me from my room the moment I'd gotten my clothing into the tiny closet. We ate at an outdoor café, where they served spiced meat sandwiches rolled in flat bread with cooked vegetables. I liked what I had—it was lamb and cooked tender. I always enjoyed eating new things—it gave me ideas for new recipes in my kitchen.

Yes, I was thinking of the post's kitchens as mine. Everybody looked to me for recipes and preparation instructions. I realized then that I was happy for perhaps the first time in my life, though I did walk a knife's edge, worrying about whether I'd be discovered or if demons were going to come crashing through my door at night. I hadn't heard the voice in my head for a while, too, and figured that a hallucination was exactly what it had been.

"Come on, spend a little money," Delvin cajoled later as I admired a blue tunic and matching trousers, embroidered in silver around the hems. The outfit cost more than half the money I had and I dithered over it. What if I needed money for other things—such as traveling funds in case I was discovered? My heart eventually won out over my head, urged along with teasing from Delvin. I bought the outfit. The set was sized for a young woman and perfect for my height. The shop's owner smiled as she wrapped it carefully for me in thin paper. The Alliance shops would have shoved it into a recyclable bag and sent me on my way. This world was such a fascinating mix—half technology, half not. I enjoyed seeing both sides of it, actually.

With the good, there was bad, too, as someone attempted to take Delvin's small purse of coins he'd brought with him. As fast as the thief had lifted the purse, I had it back in my hand. It wasn't the first time I'd done something like that—we'd had shady kitchen workers while I was growing up. They didn't last long—it was the one thing Edan actually listened to me on.

"Reah, I might have cast a finding spell, but you saved me the trouble," Delvin pocketed the small bag. I just shrugged at him. Bel put his hand on top of my head and ruffled my hair, declining to comment. At least I wasn't shrinking from his touch, now.

"Come on, Reah, let's get in the hot water." The military station had baths, just as the outpost did. Bel was coaxing me, now.

"But I don't know who'll be there," I complained, my voice petulant.

"Then you'll never have to see these people again," Delvin chuckled.

"And the odds are good that no demons will come bursting through the door," Bel bumped my shoulder.

"Fine," I muttered. Hot water did sound good—it was late now and the trip, coupled with wandering around the city had worn me out. If I fell asleep, maybe Bel or Delvin would keep my head above water so I wouldn't drown.

This pool was three times as large as anything the outpost could offer, and there were people—male and female—already there when we arrived. Delvin was half undressed by the time we reached the bench and the clothing hooks hanging over it. "Reah, you'll be jumping in alone if you don't hurry up," Bel laughed and shrugged out of his shirt. Hurriedly I removed my clothing, hanging it on a hook quickly and grabbing a towel right behind Bel.

Yes, you could tell that Bel and Delvin got plenty of exercise. I'm not sure I'd ever looked that closely at the male form before. Mostly from the back, still—I couldn't bring myself to glance at the lower front. I swallowed a squeal as Delvin put his hands under my arms and dropped me into the water. He and Bel slipped in on either side. I noticed a couple kissing not far away and was determined not to look in that direction again.

Later, when I was about to fall asleep and Delvin and Bel were talking about getting out of the pool, the whispers started. A new party had come in, so of course we turned slightly to see who it might be. "That's the Prince Royal," Bel whispered close to my ear. The Prince wasn't as tall as Delvin, had dark hair and eyes and was dressed in robes of a deep red silk, I think. He was accompanied by four guards and three women. The prince and the women undressed to climb into the water; the guards stood near the edge of the pool watching over their charges.

"Ready to leave?" Bel asked quietly. I'd started shaking the moment he'd identified the Prince. Nodding, I allowed Delvin to help me out of the pool. We pulled our towels around us and walked quietly toward the pegs holding our clothes. I never looked at the Prince or any of his party the whole time I dressed and Bel and Delvin walked beside me on our way out of the bathhouse.

"I have no idea why the Prince Royal would come to the military baths," Bel paced inside Aris' room later. "And he didn't take his eyes off Reah even once after we got out to dress."

"Her hair color is unusual. Perhaps that's what he noticed," Aris attempted to calm Bel. "His wives were with him. That should slow him down a bit."

It was Bel's turn to growl, although he couldn't do half as well as Commander Aris when he was angry. "At least we're leaving in a day and a half. Surely he won't come looking for her."

"He won't." Aris sounded sure of himself. Bel wasn't so sure but didn't disagree with his superior.

"How many did you lose during the attack?" Commander Aris was having lunch with the Prince Royal and the High Commander. Aris sipped his wine before answering the Prince's question.

"Six, with another twenty-seven wounded. Four of those were women," Aris replied.

"You didn't have them fighting as well?" The Prince lifted an eyebrow at Aris.

"Of course not. They were hit by flying glass when a window was shot out. Nothing serious; a few cuts with a little blood and fainting." Aris didn't add that if it hadn't been for Reah's actions and quick thinking, those women could very well be dead.

"Speaking of women, I saw a girl with two of yours at the baths last evening," the Prince lifted a tiny cake and bit into it. Aris knew the Prince had done everything possible to discover who the men were— he shouldn't have recognized Bel or Delvin for any reason. Reah wouldn't have any records—except at the outpost.

"If it's the two I'm thinking of, I'm not surprised they brought a female with them to the baths."

"Yes, but this one was delectable. Beautiful. Fragile. Long, white-blonde hair. You don't see that often, do you? I might be persuaded to pay for information on her." Aris wanted to reach across the table and strangle the Prince as he spoke. Aris held back.

"None of you will come looking for her," he said, power thick in his voice. "You will forget about her and not trouble me about it again. Do you understand?" The Prince and his High Commander nodded their heads like puppets at Aris' command.

"We're having dinner with Commander Aris tonight. You're invited," Bel informed me after we'd seen more of the city on our second day. At times, I saw the Prince lurking around every corner, but eventually pushed those thoughts aside—they were foolish. They only served to frighten me and make me jumpy when I should be enjoying myself.

"Where are we going?" I asked.

"The nicest restaurant in Crown City," Delvin teased. His words made me sigh. If things were different, I might have taken him to the best restaurant on all of Tulgalan. That option was now closed forever.

"What's their specialty?" I asked instead.

"They serve a great lamb rack with a fruit sauce," Bel replied. "Look, there's an outfit you'd look nice in." He steered me toward another clothing store.

~

"Little cook, do you think you might do something like this if we obtained the proper ingredients?" Aris was enjoying the lamb, as were the rest of us. If I had the proper ingredients I could do better, but I didn't say that.

"I think so," I replied. He, Bel, Delvin and I sat around a small, square table at Rodu's of Crown City. Aris wore his dress uniform, as did Bel and Delvin. I'd unwrapped my new blue outfit and worn it, braiding my hair more intricately than I normally did. I had no jewelry or I'd have worn that, too.

"Did you enjoy your trip, Reah?" Aris went on, smiling at me.

"Yes. I saw too many things I wanted to buy. I'll save more for next time."

"Next time will be in six moon-turns. Just so you'll be warned," Bel reached over and lifted the roll I hadn't eaten. He was welcome to it. The bread wasn't very good, in my opinion. The cheeses they'd brought out at the end of the meal made up for it, however. I was wishing we could get cheeses like that at the outpost. I could prepare all sorts of dishes with those, not least of which was serving them as an appetizer with fresh-cut fruit. We walked out of the restaurant later, and even I couldn't help but notice that Aris, Bel and Delvin formed a ring around me as we walked toward the public transport to return to the military station and our beds.

That night I dreamed. The dream was a good one—a comforting one. I was held against a broad chest while gentle fingers stroked hair back from my forehead. *My love, they cannot take you away. Not ever. Do not fear, my pretty one. You are safe.* I slept a dreamless sleep after that.

The women who'd come with us were laughing, talking and stowing away many bags of purchases as they boarded the transports to return to the outpost. When all passengers were settled in, Delvin right next to me just as before, we drove away from Crown City, heading toward the desert.

Perhaps we'd traveled for two clicks, more or less, while the sun beat down upon our vehicles and we saw nothing growing in the desert except the occasional succulent plant. I imagined that there were stinging insects and snakes in abundance and had no desire to find these things out for myself. The transports were cooled with solar power and we were comfortable as we made our way along. I was drifting off to sleep when we were hit. The first two transports didn't survive the blasts—all aboard were killed immediately. Our transport was tossed into the air and landed hard on its side, knocking all of us around, even though we were strapped tightly into our seats. Most of the windows shattered as our transport slid for several ticks on its side before coming to a complete stop. The six women on the transport with us were screaming or crying. At least it meant they still lived.

Unbuckling my harness as quickly as I could, I climbed out of Delvin's way as he lowered himself to the opposite side of the transport, which now lay on the ground. Bel, Aris and the other Rangers were all getting out of their seats as well. Hish was holding his hands up and I saw light form around him—I learned later that he was placing a shield. It was a good thing, too, as another explosive landed near us. We might have been destroyed in the second attack without Hish's quick thinking.

Commander Aris did something with his hands, blowing the front windows out of the transport before striding purposely out of it—as if that were his normal way of exiting any vehicle. The Rangers followed him, except for Hish, who was still holding a shield around us. I went to the women to see if any of them needed assistance. A rudimentary knowledge of medical aid was all I had, thanks to my military training, but a few cuts, bruises and scrapes were all that needed immediate attention. A medkit was supplied on every transport, so I grabbed it and treated what I could—washing out the deepest cuts first and then wrapping them to stop the bleeding. I heard additional blasts outside while I worked and hoped our Wizard contingent was safe. I didn't know what we could do without them, stuck as we were in the middle of the desert, halfway between Crown City and the outpost.

"Reah, do you know how to fire a weapon?" That was Commander Aris' question to me as I finished the last of my patch jobs—a couple of the officers had come to me after I'd treated the women. They'd gone without treatment, waiting for the women to go first. Altogether, there were nineteen of us aboard the third transport and Aris, when he'd returned with the others, announced that our communication devices had been blocked somehow, rendering them useless.

I was too frightened to go outside and see the damage done to the other transports. One of our officers had peeked out and come back inside, shaking his head. Forty-one others, dead in an ambush. Our driver, whose head I'd wrapped, looked to have a concussion but I didn't want to mention it and upset him more than he already was.

"Yes, Commander, I know how to fire a weapon," I whispered my answer while packing unused supplies inside the medkit. Who knew if we'd need it again?

"We have enough weapons for all aboard, but the other women don't have any skill. The Rangers and I will carry two weapons each in case they're needed. We should get away from here as quickly as possible. We'll have the women carry water and foodpacks. The rest of us will take what we can."

Aris' golden-brown eyes were concerned and I almost reached out to touch his face. Almost. I held back. I'd never had the urge to touch any man before and it frightened me that the idea had come now. It wouldn't have gone unnoticed, either; everyone inside the overturned transport was looking to our Commander for direction. Commander Aris had us drink from the water tank aboard the transport before we left it behind. We loaded as much water and as many foodpacks as we could carry into the backpacks stowed inside the emergency supply cabinet. The medkit went into my backpack.

I had a ranos rifle slung over my shoulder as we made our way into the blazing heat of the desert. The blasted hulks of the first two transports were left behind when we walked away. There were two more clicks until sundown and we were walking in as direct a line toward the outpost as we could, Aris leading, Bel and Delvin coming behind the rest of us. I was positioned in the middle, walking next to the women. All of them seemed weary already.

I will likely never know how Aris found the outcropping of rock where he stopped us for the night. I had become more and more frightened as we walked through blistering heat, worried that we'd be spending our night on the sand of the desert with nothing surrounding us for protection. Aris found the impossible. Perhaps it was tied to his Wizard's ability—I knew now that he had it, just as the Rangers did.

The driver was nearly delirious by the time we stopped, and that was another concern. Would he make it through another trek? It would take us at least two more days to reach the outpost if help didn't come looking for us, first. The women, too, didn't appear to be holding up well. I was used to the heat of the kitchen, but this heat was inescapable and would be followed by a shivering cold during the night.

"Reah, can you stand early watch?" Bel was there this time, asking the necessary question.

"Yes, Ranger Bel." I nodded, just as any good recruit should.

"Take the southeastern side," Bel instructed. That would be the direction from which our help would come—if they came at all. I nodded, allowed the ranos rifle to drop into my hands and went off to do my duty.

Cold seeped into my bones after sundown so I walked back and forth to keep from shivering, my eyes always on the area I was watching. I could see Delvin off to my left and Hish to my right. The other Rangers and Aris were stationed at regular intervals around our small camp. No fires were lit—I wasn't sure if Aris was expecting an attack to come but it certainly felt that way.

Officers were scheduled to relieve us later; they'd eaten first and then slept as well as they could around the boulders Aris found for us. The tall rocks were a blessing, holding the heat and radiating it out to those huddled around them while the rest of us stood watch.

Silence surrounded us for the most part—I heard the occasional skitter of some small animal or other at times but nothing more. When four pinpoints of light appeared in my sight, however, I stopped walking and blinked, making sure I wasn't imagining things. The pinpoints were still there and man-high. Clicking my tongue in the way I'd been taught, I had three Rangers beside me in moments, silently watching what I was seeing. More points of light appeared. Commander Aris came.

"Don't fire recklessly," he ordered. "Aim for the lights on my command and don't miss."

# CHAPTER 6

"Fire." Aris' command came. Sleeping officers had been wakened and now they stood with the rest of us as we shot at our targets. As quickly as one set of lights went out, they were replaced by others. I wanted to shake and shiver, but there was no time and it would have been foolish anyway. Had I ever thought as a recruit for the Alliance that I'd see combat? Even my superiors had said it was unlikely in the extreme, yet here I was, standing on an alien world, shooting at an enemy that defied logic.

Exhaustion set in and still the lights came. I was on automatic—sight a set of lights. Aim. Shoot. Another set of lights—aim and shoot. Perhaps it was a click or two before dawn when Commander Aris told us to stand down—the last of the enemy was finally gone. I was ready to drop where I stood. Wearily I followed the others to the rocks—I no longer felt cold; numbness had taken over instead. A foodpack was shoved into my hand so I sat and ate, not even tasting the mush inside the plastic. The others were doing much the same, eating and then falling asleep where they sat. The officers, fresher than the rest of us, took the daywatch while we rested as long as we could.

*Little love, wake now and eat. We must go on.* The voice inside my mind woke me with gentle words. I almost jerked awake—my sleep had been dreamless and silent until then. "Here," Bel handed another foodpack over—he sat nearby as I rubbed my eyes and accepted the plastic tube of sustenance that he gave me. It was just as tasteless as the other had been. I was hungry, so I emptied it.

Our driver died during the night—we'd been engaged elsewhere so the poor man had likely died alone with no one to tend him. The six women had huddled together beside the boulders when the shooting started, never thinking that their help might have been needed. I could see the guilt in their eyes now—they hadn't realized they might have helped the poor man. As it was, Aris ordered the body left behind—we had no shovels or tools to bury him and no rocks small enough to cover his body. He would be left to the desert scavengers. Hoping that his family never learned the truth of his death and what came after, I shouldered my rifle and my backpack, swinging into the line of trudging people as we made our way into the blinding light and heat of Mandil's desert.

"Demons like the night best, and they certainly don't like the heat," Delvin said beside me after a while. "Commander will call a halt soon." He nodded to two of the women ahead of us; both were walking drunkenly. I nodded at Delvin's assessment—I'd already gotten the two to drink some water while we walked. Heatstroke was a dangerous probability, making me think we could lose more of our party before we reached the outpost. All of us were using the white caps in our emergency backpacks to cover our heads, keeping the sun off as much as we could. The caps shaded our eyes; mine had stopped watering from the brightness long ago—a lack of moisture was likely responsible. I admit I was more tired than I'd ever been when Aris called a rest break. Nothing was available to shade us as we sat on heated sand, drinking a ration of water and lowering our heads.

We were set to guard again once we stopped for the night, but Bel and Commander Aris came to me after only a click had passed. "We think one of the women is dying—this was too much for her," Bel said softly, taking my ranos rifle away. "Can you make her last few hours more comfortable?"

"I can try, but there's not much in the medkit for this sort of thing," I sighed, following the Commander—Bel was taking my place on the perimeter.

"Reah, the killshot is in the kit," Aris informed me quietly. I stopped at his words and he did, too. The killshot was for those who were in a hopeless situation or were dying anyway, with no help or the possibility of getting any. The killshot sent them on their way as painlessly as possible.

"Aris—Commander," I stammered over my slight, "I'm not sure I can do that." My hands trembled at the thought of administering the drug.

"Reah, it will be a mercy. The poor woman is already hallucinating. How much agony is enough before you do what is right?" I gripped my lower lip in my teeth to keep it from trembling. Lowering my head, I nodded at the Commander's words. Perhaps the gods—if there were any—would have mercy for me as well. "Good girl," Commander Aris patted my shoulder and led me toward the dying woman.

It took two clicks of the woman thrashing and moaning before she became extremely feverish and comatose. The time had come—she was suffering and there wasn't anything else we could do for her. I spoke softly to her as I pulled the syringe from the kit. Enough killshot syringes were in the medkit for all of us, if needed. I desperately hoped they weren't needed. This was the limit of my brief medical training—I slipped the needle into her upper arm and pushed the small plunger. It didn't take much—only a minute amount of the medicine would ease the pain and bring the sleep from which she wouldn't wake. I wiped tears away as I placed the used syringe in a box inside the kit. In less than a click, the woman was dead. Two officers came to carry her to the edge of the camp—the other sick one was feverish but still lucid and they were giving her as much water as they could, cooling her down with wet strips of cloth. It was a kindness—I didn't think she would last through the following day.

"Reah, we all have to make terrible decisions at times," Aris brought me a foodpack later as I sat hugging myself and staring out at the darkness. I wasn't hungry, but I might be the next to fall if I didn't eat and drink enough. He handed me a canteen after I consumed my mush, encouraging me to drink as much as I could. I did, shivering as I drank.

"Try to get some sleep—we may need to wake you later to stand guard. Some of the men aren't doing very well either," Commander Aris told me as he stood up and stretched. I blew out a sigh and rested my forehead against my knees. One more day before we could hope to reach the outpost. None had come looking for us, which made me worry about what we'd find when we arrived. *If* we arrived.

I was wakened before daybreak and took over for one of the men. My eyes felt as full of sand as the desert beneath my feet while I stood my watch. Thankfully, no lights came that night.

The remaining sick woman fell after walking two clicks. She began to convulse so I pulled the medkit out of my backpack and went to her. Aris ordered the others away from us while he watched me give the second dose of the killshot. It didn't take long—she was gone in less than half a click. At least she died peacefully—the convulsions had stopped quickly.

I wondered if we would leave any other bodies behind as I trudged along afterward. The four other women were beyond weariness now, as were several of the men. Aris and the Rangers must have been cut from a tougher cloth—they strode along resolutely. I supposed they all walked miles in the heat on a regular basis. Our skin was reddened now; every bit of exposed flesh was burned. Our caps kept our faces shaded, but our hands and necks were a deep red.

I learned that Hish had kept us from burning the first two days with one of his shields, but he was exhausted now, just as the rest of us were and unable to use his ability. I hoped the outpost physicians were waiting on us to arrive with plenty of burn relief medication on hand.

One of the officers dropped four clicks later, so Aris and I did our duty again, leaving his body behind after a short break. I was beginning to stagger at times, and in my more lucid moments, I was frightened that I'd be left behind like the others. Those thoughts wandered through my mind and at first I believed I was hallucinating when an image shimmered before my eyes.

*Only a little farther—you can make it, love,* came the voice. Truly a hallucination, I knew. My mind was telling me what it wished to hear. I struggled to keep up with the others.

"Drink the water you have left and drop everything you're carrying except your weapons—the outpost is in front of us," Aris' voice sounded as dry as the sand beneath our feet as he walked down the line. Fifteen of us had made it this far, and it was a miracle that this many had survived. We did as Aris instructed, emptying our canteens and leaving our backpacks behind. It took the better part of a click to reach the outer walls of the post, but we did it. Troops waited inside the gate and they were helping us as quickly as they could. At least half were carried to the hospital on stretchers. The physicians were there, waiting with water, burn relief and other medicines. Our faces were washed with cool cloths, clothing was removed and many of us were slathered in the gel made from the cooling plant.

"Commander, we were too afraid to venture out—we have been attacked every night for the past four nights," the captain raked fingers through his hair as he paced. "And since we could not contact you, we were worried that everyone had perished."

"You did right," Aris sipping the juice he'd been given while the physician worked on blistered skin. "Physician, are the others going to make it?"

"Your Rangers for sure. Most of the officers. We may lose one of the women—she is not responding well."

"Which one?" Aris almost came out of his chair.

"The tall, red-haired one," the physician replied, causing Aris to relax. "I hear you lost two women and two men in the desert. An amazing feat—only losing four. I'd have guessed at least half would go down before you walked the distance."

"I too, am surprised," Aris muttered.

"Now, you will rest or I will administer a sedative," the physician said, sending Aris to his bed for some much-needed sleep.

~

An eight-day. That's how long the physicians insisted I rest before taking up my duties. Others got more time than that to recover. Another of the women died, too, despite the physician's best efforts.

"It happens, at times—they stop fighting to live," the oldest physician—the one who'd treated me for the sickness before—informed me as he examined my burns. My fair skin would show signs of the sunburn for a long time, and I was miserable while it was healing. When I saw Hish in passing on my way to work in the kitchens again, I thanked him for the shields he'd supplied. He smiled and nodded his acceptance. I made the best midday meal I could for everyone when I went back to work. Even Stef seemed happy to see me.

~

"The High Commander is coming," Widnal announced three days later.

"I hope he makes it," I slapped a hand over my mouth after the words left it. Too late; by that time, I'd already spoken my mind.

"I am in complete agreement," Widnal nodded at me as we put vegetables on to cook. We hadn't seen any of the locals since the fifteen of us walked out of the desert, and Widnal told me it had been longer than that since they'd come. We had no fresh vegetables or fruits—relying solely now on what was in the freezers. The High Commander was coming with the food shipments from Crown City. The Rangers had gone out again—twice I think, since we'd gotten back. They didn't get as much rest as the others, including me. I felt guilty about that. Aris drove his Rangers harder than anyone else at the post.

We hadn't been attacked again by the demons, but it was whispered that some of the villagers had thrown in their lot with the monsters in order to save their lives. I just shook my head—you didn't throw in your lot with something that would likely eat or turn you before everything was done. I remembered, too, walking past piles of dark dust after the night of our attack in the desert. Some of those piles were deeper than others, as if many of the creatures had died in the same place after we'd shot them with our ranos rifles. No humanoid bodies were found among them.

The outpost underwent a concentrated campaign of cleaning—we barely had three days before the High Commander was supposed to come. The kitchens were in fine shape but the pink wing and the barracks had to meet the Commander's expectations. I didn't have any part of that, but Stef and Nedis were right in the middle of it. Widnal grinned at their moaning whenever they weren't looking. All was made ready, having passed the Commander's inspection on the day the High Commander was to arrive. We all waited. The kitchen had produced a good meal for our visitors but the time for their arrival came and went. Darkness was falling and we held our breath. Commander Aris, Bel and two captains walked into the kitchen as I was putting uneaten food away.

"Reah, come with us," Bel said. Struggling to hide my concern, I removed my apron and followed them to Aris' office. "This should fit," Bel handed a uniform to me. The shirt and pants were in the regulation colors of the desert—just as theirs was. The uniform had been sewn to fit me. It looked as if they'd planned this.

"We have to search for the High Commander and his officers," Commander Aris said after I'd returned from his private bath wearing the uniform and boots they'd given me. "Reah, it didn't get past us that you didn't miss when you fired your rifle while we were under attack in the desert. We won't ask questions, we're just happy to have someone so accurate with her shots. We'll take two of our armored transports—Hish is fresh and can provide shields for a while. I expect you to help watch on our way to retrieve the High Commander. You'll let us know if you see anything."

That was a command, so I nodded at his words. I followed the others from Commander Aris' office and we picked up charged ranos rifles, a backpack filled with foodpacks and water before climbing into the armored transports. The Rangers were split between both vehicles; I saw that right away. I rode with Commander Aris while Hish, Bel and Delvin climbed into the other transport.

The window through which I kept watch was bullet and fireproof. Wondering how strong a blast it could sustain without shattering, I kept careful watch as we drove along, the second transport right behind us and in continuous communication. Commander Aris repeatedly attempted to get the High Commander and his convoy to reply to his communications. Only silence met his queries.

"Commander," I hissed—I'd seen movement from my window. Aris heard and was beside me quickly.

"They're out there," he agreed, peering through my window. I'd seen tiny lights, just as before. It must have been the reflection of the moonlight in their eyes—I was afraid to assign any other explanation to it. "Reah," Aris whispered, "only the wizards and I can see what you see. I am still attempting to puzzle that out. In the meantime, don't discuss this with anyone other than the Rangers or me." His breath stirred the hair at my temple—I had it braided tightly otherwise. I nodded at his instructions. How could I see what only the wizards saw? I didn't have a drop of talent—nobody on Tulgalan did.

We drove on for a while, though the lights seemed to be following us. We came upon the transports that had been hauling the High Commander and his escort. Most were dead; we discovered that quickly after climbing out of our vehicles. The High Commander was severely wounded and what was left of his troops formed a ring around him, all equipped with ranos rifles. Altogether, seven of what had once been fifty-six were alive, while no working communication remained.

"Reah, do what you can," Bel and Delvin hauled the High

Commander into our transport so I pulled out the medkit. The High Commander had a concussion and the heat of the day hadn't done him any good. I convinced him to take some of the painkill and then gave him as much water as he would willingly drink.

"Just rest, we'll take care of this," I patted his shoulder. Delvin had stepped inside the transport, motioning me outside. It looked as if we were going to be attacked again.

If Hish hadn't saved some of his strength, I don't think we would have made it out of there alive. As it was, I ran my ranos rifle out of power and Aris slapped another weapon in my hands quickly. The non-wizard officers the High Commander had brought with him were firing blind—I discovered that quickly. They couldn't see what the rest of us were seeing. They were spaced out so they'd be near a wizard. Explosives burst all around us for at least the first click. I think Hish was exhausted when the explosives finally stopped coming and we began to shoot at the approaching enemy. I have no idea how many we killed. Dawn was breaking when Commander Aris ordered us to stand down.

"They emptied both our other outposts," Aris grumbled angrily as we piled into the two transports. I was just as exhausted as the rest of them and hoping that we wouldn't be attacked on the way home— Hish didn't have anything left to give and none of the other Wizards seemed to have the shielding talent.

"Reah, are you all right?" I was wedged into my seat, making room for two others on a bench built to hold only two. Bel had leaned over the seat in front of me to ask.

"I'm good," I mumbled, half asleep.

*Close your eyes and sleep, love.* Those words felt like the softest of touches against my mind and I did close my eyes. I didn't remember another thing until the transport stopped and someone unbuckled my harness.

"How much food do we have left?" That was Commander Aris' first question to me as I stood in front of him and the High Commander two days later. The physicians had only let the High Commander up that morning, and he was grumpy as a bear wakened in winter.

"Perhaps two eight-days, if we stretch it. Another eight-day with the foodpacks." I'd gone looking at exactly that the day after we'd rescued the High Commander. Three eight-days we could survive, feeding the entire outpost. The supplies the High Commander brought with him were destroyed in the attack; there wasn't room for it inside the two transports we'd taken even if there'd been anything to bring back.

"Then we leave in two days. I don't care if we're attacked on the ride to Crown City—we'll be attacked anyway. I'd rather die trying to get back to civilization." The High Commander's words made me realize that he didn't like where he was. Not even a little.

I watched Aris' face. I think that he'd made the suggestion— perhaps long ago, to move the troops. With this blusterer for a High Commander, I think Aris' words had fallen on uncaring ears until now.

"Reah, have your staff pull out all the foodpacks and divide them evenly between all the transports," Commander Aris told me. "We have thirty vehicles and we'll have to use all of them to move everyone out. Have Widnal go to the pink wing and inform the women that they can only take what they're wearing the day we leave. I suggest it be something serviceable with appropriate shoes in case we end up walking through the desert again."

"I will, Commander Aris." I nodded to him before stepping out of his office.

~

"They're not going to like it, but orders are orders," Widnal told me later when I passed the Commander's words along to him. He dried his hands on a towel and went to inform the women.

The next day and a half bore witness to a great deal of activity. Transports were checked and then checked again to make sure they would survive the trek to Crown City. It hadn't escaped my notice either that the attacks had come nearly halfway between Crown City and the outpost.

"Bel, how many do you think we killed—out in the desert, I mean," I asked him quietly during our midday meal on the day before we were to leave. He'd wandered into the kitchen and sat down to eat with the other kitchen workers.

"Aris thinks we killed a thousand, perhaps more," Bel cut into the fish we'd served for the midday meal. The precious stream-trout had been in the freezer, and I'd hoped to serve it for a special occasion. Now it was lunch—I couldn't bear to let it go to waste when we left.

"How many were in the other outposts?" I was nearly afraid to hear the answer.

"You're asking the question that has been the main topic of discussion inside the Commander's office of late," Bel answered. "This fish is exceptional, Reah. Someday, you'll have to tell me how you learned to cook as you do."

"That will be a tale for a day long in coming," I muttered. At times, I still wondered if it were his voice that I occasionally heard inside my head. Yes, I liked Bel but more and more I hoped that the voice was real and not his.

"Reah," Bel reached over and patted my hand, "we'll either make it or we won't. They think to starve us and then attack. They won't expect us to leave this quickly. I'm hoping we get past them."

"Then I'll hope, too." Turning back to my fish, I didn't tell Bel that my hope was far outweighed by my fear.

"Reah, you'll come with me and Bel this time," Delvin hustled me onto the transport with him. He handed me a rifle once we were inside—I noticed that none of the High Commander's troops were on the transport with us. Bel told me earlier that he had my uniform and boots and asked me to dress in light-colored trousers and a tunic with the sturdiest shoes I had. I did as he asked. Somehow, although the

High Commander and his men had seen me the night we'd rescued them, Bel and Aris didn't want me to come to their notice again. I did my best to stay away from all of them.

Our transport jerked as we began to move a half click later. "Keep your hopes alive," Delvin whispered as we jostled in our seats while going through the gate and leaving the outpost behind.

"Where will we stay—in Crown City?" I asked, quelling the uneasiness settling in my stomach.

"At the military station. It's quite large and we'll have our own section, most like," Delvin answered. That made me nod. What was I going to do, though? Were the women going to have their own wing, as they did at the outpost, or would they be scattered throughout Crown City, as they probably were before? And would we have our own kitchen or would there be a centralized mess where all the troops ate? Not only were we facing death, driving through a desert that had been taken over by the enemy, but my place upon this world had grown increasingly perilous. Too many questions and I'd be waiting for judgment in the Prince Royal's prison.

"Re, stop worrying," Delvin bumped my shoulder with his. I just shook my head. Telling me to stop worrying was like telling a baby not to ever be hungry. It was something that came, whether you wanted it or not.

We passed the point where the High Commander had been attacked. My fear rose several notches higher—this was the section where the attack was likely to come. We passed the spot where we'd first been attacked. My mouth was dry and remained so for another click. An attack hadn't come. I was attempting to loosen the knots forming in my neck and shoulders. Then, when the high walls of Crown City appeared in the distance, I did my best to breathe deeply for the first time since we'd departed. Some of the others, too, had been holding their breath. Did we think to arrive unscathed? If any of us did, those hopes were dashed ten ticks before we reached the gates of Crown City.

The last six transports in our convoy were hit, exploding into debris that rained around us. The vehicle in which I rode was near the center and every driver who still lived hit the accelerator, rushing toward Crown City. What do you do when an enemy you cannot see tosses explosives at you from far away? We had no cannon and apparently no way to fire it at a hidden target anyway. Is that what they did? Hide, somehow, so we couldn't hit them back? More transports exploded behind us. The gates were closer but still not close enough. Terrified, I was tempted to fling off my harness and leap out the door of the transport. I have no idea what good that might do —if anything was hit anywhere nearby, I'd still be just as dead.

Crown City was sending out answering fire, but surely they were firing blind, just as the non-wizard troops did during the attacks at night. An explosion occurred to our left, sending fountains of sand flying into the sky. Clumps of sand and desert rock slammed against the windows of our transport, causing all of us to duck. Two women were on board the transport with us, and they were crying. Our driver pushed the vehicle to its highest speed. We were running evenly with two other transports, all racing toward the gate and the perception of safety.

"The Prince has his own wizards," Delvin shouted next to me as another explosion came and we ducked instinctively. "They protect what's inside the walls. If we make it, we'll be safe." By that time, I was so frightened I had no idea if I might conjure faith in any wizard to fight this. I'd never seen explosions such as these, before. Someone was quite determined to kill all of us.

"The first transports are through the gate," Bel stood at the front of our vehicle and made the announcement. He'd been in contact with Commander Aris and the High Commander—their transport had been second in line and most likely they were safe, now. The transport in front of us was hit, causing our driver to swerve and our transport to lurch dangerously to avoid the hole in the ground. We were hit by the debris anyway and Bel almost lost his footing, holding onto the metal pole at the front directly behind the driver. The gate was closer now, but still a lifetime away. I couldn't even spare a thought for the lives lost already—I wanted to weep for them and perhaps for myself, too—I and the ones seated around me might be next. Two more transports were hit before we reached the gate; some of our passengers cheered when we drove inside, steering out of the way immediately to allow any behind us to come inside as swiftly as possible. Delvin had me unbuckled and hauled out of the transport in very little time, following Bel, who had some destination in mind.

Delvin carried me under his arm, like a bag of vegetables. Aris was standing next to a building as the High Commander climbed into a waiting vehicle and drove away. Delvin skidded to a halt beside Aris. If I'd ever though it before, it was confirmed now. Aris jerked me away from Delvin and held me so tightly against him I could barely breathe. He was murmuring words into my hair that I didn't understand. My face was buried against his shoulder and I shuddered before wrapping my arms around his neck and holding on as if my life depended on it.

"Reah, walk with me and hold your head up," Aris pulled me along beside him. We didn't touch while we walked—other transports were waiting to take us to the military station. Again, I rode beside Delvin; it was perhaps one of the longest journeys of my life—sitting with him —wondering how my life had made yet another turn. What did this mean? I trembled again—delayed shock, I'm sure.

"Delvin, how many are gone?" I wanted to cry and couldn't. Not here—it was a sign of weakness.

"Reah, the numbers will be given to us," Delvin pulled my head against his shoulder and kissed my temple. "Don't fret, we'll be there soon."

But what was I supposed to do when we arrived? I suddenly had no purpose. There I was, trapped on an alien world, cut off from everything I'd ever known in my short life after nearly being killed on at least three occasions. The trembling became worse.

"Aris, we'll need a physician," Delvin said quietly. Aris and Bel sat in the seat in front of us, directly behind the driver.

"No," Aris said flatly. "Bring her. I'll take care of this."

Delvin held me up most of the way to our new quarters; Aris and Bel strode determinedly ahead of us while we walked a lengthy corridor. I couldn't stop shaking; it was getting worse. Physicians had met some of the others, but Aris had waved them off, settling for asking an officer who met us to take us to our assigned barracks. My head hurt, my vision blurred and I was having trouble keeping myself upright and walking. I couldn't have told you until later what that corridor or the room we were led to looked like; I was lost in a narrowing world of fear and misery.

"This is your new office, Commander Aris," the officer told him, his voice sounding muffled. "Your suite is next door. The officers' quarters are farther down this corridor."

Aris said something to him and the man left. "Reah," Aris said. Bel and Delvin left—I have no idea where they went. Aris shut the door of his office behind him and took my arm. "There is no need to be frightened," Aris told me, sitting me down at the chair behind his new desk. If he hadn't set me down, I would have fallen when the blue giant appeared from nowhere. Strange, I know, that the name of the blue giant's race came to me while I sat there staring up at him. Most people lived their entire lives without ever seeing one of the benign blue Larentii. He knelt before me.

"Little one," the Larentii said, "you are experiencing shock. I will place a healing sleep and you will wake later in much better circumstances. You will not speak of me with anyone except the Commander, here." Large blue fingers reached out to touch my forehead, sending me into darkness.

I woke alone later, with no clock or window to tell me what time it was. The room was small, much like the one I'd had when we'd visited Crown City before. That short trip now seemed a lifetime ago. I was dressed in a rather large nightshirt to sleep, wondered how that had happened and stretched lazily in the narrow bed I'd been left on to rest.

Had a Larentii truly been here? What had he done to make me sleep like that? Precious little information was available on that race; all were tall and blue-skinned, with some variation of blond hair and blue eyes. Rumor had it that they fed directly from an energy source but I didn't know whether to believe that or not.

I slid out of bed and got a bath in the connecting bathroom—I wasn't supposed to have that—only the officers got separate bathing facilities. Nevertheless, I made use of it, finding soap and other toiletries already in the bathroom. I dressed, too, after finding three outfits of suitable clothing inside the small closet. A knock came on the door just as I was putting my shoes on. Those were the same shoes I'd worn away from the outpost; they were the only ones I had at the moment.

Bel stood outside the door when I answered. "Good, I was afraid I'd have to get you up and around," he grinned. "Feeling better?"

"Yes. Much," I replied.

"Good. Commander Aris wishes to speak with you," he motioned me to follow. We walked down a narrow corridor before coming to the Commander's new office. I did my best to get my bearings as we walked along. The halls were painted white, else it would be quite dark there—lights were spaced far apart in the ceiling. The floors were a dark, reddish-brown tile that echoed with our footsteps. Bel knocked on Aris' door—his nameplate was already there, I noticed.

"Come," I heard Aris say. We walked in, closing the door behind us.

"Reah, sit," Aris nodded toward the standard chair in front of his desk. I sat; Bel remained standing. "Reah," Aris sighed, studying my face carefully, "You know that we cannot have a relationship as long as you are a subordinate." That was true in the Alliance as well. I nodded my head, feeling cold, suddenly.

"Reah, don't look like that. I hope this conflict we are experiencing will be over soon. As quickly as that happens, I will be free to court you. Please be patient and wait for me. That is what I ask. Meanwhile, I have made arrangements to place you with my Rangers. The problem with this is that the Prince Royal doesn't allow women to serve. Because of this, we must cut your hair, and then Bel and I will make you appear to the others as a young male recruit attached to the Rangers. You will run errands for us and deliver messages. You will also go out with Bel and the others on scouting trips into the desert. Do you understand? We need your marksman's abilities, and we cannot pass up this opportunity. You will be known as recruit Re Nilvas from this point forward. Answer to that name and no other. Is that clear?"

"Yes, Commander." I lowered my eyes. My situation had taken another, unexpected turn. I felt like weeping—they were going to cut my hair. I'd gotten special permission from the Alliance to keep it long during my training. I'd had to sign a paper, promising to keep it braided and out of the way, else it would be ordered cut. I'd carefully followed those instructions. Now it would be whacked off and there was nothing I could do about it.

"Re, do not show me that pouting lip again," Aris' voice was stern and held a warning. I couldn't give myself away as a female. He wouldn't tolerate it and it would put me in danger of discovery. I nodded again and schooled my face. "Bel," Aris said. I still wasn't looking at him. If this kept up, I didn't know if he had any hopes of a relationship after our ordeal with the enemy was over. At the moment, I had no idea how long that might take.

Bel opened the door and called out to someone. A man came in with shears and a comb in his hand. My hands were clasped tightly in my lap as he proceeded to cut my hair, initially snipping right through the top of my braid and setting the length on the edge of Aris' desk. If Aris hadn't warned me before, I might have been sniffling like a baby when the barber did that. He went on to cut the rest of my hair—just as short as the other Rangers wore theirs. I was light-headed when he finished—I couldn't remember ever having short hair. Bel dismissed the barber, walking out of Aris' office with him. Perhaps he would deliver a warning of some kind—I didn't know.

"Re, it will grow back." I hugged myself and didn't lift my eyes to look at Aris. "Your uniform is inside the bathroom in the corner," Aris went on. "Get dressed and meet Bel in the hallway. He will assign your duties. I have your paperwork in my files. Do not disappoint me and do not give yourself away. Much depends on this. I have three more uniforms ordered for you—they should be delivered tomorrow. The room you woke in is yours, as an attachment to my Wizard Division. You know how to behave as a recruit."

I nodded at Aris' words, still refusing to look at him as he rose from his desk and walked toward the door. He didn't come near me and I didn't expect it, now. Aris was too good at his job to give himself away. I was under his command and that was how it would stay.

Bel was waiting for me and took me to the mess hall attached to our section. Widnal was there, serving breakfast. I wanted to hug him —until that moment I didn't know that he'd survived. He didn't recognize me—whatever Aris and Bel had done was working. Bel pinched my elbow as we picked up our trays of food. Widnal had done his best—the breakfast was probably better than the rest of the station was getting. I ate my meal without speaking to Bel even once, keeping my head down and doing my best to consume what suddenly tasted like ash.

"This is my office—your desk is in that corner," Bel informed me later. His office was next to Aris' and my desk was tiny and crowded into Bel's space. It had a wooden chair placed behind it and writing utensils in a small container on the corner. Three drawers held paper and other supplies.

"Here's a map of the station," Bel handed a large paper over. It held a drawing of the station with the buildings and such represented by square and rectangular lines, each neatly labeled. I studied the map briefly. "I'll need a message carried to the Station Commander as soon as I write it," Bel sighed. I got the feeling he didn't like writing messages. He ended up dictating the message, I wrote it down, making a correction here and there, let him read the finished note and upon getting his approval, sealed it inside an envelope and dutifully carried it to the station Commander's office.

His assistant was there to receive it, saying he'd deliver it right away, so I returned to Bel's office. Aris' accounts were waiting for me, too, and I was glad I had experience with that. I'd done accounts for Desh's number two and for the Governor of the Realm on Tulgalan when I worked in his kitchen. Figures were totaled and entered, with a copy made for the station Commander's records. Bel said I could deliver those the following day.

I also wrote down Bel's account of the move from the outpost to Crown City after the midday meal. I learned then that nineteen of the thirty transports had perished, and all inside were dead. Stef was one of those, I saw, as a list of the dead was handed to me. "We'll work on condolence letters in the next few days," Bel muttered. I nodded, doing my best to hold tears back over Stef's death, as well as some of the others I found on the lists.

Wrung out might have described me after my first day as a recruit assigned to Bel and the others. I knew what I was doing in a kitchen. This was a new experience and the names I recognized on the lists of the dead didn't make things easier. Bel's "Can you find your way to the mess hall," was somewhat curt. What was I to expect? I was just another low-level recruit, now. Aris' promise to court me after this was over was having less and less appeal as the day wore on. I suppose I should be grateful—it wasn't likely that I'd be hauled in front of the Prince Royal, now, since nobody recognized me.

I wondered again what it was that Aris and Bel had done. I was no longer female in anyone's eyes. I was a young man and a small one. Nobody looked at me except with contempt or ridicule. I got three insults from others as I made my way into the low-rankers' mess. Bel, Aris and the others were likely having their meal (and a better one) served elsewhere.

The sliced fowl was dry, there was no sauce with it and the vegetables were soggy and overcooked. The bread I didn't even touch —it was an insult to the flour it had been made from.

"Not hungry?" I slid my tray into a slot for the kitchen help to dump and wash. I looked up at the one who'd spoken.

"Not today." I wanted to sigh, but that might be a giveaway, too. He was taller, of course—they all were. This one stood at least seven handwidths above my head, had brown hair, muddy brown eyes and a crooked smile.

"New?" he asked.

"First day," I nodded.

"We're all going to a bar outside the station tonight. A few others are new, too," he grinned. "I'm Nods," he held out his hand.

"Nods, this wouldn't be a hazing, now would it?" I took his hand. I'd seen the same thing after my Alliance military training had been completed.

"Now why would I do something like that?" He feigned innocence, tapping his chest with a finger.

"Because it was done to you," I muttered, going around him. He caught my arm.

"If you don't go, you'll be outcast. Here at the station, that's a bad thing."

"Of course it is," I said, staring at the fingers wrapped around my upper arm. If he knew how quickly I could get past his guard and toss him to the floor, he wouldn't hold onto me like that.

"Show up or there'll be worse for you later," he threatened, refusing to let go of my arm. Everyone else chose to ignore our exchange.

"Fine," I grumbled, jerking my arm away from him. "Which bar and where?" I got directions—it was a place not far from the station, just outside the eastern gate. We were scheduled to be there in two clicks. I went back to my room feeling shaky. Why couldn't my life be stress-free for even one day?

"What do you think they'll do?" A recruit, whose face bore acne scars, asked as I walked into the designated bar at the appointed time. I looked up at the ceiling—there was cloth rippling overhead.

"My guess is they'll drop an unsavory substance on our heads," I leveled a gaze at my fellow recruit. "That's why I wore my worst clothing." I did wear the worst outfit I'd found inside the closet—it was a loose-woven tunic and trousers in an ugly orange. I never wore that color if I could help it. The recruit I spoke with had worn his uniform. If my guess was correct, he might never be able to wear it again.

"Can you get by on only a click or two of sleep?" I asked him. "I'm Re, by the way." I held out my hand.

"Dane," he took my hand and nodded.

"Ever work in a kitchen, Dane?"

"Just my mother's."

"Know how to clean?"

"Yes."

"Good. When they dump the excrement on our heads, we'll make sure the bar is clean afterward. The rest will run like hares away from here."

His eyes were wide as he stared at me and he swallowed nervously before nodding.

Nods showed up a few ticks later, three friends and a pack of new recruits at his back. He left all of us in the middle of the floor while he and his followers went to make an announcement from the bar. They stood well away from the cloth that covered part of the ceiling over our heads and laughed when the contents in barrels above were dumped all over us.

"That's to remind you of what you are," Nods had a high giggle as he laughed. "You're all shit. Don't forget it." He and his friends walked out the back way while the bartender and barmaid gave him dirty looks. Probably wasn't the first time this had happened. Wiping as much of the smelly mess off as I could, I removed my orange tunic, revealing the yellow undershirt I wore. Pulling Dane with me while the others deserted the bar, I went to offer our services to the bartender.

Cleaning the bar took five clicks and cut deeply into our sleep time, but we got the entire mess cleaned up. The owner had taken a small payment from Nods to do this sort of thing, expecting his employees to clean up the mess. That night they had two recruits working alongside them, making sure the bar was presentable for business the following day. Rags and disinfectant were used to mop the floor after the last of the mess had been lifted and tossed into barrels. Dane and the bartender carried those out while the barmaid and I got down on our knees to scrub. Most likely the bar was cleaner when we left than it had been when we arrived.

I was thankful I had a shower in my quarters when I got back. Tossing my clothing into an old cloth bag that could be tied up and thrown away, I scrubbed myself in the shower four times, I think, just to make sure I got every bit of the mess and the stink off me. I carried the bag of ruined clothing to the communal throw-away and hefted it over the side afterward. It took some effort; the bin was taller than I was.

"Late night?" Bel carried a cup of tea into his office the next morning. He looked fresh—I didn't. Dark circles showed up quite well below my eyes. I didn't say anything. This was his military after all, not mine. I never curse or I might have been persuaded to that morning. Dane most likely was feeling the same way.

Bel and I wrote condolence notes. Then went to midday meal and then wrote more notes afterward, folding them carefully and sealing them inside envelopes with wax and a military seal. It was a different experience, working with paper instead of a comp-vid. How did they survive like this?

"Sleep late tomorrow," Bel told me at the end of the workday. "We'll be going out tomorrow night, right at sundown. Drink plenty of water and eat as much as you can between now and then." He dismissed me without saying exactly what we were going to do when we went out. I sighed as I walked out of his office, heading toward the mess hall. I wondered if I'd meet up with Nods again and hoped I wouldn't. Thought about Dane and found myself hoping I'd see him again. He hadn't shirked his duty the night before, cleaning just as hard as the rest of us. Sadly, his uniform was a total loss—he'd discarded the jacket before he ever lifted a rag to clean.

~

"Word has it that our girl went through the hazing last night with the other new recruits," Bel sat on Aris' guest chair and crossed his legs comfortably.

"How did that go?" Aris frowned as he went over reports, barely sparing a glance at Bel.

"Re and one other recruit stayed behind to help clean up the shit afterward," Bel replied. "She was half asleep when she came to work this morning."

"If it happens again, we'll provide payback," Aris muttered, signing his name after approving a report.

"They should know better than to pick on the recruits assigned to the wizards," Bel grinned.

~

"Re." Dane nodded to me as he sat across from me at the table. Two others came, sitting next to Dane.

"You should have told us you were staying to help clean up last night—we would have helped," one of them said to Dane. Dane just shrugged and tore his roll open to butter it.

"Re, this is Gin and this is Dory," Dane introduced me to his friends. I nodded to them. Gin had blond hair and brown eyes. His blond hair was cut quite short and stood almost straight up. He was also shorter than Dane by about a hand. Dory had black hair and nearly black eyes, was only a hand taller than I was and had a thin build. It seems the Mandil Crown had no height restrictions, just like the Alliance, although the Alliance often sent the smaller ones home during their initial training; they couldn't compete with the others. My completion of basic training was a testament to my quickness, strength and determination. I'd been allowed to stay, although most of my instructors had shaken their heads the first time they'd seen me.

"Look, it's the smallest pile of shit." Nods walked by carrying his tray, followed by three others. How juvenile could you get? They resembled the bullies I'd known from my dayschool classes. These hadn't grown up—they'd just gotten older. I didn't look at them past the initial insult—it was better that way. Keep your head down. Don't seek revenge. It never worked out if you did. None of my companions said anything either, and I think Nods knew if he started something he'd be facing the mess officer on duty. I had a feeling he was watching anyway. Nods and his followers moved on.

"You think they'll hit us again?" Gin's voice held worry.

"Probably." Dane held no hope that we'd escape the bullying. We were the smallest ones at the gathering last evening. The others were all bigger and might be convinced to organize and fight back. Dane and his friends didn't have enough in the way of strength or support.

Lendill Schaff sat across the table from Norian Keef, Director of the ASD—Alliance Security Detail. Lendill was Norian's second-in-command. "Here are the records. I pulled everything I could find, including her military papers." Lendill handed the comp-vid to Norian. Lendill had dark hair and eyes, was considered quite handsome and occasionally wished it weren't that way. He had attention at times he had no desire to have. Norian wasn't quite as handsome, with brown hair and eyes, but Norian wasn't only the Director of the ASD. He was heir to Ildevar Wyyld, founding member of the Alliance and one of the mates to the Queen of Le-Ath Veronis. The fact that he was also a shapeshifter was known only to a very few. Norian kept that information hidden from nearly everyone. Lendill knew—that knowledge had been given only recently.

Norian skipped most of the information on the comp-vid, finally coming to what he wanted. "Here it is—they *ranked* her because of her height."

"Ranked?" Lendill was unfamiliar with the term.

"Put more on her than the other recruits—it's a way of sending undesirables home if the officers don't think they're good enough to stay. Usually those don't last when they're loaded with extra weight on marches or given additional duties. Reah Desh was carrying three times the load the others carried and still made it." Norian made a face as he studied the other records—Reah's medical records in particular. "Did you see this? All the broken bones and accidents she had under the age of fifteen?"

"I did. Director, I don't think those were accidents. I'm having her brother investigated—the one who supervised her after the age of eight. Edan Desh is his name."

"We'll have to have her cooperation to lay charges," Norian sighed. Both Lendill and Norian knew where Reah was—someone they knew had passed that information along to them. Someone currently stationed on Mandil. Not one of their operatives, but someone they knew anyway, who was there to help with a problem that was likely to spread into the Alliance if it weren't stopped on Mandil.

"If we can get her out of there when this is over," Lendill observed. "I know Aurelius plans to bring her out, but anything can happen."

"How long do you think that will take?" Norian asked, sipping his tea. He and Lendill had met in a coffee shop in Lissia, the capital city on Le-Ath Veronis.

"No idea—last I heard, Aurelius thinks the vermin have allied with the hedge wizards in a few of those small desert villages. That doesn't bode well for the others."

I carried my weapon and my backpack. I also had something new—a long knife in a sheath clipped to the back waistband of my trousers. We wore black; Commander Aris had given me two black uniforms, in addition to three desert regulation uniforms. The black was to be worn only at night in the desert.

"Re, I shouldn't have to tell you to keep your eyes and ears open and let us know if you see anything," Bel told me before we set out. Aris wasn't coming—he seldom went out with his Rangers. These were the only Rangers the Prince Royal had besides those commanded to guard the Royal city—the other two outposts taken by demons had no Ranger Wizards at all. That had made them vulnerable, according to Delvin. He and I had talked after Bel sent me to the gathering room. The others were already picking up weapons and waiting for instructions. Hish arrived and gave out information, too. Seven wizards and I—that's all that slipped through a small, hidden gate after dark. Bel, Delvin, Hish, Lin, Jorvis, Max and Pell; those were the seven I now walked beside.

"We'll walk for two clicks—those hits came from the northeast when our convoy was attacked," Bel said softly as we walked along. I was just to his left, Hish on his right. I figured Hish was already providing some sort of shield around us. Delvin and Max came behind, leaving Lin, Jorvis and Pell in the center, spaced out to watch carefully for any signs of the enemy.

We'd walked for nearly the entire two clicks, only seeing or hearing small desert animals. I almost jumped when a predator captured a small rodent, causing the rodent to squeak out his last breath into the cooling desert air. Bel gave me a look and I nodded— we both knew if I'd given the least sound, Bel would have had a hand over my mouth immediately. Working to steady my nerves, I turned back to searching for any signs of the enemy.

Hish clicked his tongue and we turned swiftly in his direction. I saw them—at least six points of light in the distance. Bel had given instructions before we left the station—he would give a hand signal when we were to shoot. We all waited for that signal—right then, the lights were too far away for our ranos rifles to be as effective as they should be. I waited, holding my breath, almost, my rifle at the ready.

None of us expected the lights to turn away from us. Had they seen us? Bel still held us back. I wondered what he was waiting for. Did he want to chase them? He gave the motion to move together in a tighter knot. Hish had his hands up—the sign that he was building a stronger shield. I was in the center of the knot that drew together quite tightly. If I hadn't been so frightened at the moment, I might have been concerned at the press of male bodies all around me.

The first blast came and was diverted to the desert floor around us, outlining Hish's shield that he held. Sand and earth sprayed high into the air and then splattered across Hish's shield and the desert surrounding us, causing me to duck reflexively. These beings, whatever they were, seemed determined to kill us.

Another whistling blast was hurled against us—stronger this time, followed closely by another. Both exploded with a deafening boom. Hish groaned with the last one—the earth was cracking beneath our feet with the power thrown at us. I, never having any experience with power wielders of any sort, was frightened out of my wits. What would we do if Hish could no longer protect us? Two more blasts came and it felt like an earthquake. I'd never experienced one of those either, but had read about them and been in simulations. This was worse.

Delvin shoved me closer against Bel's back. The others were crowding in too—Hish was making his shield smaller. Perhaps it was easier to hold. I hoped so—for his and our sakes. We all nearly fell, the ground shook harder and two more blasts rocked us, spaced closely together. Hish fell, even with Max attempting to hold him up. The last two blasts had clearly broken his shields. We stood there, then, waiting to die while Bel prepared a send-off of his own.

Bel aimed his hands at the last place we'd seen the lights and sent out a blast of light. An explosion boomed and hit, but it had fallen short. Now I knew why he hadn't done this earlier—the enemy had been out of his range. Had this been planned? Had the enemy known what the range of our Wizards was and acted accordingly? I would likely never know. Would Aris know what had happened to us? I barely had time for that thought when another blast came our way, whistling through the air before it hit, knocking all of us to the ground and exploding into thousands of stars around us.

# CHAPTER 7

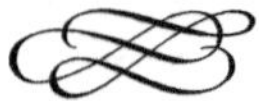

"We're still alive." Bel whispered while Max attempted to wake Hish. Hish was unconscious from his failed attempt to cover us earlier. "How are we still alive?" Bel added, his voice so soft I barely heard. Another whistle was heading in our direction. We all crouched down, expecting to die this time. The enemy wanted to make sure we were dead.

This blast when it came blew up the desert around us in a huge ring. We should have been at the direct center of that blast. Instead, we sat on a small island of undisturbed ground—sand, pebbles and bits of earth raining down on us. Some larger chunks made me whimper in pain as they hit. How were we still alive? How? "Get up," Bel ordered quietly. We all rose—Max, being the tallest and strongest of the wizards, hefted Hish over his shoulder after he stood.

"Stay as close together as you can and walk," Bel hissed, and we began to walk behind him, still in the tightest of knots. More blasts came, some almost causing us to stagger and fall, but we remained upright, marching the entire way back to the military station. When Max grew tired of carrying Hish, Pell took over, carrying him the last half click. Aris must have heard or known somehow—he was waiting at the gate for us with a physician and a stretcher for Hish. We hadn't been attacked for at least a click before getting back to the gate. We were all covered with sand and filth when we arrived—I could see it clearly once we were in the artificial light.

"How did this happen? How are you alive?" Aris demanded, once Hish had been taken to the hospital at the station and we'd gathered inside Aris' office; all of us dirty, sand-covered and puzzled.

"No idea," Bel rubbed the back of his neck. "I was hoping the Prince's wizards had followed us. Now I know that isn't the case." Aris had blown that idea away immediately as we walked toward the gathering room. He said that there hadn't been anyone leaving the walled city except us. I wondered how he knew that. Perhaps he was in contact with the High Commander, still.

"How did we survive?" Delvin asked, now. "The strength of the blast spells sent against us should have fried us where we stood after Hish's shields failed. There wasn't anything there to stop it from happening." That statement told me what Delvin's ability was—at least in part. He could sense and gauge the strength of wizard's spells. I wanted to ask him how he did that. Sometime. Not now—I was still shivering from our unexpected escape.

"Let me work on this," Aris sighed, rubbing a knot between his eyes. He was just as surprised as the rest of us that we still lived. I sat in a chair at the end of the row where six other wizards sat. Had the enemy been testing them all this time, waiting for enough information and the right time to strike, killing all of them at once? If so, they'd failed miserably. For tonight, anyway. "Go to the physicians if you have injuries or trouble sleeping." Aris dismissed us—there wasn't anything else to be learned tonight.

"Sleep as long as you can tomorrow—we'll meet after dinner in Aris' office," Bel told me as we walked out the door. I was scrubbing myself in a hot shower when the message came and it was wordless this time—an expression of fear and concern that sent me to my knees in the tiled cubicle. Hugging myself while it lasted, it eventually subsided, leaving me with a tender caress as if someone had physically touched my face.

~

"You know I cannot interfere except as required as Liaison," Renegar the Larentii sat in a chair enlarged with power and spoke with Aris.

"At least tell me how they all survived—I had nothing to do with it." Aris rose from the chair behind his desk and paced, raking a hand through his thick mane of hair.

"What was different this time?" Renegar's blue eyes twinkled with humor.

"Nothing. Nothing other than Reah going out with them. She's the best marksman I've ever seen," Aris mumbled. Renegar shrugged his wide shoulders—a humanoid trait that he found enjoyable. Most Larentii found no need for gestures, but then most Larentii conversed in mindspeech, so gestures weren't necessary.

"Then I cannot help you past that," Renegar replied.

"That's all you're going to say—what was different?" Aris' voice held a note of incredulity.

"I cannot interfere. You hold the answer; you just do not realize it." A smile tugged at the corner of Renegar's mouth. He smiled easily at times, contrary to most of his race. Renegar attributed it to his mother, who had a fine sense of humor. Most Larentii didn't know their mothers, or their mothers were deceased. Renegar's was neither deceased nor unknown. In fact, he'd spoken to her only that morning.

"You're going to make me puzzle this out, when I have the worst headache in centuries," Aris grumped.

"Now, the headache I can remove," Renegar stood, reached out and placed a hand on Aris' forehead. The headache was gone in seconds. Larentii were likely the best healers among all the races, they just kept that information to themselves.

"But what am I to do about Reah?" Aris flopped onto his chair again. Renegar didn't fail to notice and knew anything of that nature coming from Aris was unusual in the extreme—he always held himself properly.

"You have to make her yours before I can interfere any more than I have already."

"But she won't be able to make that decision for herself until she knows me better, and there's no opportunity for that here." Aris gripped hair in both hands and stared at the top of his desk.

"A conundrum," Renegar nodded, holding back another smile.

"I should know better than to ask any Larentii for advice," Aris muttered.

"*That* I have heard before," Renegar chuckled and disappeared.

Sleep was long in coming; the night's events kept repeating themselves in my mind. How were we not dead? And Hish—was he all right? Those creatures in the desert—whatever they were—did all of them hold power like that, or did only a few? Bel, Aris and the other wizards, did they have a way to fight this or would Crown City be next to fall under attack? I wondered how strong the Prince's Wizards were. Until this night, I'd thought Hish quite capable. His shields had fallen quickly. Delvin had said there was a lot of power thrown at us. Wizard's power. Who wielded it? Midmorning arrived before sleep came, and I found myself thankful that I had no windows in my small room. No light filtered in to disturb the sleep I managed to get.

"So, what do you think of the food in the mess hall?" Delvin sat next to me for our meeting in Aris' office.

"It makes me suicidal," I said without thinking. Delvin laughed. Laughter was a good sound to hear after our experiences the night before.

"Re, what are you saying?" Aris was behind his desk quickly and frowning at me. He'd overheard my statement to Delvin. A worried crease appeared on Aris' forehead as he studied me closely.

"Mostly that the food is terrible in the mess hall," I said, lowering my eyes.

"Ah. Well, not everyone is a master cook," Aris observed. His frown disappeared.

I wasn't a master cook—on Tulgalan you had to be certified to be a master cook. I had no hopes of that, now. My current desire was to I live through the day, considering recent events. The rest of the wizards wandered in with the exception of Hish—he was still in the infirmary. A few held cups of tea in their hands. I wish I'd thought of that—tea sounded good after the quality of the meal I'd gotten at the mess hall.

"Any ideas on last night's survival?" Aris asked right away.

"There's only one thing different about last night," Bel said. "We all know it, we just can't determine how it's significant." I was leaning forward in my chair so I could see Bel as he spoke. Bel had turned to look at me at the same moment. Cold and fear held me immobile. I was the different thing. Blasts had been leveled at me before, while I was inside the transports. I swallowed nervously. I'd survived every one of those attacks, when many others hadn't.

"But I don't have anything—what you have," I stuttered.

"We know that—do you think I couldn't tell?" Delvin huffed. I should have remembered that about him. He could gauge a wizard's power. He didn't get anything from me. I wasn't a wizard. I breathed a shaky sigh.

"Bel, stand." Aris had Bel standing in a blink. "Re, stand up as well." I blinked at Aris, looking into his golden-brown eyes in shock. What was he doing? What was he going to do? "Bel, I have the disguise spell in place. I'll remove mine. You place one of yours," Aris said. I thought Bel already had one on me. As it turns out, I was wrong. Aris did something with his hands; I have no idea what. Delvin was nodding— he'd registered the removal. Now Bel came forward and light formed around his hands. Delvin was still nodding—he felt Bel's power. The other wizards, Bel included, gasped in shock.

"What happened?" I couldn't tell. I hadn't felt the one Aris had placed on me to begin with.

"Re—nothing happened—Bel's disguise spell didn't work, and his is almost as strong as mine," Aris was standing behind his desk, now.

"It's as if the spell is being deflected—I feel the power around her, it just isn't settling *on* her," Delvin breathed. Max was on his feet, now.

"That's how it happened—we were all in a tight knot so Hish could cover us. That spellwork was deflected around Re. She—he—was right in the middle of the rest of us. We thought to protect him. The opposite happened instead."

"I've only known a few races that can do this," Aris breathed, coming to stand in front of me. I looked up at his face—it was a good face—a handsome face. "Re, what can you tell me about your family? Bear in mind everyone inside this room is safe. Your information is safe with them."

Delvin nodded encouragingly at me. They all knew. Aris had told them. It frightened me.

"Re, it will be all right," I blinked up at Aris as he spoke.

"M-my father is Addah Desh," I muttered.

"Addah Desh? Master cook Addah Desh from Tulgalan?" Bel had heard of him.

I couldn't answer, so I nodded.

"Re, what about your mother's family?" Aris pushed for answers.

"My mother died when I was born. They tell me I look like her. That's all I know—nobody would give me information on her side of the family."

"Your father withheld this information?" Delvin couldn't believe what he was hearing.

"My father still has seven wives and twenty-six sons. I was his only daughter. I got nothing from my father. He shipped me to my second oldest brother when I was eight. I was working with him when the conscription notice came." I slapped a hand over my mouth at the last admission—I hadn't meant to say that.

"Reah, it's all right," Aris' voice was mesmerizing. "How did you come to be here?" Somehow I was compelled to answer him.

"I was assigned to work in the kitchens of the Governor of the Realm. The master cook was jealous. I think he tampered with my pod during a drill, sending me into space as fast as the pod could travel. If he programmed as well as he cooked, then he likely didn't know what he was doing," I muttered.

"So, not a misfire but close enough," Bel sighed.

"I almost died—the oxygen was running out when I hit this atmosphere," I added. "The next thing I knew, Chlind and Seval had me on their transport and Chlind was telling me I'd die in the desert if I tried to escape and to keep quiet or I'd die anyway."

"I'm going to thrash Chlind if I ever see him again," Bel said angrily.

"Don't be so hasty," Aris said, turning to Bel. "If he'd turned her over to the crown, you'd all be dead now."

"Well, there's that," Bel agreed, taking his seat.

"Now, I'll have to do some research on which races have the ability to deflect a wizard's power," Aris returned to his desk. "Re, sit down before you drop."

He was right—my legs felt as if they would collapse beneath me. "You know," Bel said, "the ones trying to kill us won't be expecting us out again tonight." I jerked my head in his direction. Surely he couldn't mean going out again—now?

"Bel, you are more devious than I thought," Aris was smiling. "Who can hold Re up if she can't walk?" Every hand went up. That's how I found myself dressing in my second black outfit, my fingers shaking and tears threatening as we made ready to go into the desert for the second night in a row.

"Keep close to Re," Bel commanded as we walked through the small gate again on our way into the desert.

The enemy wasn't prepared when we found them, just as Bel suggested. They lobbed a few power blasts at us, but the knot of wizards tightened around me and everything burst and exploded ineffectively around us. How was I doing this? It was involuntary; I knew that. It took no effort from me—I was terrified, not just for myself but for the others as well. When the blasts stopped, Bel had us running in tight formation, firing as we went.

That was the first time I saw what the demons became when they were older. Their façade of humanity had fallen away, revealing an ugly, mud-gray creature with a wide mouth and fangs. I killed at least thirty of them—there was a pod of them behind three rogue wizards. Bel killed the wizards with power. The rest of us were firing into the creatures who'd rushed forward to attack as soon as their wizards were down. They died too, as quickly as we could shoot them.

"Re, put your rifle down." Bel pushed the barrel of my rifle downward. I was frozen in the firing position, waiting for the next creature to appear. I nodded eventually and lowered my head. "Here," Bel offered me his canteen. Mine was in my backpack, but I wasn't even thinking about that. He stood by and watched while I drank.

We trudged back to Crown City, going through the gate a half click before dawn. Aris was waiting on us again. "Success," Bel grunted as he passed Aris. We were all looking for our beds. My head was empty of thoughts—weariness had taken over. It didn't occur to me until later that not once had anyone been forced to carry me. I discovered I was proud of that.

*Love, I'm sending a tray. Wake and eat.* Those words woke me from a sound sleep around midday. I barely had time to throw a tunic and trousers on—I'd gone straight to bed when I'd arrived at my room, just slipping out of my clothing and crawling into bed naked. I found a recruit on the other side of my door, holding a tray in his hands. I thanked him, took the tray and pushed the door shut with my foot as the young man walked away. I didn't recognize him, except to note that it wasn't Nods or any of his pack of followers.

The tray held food; that's the best compliment I could pay it. I bemoaned the fact that I wasn't likely to get a good meal ever again unless I could cook it myself. I ate because I was hungry and because Aris had wakened me to eat. I'd only had three meals in two days instead of the usual six. I couldn't go haring into the desert on short rations.

"Where are we going?" Aris had pulled Bel away after they finished their evening meal.

"Shopping," Aris grinned. Bel stared at Aris—he seldom grinned or laughed.

"Commander, that is so unlike you," Bel grinned back. "Where and for what are you shopping?"

"Clothing," Aris replied. They walked through the eastern gate and into the shopping district next to the military station. The shops stayed open later, hoping for the troops' business. They were getting Aris' custom that night.

"Those aren't going to fit you," Bel teased as Aris looked at young men's tunics and trousers.

"Re doesn't like orange or red," Aris muttered to himself, setting those colors aside. He lifted blues and greens instead. Black went into the pile. A dark gray. Shoes came next—two pairs of good leather boots. Aris' purchases were wrapped and bagged.

"Now what?" Bel asked as Aris continued his journey, carrying the bag of clothing.

"This," Aris breathed, stopping at a shop that sold women's clothing. "She lost something like this when we got hit the first time." Aris was fingering the cloth of a lovely aqua tunic with rich embroidery.

"Aris, Delvin and I were with her when she bought that other outfit. It didn't cost nearly this much."

"How much is your life worth?" Aris turned his eyes to Bel.

"I'm buying," Bel pulled out his money pouch.

Dane, Gin and Dory had become regular dinner companions. When

Nods and his bunch came by, the abuse was spread among the four of us.

"I'm surprised the military accepts babies," Nods taunted as he passed.

"That's why they took him," I muttered as soon as he was past us. Dane burst out laughing and then slapped a hand over his mouth.

"They're looking this way," Gin whispered urgently. Feigning innocence, we turned back to our food.

"That'll cost us," Dory said as we dropped our trays off and walked away from the mess hall.

"Yes. I should learn to keep my mouth closed," I said. We wouldn't know any details before it happened, but my money was on a swift plot hatching between Nods and his friends to get back at us.

~

Bel and I were back to accounts and other work the following morning. He called it paperwork. I just shrugged and accepted the new term. We also turned out for inspection in the afternoon—a regular occurrence there at the military station, I learned. Every second eight-day, according to Bel. The Station Commander came through Bel's office, looked around, didn't find much in the way of dust or clutter, told us to clean anyway and then stalked off. If I were he, I wouldn't insult Bel. I'd seen him fry three wizards with the power he had.

"This is for you," Bel handed a large bag to me before I left his office to get dinner. "Aris sent this." I nodded and carried the bag to my room. Clothes were inside; a young man's clothes. What else would I get? These added to my meager closet and were colors I might choose for myself, including two more black outfits. I wondered if that meant there were more treks into the desert soon. Shaking my head, I headed toward the mess hall.

"Nods and his private military didn't even stop by our table," Gin noted later as we sat eating.

"Lulling us into thinking he's backing off," I said quietly. "The calm before the hurricane comes."

"You think he's got something planned?" Dane sounded worried.

"Yes. I think that," I said. "The questions are what, where and when." We kept eating, our thoughts chasing each other over what Nods would do when the evacuation drill sounded. These weren't scheduled like the inspections—they came irregularly. We had to turn out wherever we were. Dane, Gin, Dory and I had to leave our unfinished dinner behind and rush out of the building—in an orderly fashion, of course.

"New recruits this way," someone shouted. A rush of newly trained troops followed that voice. Dane and the others hurried along behind the others. I went but more slowly. I didn't trust that voice—it didn't sound like one of the officers to me. I found recruits crowding into a space between buildings. It resembled a blind alley; the buildings were so closely spaced. I didn't see signs of officers anywhere. Later, I attempted to puzzle out how Nods had learned of the drill. Unless he was behind the drill itself. I learned that with Nods, almost anything was possible.

None of the recruits were prepared for what happened—the hoses that gushed water with extreme force were built to put fires out quickly. These hoses were now aimed at the recruits and they were soaked and slipping in the muddy sand between buildings in very little time. I backed away as quickly as I could—I hadn't gone into the alleyway to begin with—it looked too suspicious to me.

Officers were arriving quickly, shouting for the water to be turned off. I watched from a distance as all the recruits were dressed down as if they were at fault for the entire incident. None were allowed to speak. I'm sure the officers knew—they did it anyway. It made me angry, but what could I do? Aris would certainly have something to say if I called attention to myself. I slipped away, unwilling to watch even more injustice that evening.

❧

"Take the afternoon off and sleep if you can, then get dinner and meet in Aris' office," Bel told me the following morning. That meant we'd be heading into the desert again. I nodded and went to deliver messages for Bel and Aris.

"You knew it was a trap," Dane muttered over dinner.

"You ran off; I was trying to get you to slow down," I pointed my fork at him. "Next time, look for the officers issuing the commands. If you don't see any, that could be a problem."

"We have extra duties for an eight-day," Dory grumbled.

"And a lot of embarrassment," Gin elbowed his friend.

"This could stop with your class, you know," I said. "If you all decide that the next batch of recruits gets left alone, then it may stop. It's a stupid practice and only allows the bullies to do what they like with very little chance of punishment." I'd seen some of the officers the night before, grinning and laughing at the recruits as they slipped and slid in the mud while trying to exit the alley at the same time. Nods had given the officers and other troops fine entertainment. I'd seen him off to the side with his group. They hadn't been given extra duties—I'd bet money on it.

In a way, I had extra duties myself—they just weren't handed out as punishment. I hadn't slept well during the afternoon so I'd dropped off clothing to be washed at the station laundry. I was to pick them up in two days. The Alliance did your laundry for free. Here, you were charged if you had anything other than uniforms. My pay would be docked for laundry services. I'd signed the slip pushed across the counter at me, describing the clothing to be laundered and what the charge would be.

At least the trooper at the counter wasn't one of Nods' level—he was older and looked as if he'd been doing his job for several turns. Nods hadn't been at the station for a turn, even. Classes of new recruits were turned out every three moon-turns here, just as they were with the Alliance. Half a sun-turn might describe Nods' length of service. It might describe his maturity level, too.

"What are you doing tonight?" Dane asked as I placed my tray in a slot to be washed.

"I have extra duty, too. Ranger Bel has things for me to do," I replied.

"You work with the Rangers?" Dane's voice was almost breathless and his eyes were wide with something close to awe.

"It's not that exciting," I said, trying to cover what might have been a gaff. "I deliver messages, run errands and do paperwork."

"Oh." Dane's face fell. I wondered what he'd do if I told him that I'd gone out to the desert twice in the past eight-day. I didn't mention it and resolved not to talk about my duties again. Working with the Rangers sounded exciting to the others. They had no idea how dangerous it was.

Did I expect the attack on the way back to the Rangers' quarters? I'm afraid to say I didn't. I should have been paying more attention, rather than allowing my thoughts to distract me. I wouldn't allow it to happen again.

The first punch landed before I had a chance to react. Nods delivered it himself. He and his followers didn't land another—I pushed him down and ran. They might have been fast—I was faster. They didn't catch me as I slammed through the door into the Rangers' quarters. Nods and the others wouldn't follow me into a building— there was too much opportunity for them to be caught. Nods would never take responsibility for his actions—not if he could help it.

"Re, what happened?" My right eye was already turning purple when I walked into Aris' office a few ticks later. I'd put a cold cloth on the eye where Nods hit me, but ice would have been better. There was precious little of it at the station and I knew not to ask for any.

"The bullies. I didn't fall for their water trap last night, so they made sure to get me tonight," I said, sitting down in my usual spot.

"Is this going to affect your ability to spot the enemy?" Bel asked, coming closer to examine my eye. At the moment, I could still see out of the eye. He placed fingers on the darkening bruise anyway, checking it carefully. "Let's hope it doesn't get much worse," Bel sighed and went to sit down.

~

We were heading out the gate in a quarter click, going northwest this time. A group of stragglers had arrived at the gate the day before, telling tales of monsters that had attacked their remote village. Most of their fellow villagers had been killed. Aris had gone to their questioning himself, just to see if they were being honest. Could he tell that? Some wizards could test your honesty? That could be frightening. I didn't like to tell lies, but small ones came now occasionally, like the one I'd told Dane earlier, making my work for the Rangers sound boring and dull. Much of it was—that wasn't an untruth. I just hadn't mentioned the occasional trek into the desert.

"Max is going to get us part of the way," Bel announced after we'd walked perhaps a click. I didn't know what he meant. Somehow, Max could transport a few people. That was his talent. He just needed to know exactly where to transport them, and his range was limited. That's why we'd walked the length of time we had. The villagers had given Aris their location in the desert, so Max knew where to take us. He had a target to hit. He couldn't do this without a specific location.

It felt as if I were being squeezed—all the breath was forced from my lungs when Max moved us. I was trying to catch my breath when we were set down within sight of an abandoned village. Feeling much as I had the few times I'd fallen hard on my back, gasping for breath when the air had been slammed out of my lungs, I worked desperately to draw air into my body. Max walked over and straightened my cramping frame. I'd bent over in agony, desperately trying to pull in air.

"Slow, Re," he said, holding my arm to keep me upright. Thinking that I might never breathe again and considering smacking Max if I did, I kept trying, eventually getting the much-needed air through my nose and mouth. I coughed.

"First time's always the worst," Pell said, walking past me with a grin on his face. He just got added to the smacking line.

Our rifles were up and Bel was at the ready when we approached the village a few ticks later. Lights appeared. Bel gave us the signal to be prepared. We moved closer and pandemonium came.

~

Nods was on his way to the barracks with the three who followed him constantly. They made a turn to walk between the exercise facility and the bathhouse. It was a shortcut they weren't supposed to take—there was a garden there planted by the Station Commander's two wives. Cautiously they made their way around the plants—the vegetables and flowers were watered daily, just to keep them alive. Nods and the others were halfway through the garden when something dropped from above.

Nods jerked backward with a curse, bumping into his three friends. Whatever had fallen didn't hit them and Nods realized it was someone instead of something rather quickly. The buildings were quite tall on either side and Nods, if he'd had more intelligence, may have wondered how any person might have survived the leap from the rooftop to the ground. He didn't—he was backing away from the one in front of him.

"You're the one doing all the mischief, aren't you?" Nods stared at the one stalking him. He moved like one of the big jungle cats—silent and deadly. Nods knew who it was—Commander Aris of the Rangers.

"No—we did nothing," Nods stammered.

"That's a lie," Commander Aris growled. Nods didn't know to be more frightened of the growl—he was already quite frightened. "You attacked my recruit earlier. Punched him in the face." Aris reached out and gripped Nods by the throat, lifting him high in the air with only one hand. Aris growled again. Nods' three friends cowered behind him.

"He-he's your recruit?" Nods didn't have much control over his voice now, and he squeaked.

"Yes. And he needs both his eyes and a healthy body to do his chores. Interfere with that again and I'll make sure you and your friends suffer." Nods could only gurgle at Aris' words—Aris had him gripped quite tightly.

"We understand one another—good." Aris let Nods drop. The

sophomore recruit dropped like a bag of sand to the ground, crushing several of the Station Commander's prized tomatoes.

"Who's there?" A guard shouted as Nods attempted to get his breath back. Nods' three friends tried to run, but another guard at the opposite end of the alley blocked them. Commander Aris had disappeared like wisps of fog in bright sunlight, leaving Nods and his followers to face the Station Commander's punishment.

# CHAPTER 8

We gathered into the designated tight knot, guns pointed outward and firing, even as the blasts rocked all of us on our feet. Hish hadn't come with us—he was still recovering. I was their protection. My eye was swelling, I could barely see as I fired. The next blast blew everything up around us, leaving a crater behind. We stood on a small island of desert sand, gaping at a trench ten hands deep around us. The outer edges of our circle were irregular—the explosion had seen to that. Our island was perhaps thirty hands across—two tall men might have fit lengthwise across that distance. The circle was large enough to hold all of us, with a bit of extra room. We were covered with dust, sand and detritus as we went back to firing at the points of light coming in our direction.

The number of the enemy killed may remain a mystery—we fired until our rifles ran out of power. We hadn't brought extras—Max could only transport so much. He had to transport us back to the site from which he'd taken us in the beginning when more of the enemy poured out of the village, intent on taking us down. I didn't think whatever I had protected against a physical attack—only one sent by wizards. That's why I now had a black eye. Again, I was gasping for breath after we landed, but I wasn't as frightened this time. That helped and I was able to breathe faster. Aris was waiting for us at the gate when we returned three clicks before dawn.

~

"How many do you think were out there?" Aris sipped a cup of tea while he questioned us.

"We killed around six hundreds—we had power for eight hundred shots, and using the normal figures for the miss ratio, I'd say that's how many dusted. We didn't get close enough to do anything about the two wizards. That's how many Delvin sensed." Bel drank a cup of water while Aris considered his words.

"So, how many do you think were left?" Aris steepled his fingers. His eyes were on Bel as Bel calculated.

"At least a thousand," Bel replied. "Maybe more. We might have taken them all down if we'd had extra weapons."

Aris nodded—he knew Max had stretched his talent to the limit, taking what he did.

"We can try again tomorrow night," Bel suggested.

"No, they'll be waiting," Aris waved Bel's words off. "We did what we could with the information brought to us. I'll have to do a location spell."

"They may still have a blocker—we don't know which ones we killed last time," Delvin pointed out. Delvin could only sense the level of power or talent; he couldn't discern individual abilities.

"And we now know the limit of Re's ability—we stood on an island about thirty-three hands in diameter," Bel added. "A ten-hand deep ditch lay around us, after they threw their best in our direction."

"Amazing." Aris still wasn't looking at me. I didn't mind—my eye was now swelled shut and I'm sure the bruise around it was so deep a purple it looked black. It made me wonder how many times I'd missed while shooting earlier. I wanted to curse Nods—he might have cost us in our attempt to take down the enemy.

We were dismissed shortly after that. I was just out of the shower and dressing in a nightshirt when the knock came. Aris was at the door with the old physician from the outpost. My eye was swelled so the physician had a pack of ice and herbs with him. "Keep this on as much as possible, it'll help with the swelling," the physician had me lie down on my bed and place the pack over my eye. "It won't matter if you fall asleep with it on there." He and Aris left shortly afterward. Aris hadn't spoken the entire time.

Aris growled and fretted while he dressed for bed. He'd been afraid to open his mouth—all kinds of endearments wanted to fly out. He couldn't let that happen. But his silence might make Reah think he didn't care. Aris eventually had to shut his mind off and go to bed—he had a meeting with the High Commander in the morning.

"That's new." Dane examined the black and purple flesh around my eye.

"Compliments of our good friends," I blew out a breath after sitting at our regular table with my dinner tray.

"Nods did that?" Gin was leaning halfway across the table to take a look. Dory just stared.

"Yes. I was thinking about something else and wasn't paying attention. He jumped me between the officers' barracks and the wizards' wing."

"Did Commander Aris see that?" Dory asked.

"Commander Aris, Bel and the others all saw it." I dipped into the chopped pork we were served for dinner. They'd butchered it in many ways.

"Did they say anything?" Dane asked. By that time, I was hoping my eye would lose its novelty soon. If Nods came by, I would have to keep myself under control—I wanted to hit him.

"Only that they hoped it didn't interfere with my duties, and Commander Aris sent a physician who brought an ice and herb pack."

"As black eyes go—it's impressive," Dane nodded, stuffing a forkful of pork into his mouth.

"It isn't my intention to stand out," I said. "I'd prefer to not have the bruises, I assure you."

"Where is Nods, anyway?" Gin quietly looked around us.

"He's at his usual table, with his horde," Dory said, purposely not looking in that direction.

"You mean they didn't stop and gloat?" Dane couldn't believe it.

"Maybe he thought he'd get in trouble—gloating might be an admission of guilt," Gin smiled. "And you know he won't admit any of his misdeeds. That would mean taking responsibility."

"Nods and responsibility have never been in the same room together, have you noticed?" Dane was snickering. We made it through dinner without a single word or even a glance from Nods. I wasn't foolish enough to think that he was through with us, though.

"How's the eye?" Bel looked it over carefully.

"Sore." That word said everything. It was tender, too, and I could barely touch it without wincing. The ice pack had helped and made me wish for more ice on subsequent days.

"Can you see all right?" Now we came to the real question Bel wanted answered.

"I can see."

"Good. We're going out again tonight, so the afternoon will be spent resting. Max will move us again, so dress as lightly as possible. Your shoes will be the most important thing—make sure to wear your sturdy boots."

"Yes, Ranger Bel."

"Re, this won't be forever." Aris had walked up and I'd failed to hear him. I wanted to argue with him. Ask him how long, then. Would it be days, moon-turns, full turns?

"Tired of taking my orders so soon?" Bel tousled my short hair affectionately. I was reminded of my place every time I looked in the mirror at my haircut. Likely it would have to be cut again soon—it was growing out quickly.

"Ranger Bel, if you had ever worked with my brother Edan, you would know what a silly question that was." I gave him a quick nod and went to deliver reports to the Station Commander's office.

"I don't think her brother treated her very well." Aris sipped tea from the mug he held. The mug looked small in his large hand.

"You think that's where that timid manner came from?" Bel sent Aris a questioning look.

"She's better now, but yes. And the military training didn't help much, I imagine. My guess is that they tried to get her to wash out because of her size. I think they discovered she's tougher than she looks."

"Definitely that. She hasn't slowed us down when we take our trips into the desert. Even with that shiner she's wearing." Aris growled at Bel's assessment. He growled every time he thought of that idiot recruit who'd hit her. Bel could almost read Aris' mind on this. Nods Whitlin had better watch out if he ever touched Reah again.

"It may have begun as a practical joke, but you are no longer a young recruit, too stupid to know better." The military tribunal stared down at master cook Vyn Bralnon. "Although the last word we had from the ASD is that recruit Desh is still alive on Mandil, that could change at any time. You sentenced her when you allowed her to get inside that pod. Didn't you? Over what? Jealousy?"

"I have no excuse," Vyn mouthed the proper response. Master cook Vyn hated Reah Desh. He'd been jealous before and he'd allowed Leetha and Morane to convince him to get back at her for imagined slights. He hated them and he hated Reah. Had she not come into his life, he would still be enjoying his comfort as the master cook in the Governor's kitchen. Now he would be sent to prison. The military tribunal would set the sentence today. Leetha and Morane, as accomplices, had already been sentenced to three turns each in the military holding and forced to work while there, laundering new recruits' clothing.

"Don't lay the blame on anyone except yourself." Someone new walked into the room.

"Who are you?" Vyn snarled, realizing immediately that he'd spoken rudely and out of turn. It wouldn't help him at all when the sentencing came.

"I am Norian Keef." Vyn cringed. The Director of the ASD was here. "I can see you wonder why I came," Norian glared at Vyn. "You might have caused us all sorts of problems, sending that pod to Mandil. Oh, I know it was unintentional," Director Keef held up a hand to ward off Vyn's attempt at an explanation. "Our treaty with Mandil is shaky at best. They have ranos technology and a cannon built large enough can destroy an entire planet. You should know that. Yet you decided to reprogram the pod without checking to see where it might land. You are sixty turns in age, Vyn Bralnon. You attack a nineteen-turn kitchen helper. Someone barely out of childhood, by our standards. Defend yourself against that, Master Vyn."

"He can't, and there is no remorse in him," the military tribunal said. "Therefore, unless you have other evidence to offer, Director Keef, I am prepared to pass sentence."

"I don't—you have what I sent," Norian nodded at the tribunal.

"Very well. Vyn Bralnon, I sentence you to fifteen turns in the military prison. You will not be allowed inside a kitchen during that time. I can only imagine that you would attempt your petty revenge there, if allowed. I think cleaning the facilities and doing laundry for that length of time might better serve the military you betrayed." Former master cook Vyn was led away by military guards.

"What will happen to that poor girl?" The tribunal turned to Norian Keef.

"No idea—they're using her at the moment, if my sources are correct. The ones surrounding her are keeping her secrets for now, but who knows if that will change?" Norian shrugged.

∿

"Walk for three clicks—I did the locating spell and the spawn that still lived last time are heading in this direction." Aris looked at all of us as we sat in front of him in the gathering room.

"Don't miss them when you shoot," Bel added, turning in his seat at the opposite end to look at us as well. "They're headed this way because they're hungry—Aris and I figure they've taken the outlying villages and Crown City is now the nearest food source. They'll attack the walls. The Prince's Wizards assure us that they have things well in hand, but we still don't know how many village wizards are with them, or how strong they are together. In the past, they never associated with any other tribes and refused to combine power. That no longer holds true. Aris and I are worried that they might breach the wards around the walls. Even a single demon can cause havoc if he bites anyone inside the city. They turn quickly, as you know, and can bite someone else in less than half a click."

"How many do you think are coming?" My question sounded timid to my ears. I wasn't used to asking questions, forcing myself to be content with what the others asked or offered.

"The numbers are blocked. We don't have good intelligence on this," Aris replied. "Max will come back for more ranos rifles if they're needed. Bel is prepared to keep all of you there past daylight if necessary. You'll carry extra water, foodpacks and an extra weapon each."

This sounded more serious than any of our previous missions. Were the monsters amassing to attack Crown City? It worried me that they always came at night, when only the wizards and I could see to kill them. I still had no idea how I could see them as well. "Stand," Aris ordered. We all stood simultaneously, as good troopers should. "Protect your brothers and protect yourselves. You are the Crown's best troops against the enemy. Do not allow them to win this battle."

Bel led us out of the gathering room, Aris' words still ringing in our ears. We slipped backpacks on and shouldered two ranos rifles each. Following Bel and Aris, we headed toward the small hidden door that would send us into the night air of the desert outside the city walls. Stars were sprinkled across the night sky like bits of sugar on a pastry. They twinkled and smiled down on us, just as they did upon the ones we were sent to kill. Only now was I beginning to wonder where the enemy had come from—how they'd gotten to Mandil. I'd never read anything about them in my studies, either in dayschool or while training with the Alliance troops. Surely, something would have been mentioned if the Alliance knew of their existence. It was too late to raise my hand and ask questions of my instructors now. Aris spoke as if he expected that some of us might not make it back. He was sending us out anyway.

Our footsteps were as silent as we could make them as we followed in a close knot behind Bel. We were all conscious of how much ground was safe around me. Hish had come, but Bel had instructed him to save his shields for now and only use them if there was no other recourse. To me, that meant a physical attack that we couldn't overcome. Everything was happening so fast—did they do this purposely? Not telling us so we wouldn't have time to fret over it? I had no idea. Bel gave the signal to pay attention and not lag behind; perhaps I wasn't the only one thinking these thoughts. Now I concentrated on staying near the center and watching the others—I was their protection as long as they stayed within fifteen hands in a circle around me. Unsure whether I'd ever felt such weight on my shoulders before, I trudged along, hoping we'd all make it home again.

Aris had sweated over this; his desire to have someone come to get Reah warring with the knowledge that she was the hope the Rangers had of coming back. If they didn't go out and meet the enemy tonight, taking as many of them as they could, then the spawn would reach Crown City by nightfall the following evening. The Post had enough ranos rifles to equip about a third of the troops and only the best shots would get them, but they'd be firing blind.

Only the wizards (and for some unknown reason Reah) could see the enemy at night. That is why the spawn attacked then—they had more chances of survival with the limited number of wizard Rangers available to fight them. It was a wrench, making the decision to send Reah into such peril, but the fate of Mandil might depend on it. Aris was risking his heart and he knew it.

Aris watched from the back of the large assembly hall as the Station Commander walked up the steps leading to the low stage. All the troops and recruits had been called to assemble there after the Rangers went out. The High Commander was coming as well, but the Station Commander would make the announcement. Aris turned his head; the High Commander and his guards had just arrived. The guards followed the Station Commander up the steps and sat down behind him. Station Commander Evlif Gorth stepped up to the podium. Everyone became quiet.

"The enemy is coming this way, and in numbers we cannot fully assess—they have a blocking wizard working with them," Commander Gorth announced immediately. If his troops hadn't been so well trained, they might have burst out in whispers. As it is, they kept their silence during the rest of the announcement. "They may have other wizards from the outlying villages working with them," the Station Commander went on. "The numbers could be in the thousands. I know many of you have not seen the enemy before, having merely heard about them or had them described by another. Tonight, when this announcement is over, you will each go with your section leaders and a full description of the enemy in all its forms will be given to you. Our Rangers have gone out again tonight, to see if the number of enemy troops might be pared down before they reach Crown City tomorrow at nightfall. Bear in mind that only the wizards can see them well enough at night so their shots will not be wasted. We will bend our thoughts in the Rangers' direction tonight, with hope that their mission is a success. Should that not be, we will be waiting at the gate tomorrow morning to mourn our losses and prepare for the coming attack."

"Where's Re?" Dane hadn't seen their friend anywhere, although he'd seen Commander Aris at the back of the room during the assembly. The new recruits were shuffling behind their section leader, who would be giving them information inside the barracks.

"I didn't see him either." Gin swore softly, and he never swore. "I wish I had enough nerve to approach Commander Aris."

"I'm going." Dory, smallest of the three, swerved away from his place in line, heading straight for Commander Aris who watched as the troops broke into groups and filed out of the large hall.

"My apologies, Commander Aris," Dory ducked his head respectfully to the Commander. Dane and Gin came up behind, almost breathless from bucking the crowd to follow Dory.

"Recruit, what is it?" Commander Aris gave Dory a stern look.

"Commander, we know that Re is attached to the Rangers. We didn't see him tonight. Is he well?"

Commander Aris breathed a sigh and lowered his eyes briefly. "You are his friends?" He said, looking up again.

"We are his only friends—among the recruits," Dane declared, then dropped his eyes, ashamed.

"No, we have guessed at this," Commander Aris smiled slightly. "Which one of you helped him clean the bar?"

"I did," Dane blushed.

"Then what I tell you now you may not repeat to another soul, do you understand?" Power was in Aris' voice and the three could only nod in understanding—they had no choice. "Re," Aris went on, "goes out with the Rangers. He is the finest marksman I have ever seen among my troops, and when he fires at the enemy, he does not miss. That is why he is so valuable to Bel and the Rangers. He keeps them safe."

"Re goes into the desert with the wizards?" Gin squeaked. Just the idea of it frightened him.

"Has been since we arrived at the Station," Aris nodded. "Go now, or you will be late for your gathering."

～

Bel motioned for us to stand down when the first lights appeared far in the distance. I saw only a few, and none were within firing range as yet. More lights appeared as our steps became more careful and we drew closer together. Bel, Hish and Lin would drop to their knees in front when the time came, I would remain standing right behind them, firing over their heads and Delvin, Jorvis, Max and Pell would be right behind me, firing over my head. That formation was the easiest way to stay in the prescribed circle around me and kill the enemy without harming ourselves. Aris had devised the formation and drawn it up for us before we left.

Bel was still walking forward, but Delvin had crept forward and given Bel a hand signal. Bel gave us the sign to stop. We stopped. And then stared at what lay before us. The enemy knew we were there and now knew that we'd stopped. What looked to be thousands of lights blinked into existence and I went cold.

"They've found them and the numbers are worse than we feared." Aris' eyes were unfocused for several moments before coming back to the room that held him, the High Commander and Station Commander Gorth. One of Aris' many talents was that of seeing through another's eyes—in this case Bel's eyes. Bel had given permission long ago and Aris used it when needed. It cost him little in the way of effort, and gained him and the others much-needed information. Aris would have gone out with his Rangers, but the High Commander had insisted he stay behind to feed him information. Aris had argued with him, but the orders had remained the same. Aris held his own opinion of the High Commander and of the Prince Royal, but held those thoughts back—they wouldn't be spoken aloud. At least not while the enemy threatened.

"Do you think any of them will return?" Station Commander Gorth was genuinely worried. He'd been against sending the Rangers out, preferring to keep them inside the walls and forcing the Prince Royal's wizards to aid the military in the fight when it came to them.

The Prince had refused, saying that his wizards protected Crown City's walls. Both Aris and Commander Gorth had explained that the enemy, combined with the hedge wizards they'd conscripted, could breach the walls quickly. The enemy would come pouring through, leaving everyone vulnerable to the attack.

The Prince, having listened to the High Commander and some of his cozy, well-fed wizards, had refused to consider Aris and Commander Gorth's suggestion of pooling their strength and taking the enemy down quickly. The hedge wizards had done the same thing and nearly killed the Rangers. If it hadn't been for Reah and her peculiar talent, the Rangers would be dead already. Aris was withholding that information in order to protect Reah and the Rangers.

"I am concerned for the Rangers," Aris turned to Commander Gorth. "If any of them survive this night, it might well be a miracle." Aris rose and stalked from the room. He'd seen what Bel had seen— multitudes of lights blinking in the desert. The eyes of the enemy— that's what they were seeing. Aris wanted desperately to send a mental message to Reah as she lifted her rifle with the others, preparing to shoot on Bel's silent command. Aris climbed one of the many ladders that rose to the top of the wall surrounding the military station and stared out at the darkness in the direction the Rangers had taken. A mental message now would only distract his Reah. Yes, *his* Reah. He was terrified for her and for himself.

Only a moment longer—that's what we had. The desert was completely silent around us—not even the sounds of sand shuffling betrayed the enemy's footsteps as they came toward us. Perhaps one of their wizards had done that for them—muffled the noise they made as they approached. I'd seen Delvin counting on his fingers while Bel watched, figuring that Delvin was giving Bel information on how many wizards might be with the enemy. He'd counted out seventeen. That was frightening. Bel gave us the ready signal. We lifted our rifles in unison. Bel gave the signal to fire. I set my sights and fired.

"The enemy is engaged." Commander Gorth had come to stand next to Aris on the wall. Gorth had no way of seeing what Aris could see and had to depend on Aris' description of what was happening in the desert. The High Commander and his guards had stayed inside the private meeting chamber, reluctant to come out. The High Commander would remain in contact with the Prince Royal, giving regular updates. Aris knew the High Commander would be giving erroneous information unless he came to receive Aris' intelligence.

Aris huffed out a sigh. The High Commander played a dangerous game, feeding the Prince Royal contrived messages of safety. Only the attack from the enemy while the High Commander had been on his way to the desert had forced him to give the Prince anything other than rosy accounts of their successes. Aris had attempted to inform the Prince, but the High Commander had stopped it and stopped Aris from going to the desert himself. Aris was powerful and the High Commander wanted that power under his thumb in case he and the Prince Royal required it. He was risking lives—lives that Aris knew might be too precious to lose.

Max had been forced to move us back once already, when the enemy rushed us. All of us were disoriented—we'd been firing when Bel gave the swift hand directions to cease firing so Max could move us. I still had difficulty breathing when he did that and it took several moments to get myself under control. By that time the enemy was within range again—Max hadn't moved us far. Pell, too, had employed his talent. He could cause rifts in the ground beneath enemy feet. It failed to harm them—they climbed out of the ditches easily. What it could (and did) do, was slow them down.

I was firing as quickly as I could point and shoot at a target. The enemy steadily marched toward us. Bel prepared to send out the first of his blasts—they were close enough now. I heard screams as the first hit the target and many lights went dark. Others came to take their place. I fired. And then fired again. The enemy wizards sent a blast that knocked us to our knees. We rose and began to fire again, even as sand and small rocks pelted us when they fell to the ground after shooting high into the night sky.

Jorvis was next, creating illusions of more of us. I could see through the images he made—they looked like wispy ghosts to me, but the enemy attacked them as if they were real, sending blasts to the left and right of us. Jorvis seemed quite talented if he could create two complete illusions at the same time. While the enemy focused on Jorvis' constructs, we continued to kill the lights coming toward us. Bel saw their attempts to surround us, so Max moved us backward again—a little farther, this time.

We had a few more precious ticks to recover before we fired once more. I had no time to think, otherwise I might have wondered at the sheer numbers that were coming in our direction. All I could do was fire, making sure my shots counted. Who knows how many enemies we were bringing down? It only seemed that each one that died was replaced by another. We'd been working our way through the night and emptied one rifle before shouldering our second. Poor Max was sent to gather extras after moving us twice. He had to be exhausted when he arrived with two extra rifles for each of us. He never said a word, shouldering his own rifle and firing in a smooth and practiced manner.

The enemy was attempting to circle us again, but it was too soon for Max to do anything for us. Bel pointed me to his left—he wanted me to fire in that direction. I swiveled quickly, taking as many as I could in a furious burst of shots. Had they thought I might fire that fast? I was desperate—we didn't need to be surrounded like that. We needed an escape route in case Max couldn't get us out. Bel fired another blast of power toward our right. And then another blast. More screams came. More of the enemy died. I fired as swiftly as I could aim accurately, emptying another rifle quickly. Lin tossed me another as I dropped the empty.

As a unit, we backed up slowly, still firing. Again, I wondered how many were out there, waiting. Their wizards sent another blast that exploded in front of us. That served to send a river of sand flying in our direction—they were trying to blind us. We covered our eyes and ducked as the storm of stinging particles hit. Pain bloomed against exposed skin, which meant our hands and what wasn't covered of our faces suffered from the onslaught, feeling raw afterward.

The moment the air was clear around us we began to fire again. Twice more we were hit by blasts that exploded before us and I felt as if the skin had been flayed from my hands, neck and chin—those hadn't been covered as I threw an arm across my eyes. Nevertheless, we continued to fire at the earliest opportunity after each blast. Max went back for another round of rifles, taking the empties with him. It would be foolish to leave them in the desert for the enemy to find and use. Ranos rifles were precious against these creatures and the wizards protecting them.

"More are out there than we imagined." Aris felt weary as he updated the High Commander. The High Commander had sent one of his guards out to bring Aris and Commander Gorth back to the private room—he didn't venture out.

"How are they faring?" Aris didn't fail to notice the coldness in the High Commander's voice and wanted to squeeze his throat until he squeaked. He buried that thought and concentrated on the High Commander's question instead.

"They are doing as well as anyone might expect—all are still alive at this point, but they have been hit many times by wizard blasts. The last few were attempts to blind them with sandblasts. They are tiring, I know that much. Dawn cannot come soon enough."

Dawn was little more than a click away. The enemy, in Aris' opinion, might try one last offensive in an effort to kill the Rangers before scurrying to bolt-holes to spend the day. Aris worried about that. He worried about the Rangers. Most of all, he worried about Reah.

$\sim$

Dawn was coming soon—we all knew it, tired as we were. Max was down—too exhausted to move. He huddled behind me on the ground, making himself as small a target as possible. He'd emptied himself, going for one more supply of rifles. I hoped what we had would last until the enemy went seeking their holes to hide in when daylight came. My other hope was that the enemy wizards might be tiring just as ours were. Bel expected them to hit us hard before they retreated with the dawn. What would they do? What *could* the do? That worried me as I attempted to aim at the enemy. My vision swam at times and I was forced to wait for it to clear before pulling the trigger. I had no desire to waste the power in the rifle Max had exhausted himself to bring to me.

My weariness kept me from registering Bel's frenzied hand signal for a moment, but it did register. He was telling us to back up. We began to back up, but Max didn't rise. Panicking, I moved to pull one arm as Bel grasped the other. We dragged Max backward with us, Bel setting the pace. He was worried about something—I could sense it as he hurried us along. It almost seemed to be an act of desperation.

It was then I noticed Delvin, who was gesturing wildly. He was the one sensing it. My exhausted brain just hadn't thought to look in his direction until now. Delvin sensed power. That was his talent. We kept backing up, even as the whistle in the air headed in our direction. This attack was their final effort. Delvin was gesturing for all of us to drop to the ground. We dropped where we stood and covered our heads as the explosion hit, blowing a perfect sphere of sand and soil around us high into the air.

# CHAPTER 9

"They're hit." Those were Aris' words as he ran from the room, leaving the High Commander to shout after him to come back. Aris wasn't about to obey that command—he used Max's trick of propelling himself from one point to another, landing in the desert moments before dawn. He witnessed the enemy fleeing from the brightening sky as he ran toward the scattered bodies of his Rangers. Did they live? Aris didn't take the time to send out the mental tendrils, checking for life. His fingers and other senses would tell him when he reached the bodies.

"Drink." That word penetrated my brain as a canteen was held to my lips. The sun was now shining brightly in the east and a blurry face was positioned over mine. Bel was leaning over me; I recognized him when my vision cleared enough for me to see. I drank as ordered, coughing painfully as too much liquid came too quickly.

"Re, sit up, baby." Bel coaxed. My limbs didn't want to obey. It took moments to force my feet and hands to move. Painfully I pulled myself to a sitting position. Bel was in the same condition, else he would have helped. I lifted the canteen away from him and drank.

"Jorvis and Lin are gone." Aris knelt next to me. I turned to look at him, sure now that he was a longed-for fantasy. Likely, I was still unconscious and dreaming or something.

"It's not a dream." Aris lifted a strand of hair off my forehead.

"Dead?" My voice was as dry as the dust I sat upon. We were in a bowl, I noticed. I had little memory of what had happened the night before, when the enemy wizards had thrown their worst at us, right at the last.

"Reah, they're dead. I don't think they suffered. We need to get the rest of you back to the station. Do you think you can stand?"

I didn't want to stand. I wanted to curl up right there and weep, but there wasn't enough fluid in my body to produce tears. Jorvis and Lin were dead. My body was numb, now, as was my brain. The rest of us were lucky to be alive. I nodded to Aris instead. I would stand if I had to. He and Bel lifted me from the sand. I stood. The standing was shaky, but I stood anyway, much like a newborn animal might, I imagined, as it rose for the first time after the birthing.

"I'll get you back to the station, but I'll drop you off just outside the walls. I want you to walk inside the gate. Hold each other up if you have to," Aris ordered. Bel and the rest of us nodded, too tired to speak. Aris could move us, just as Max could and he did so, dropping us off outside the gate as promised. I didn't have as much difficulty breathing this time, and that was a good thing. I might have considered never breathing again if it had taken any effort.

I wasn't expecting the crowd that waited silently for us on the inside, once we passed through the main gate into the station. Troops were lined up on both sides as we staggered in, covered in sand and filth. Max needed help, so Bel and I each had one of his arms over our shoulders, helping him. I had both my last rifles slung across my back, too. We all did. I didn't recognize any faces in the crowd as we walked past, except for one. Nods stood at the front, with his friends. If I hadn't been weary beyond measure, I might have taken pleasure in the look of shock that enveloped his face as he stared at me.

"Reah, nobody else can do this for you right now without discovering what you are." Aris and I were in a small bathroom, where he was pulling my clothing away. Crusted with sand and dust, my uniform appeared to be a dirty tan instead of the black it should be. I was inside his private suite; that information sank into my brain in a detached manner. The other Rangers had physicians tending them. Poor Jorvis and Lin had been left in the desert. I still wanted to weep for them and couldn't.

"Love, your skin is raw," Aris muttered as he pulled the cuffs of my shirtsleeves open, careful not to touch my hands more than necessary. It didn't matter—I was numb at the moment. I only felt the weariness. The pain would come later, when my body began to recover. Aris removed the rest of my clothing while I watched. Normally I would have blushed from embarrassment—no man had undressed me before. Not while I was conscious, anyway. My breasts were small— they made it easier to hide behind a male recruit's disguise. The rest of me—not voluptuous in the least. Not as men preferred their women to be.

"Love, you worry over the damnedest things," Aris whispered as he lifted me gently. I soaked in the tub in his bathroom while he washed me as carefully as he could. I was determined not to whimper or whine as he cleaned the tender parts. My face and hands felt as if they'd been burned when he settled me in the water. If I'd had the energy, I would have climbed right back out of the tub when that pain hit. Aris held me down, his voice crooning nonsense as he lifted a soft cloth and began his cleaning.

"He only needs ointment on his face and hands," Aris informed the old physician, who'd just come from tending Bel.

"This young one has seen more than any new recruit should," the old physician muttered, slathering ointment on raw skin. Recruit Re was in his own bed now, after Aris had cleaned him up and dressed him in a nightshirt.

"Yes. Too much, actually, but there is nothing you can do about such things in times of war."

"I know that," the old physician agreed, finishing his work. "Let him sleep as long as possible, then have a tray brought. All of them need to eat. Word has it that they may have to rise from their beds and help us if the enemy comes tonight."

"Yes." Aris' one-word answer said everything.

"Re, eat." I was commanded after the coaxing hadn't worked. Bel looked as if he should still be asleep—he was sitting next to me inside Aris' office. My food tray had been set on the edge of Aris' desk and now he demanded that I eat. If anything, I think I felt worse now than before I'd rested most of the day. The numbness was deserting me, leaving a mass of pain and weariness behind.

"There isn't a decent cook on this entire gods-forsaken military station," I muttered sarcastically and dipped into the beef dish I'd been brought. My comment brought an almost chuckle from Aris, but he repeated his command for me to eat so I ate. Even chewing seemed a chore better left undone.

The other Rangers straggled in while I ate—they'd already had a meal. Aris had waited until the last moment to wake me. Delvin still looked as if half his face had been scrubbed away—he'd gotten the full brunt of the sandblasts, being at the front when they'd come our way. I could see the shininess of the ointment on his skin over the raw parts.

"Sundown is in half a click," Aris announced as the Rangers took their seats around his desk. "I expect the spawn to head this way immediately. Delvin, do you know how many wizards were there before you left?"

"No true idea—Bel took six down, and I counted seventeen different levels of power in the beginning. That doesn't mean that a blocker wasn't employed somewhere, hiding some of them." I listened carefully, not even tasting my vegetables as I ate them. It was probably for the best.

"Re, how is your eye? Can you see well enough?" Aris turned to me as I had my fork halfway to my mouth. I set it down. At least my mouth wasn't full of food.

"I can see my food just fine," I mumbled, feeling embarrassed.

"Our recruit here was killing the enemy as fast as the rifle would shoot," Bel said. I just shrugged and stuffed food in my mouth so I wouldn't be forced to answer.

"I want to know what happened there at the end," Max said.

"Lin and Jorvis stepped outside the boundary," Bel sighed. That statement stopped me in mid-chew. I swallowed with difficulty. "The rest of us were blasted upward in a bubble. Re, whatever you have protects you—and us—in a sphere. We bounced when we dropped; that's what knocked most of us unconscious. If Aris hadn't come to get us, we might have been killed then. I can only imagine that they would have rushed us and delivered physical blows. Re doesn't have any defense against those." He pointedly looked at my still blackened eye.

"Thank you for coming for us," I said, lowering my head. I was afraid to look Aris in the eye—afraid that I might cry like an infant and now wasn't the time.

"You are welcome," Aris said softly.

"We will mourn our friends after this is over," Bel promised and rose. "We have a job to do tonight, and it may well determine whether Mandil lives or dies." He rose and stretched. Aris and the others rose as well, leaving me to be the last to stand. I stood with them. Live or die. That's what tonight was about. Crown City was the largest city upon Mandil, I knew that much. If Crown City fell, it would only be a matter of time, since the enemy would either devour or turn every living being inside the city and then take the other cities, towns and villages, one or two at a time. All the wizards were in Crown City; I'd learned that from Delvin earlier. There weren't that many with talent living upon Mandil, and we'd lost two of them last night.

"They're headed this way." The High Commander was walking down the hall toward Aris' office as we spilled out of it. His words didn't surprise any of us. I'm sure the Prince Royal's wizards had given him the information.

"How long before they arrive?'" Aris' gaze was steady on the High Commander.

"Less than a click, according to the Prince's chief wizard."

"Prepare yourselves, we'll pick up our weapons at the armory tonight," Bel took charge of the rest of us, leaving Aris to deal with the High Commander. I didn't envy Aris—the High Commander was sweating. We walked behind Bel just as we'd walked behind him into the desert—in a tight formation with me at the center. If anyone tried to toss wizardry at us, we'd still be protected.

We passed the rows of recruits—I saw Nods and his gang near the front of one column. They were given orders to hand charged ranos rifles off to older troops who'd emptied their weapons. They wouldn't be allowed to fire anything tonight. I wondered how that made Nods feel and if he'd concentrate on his assignment or his anger. Other troops were already gathering near the walls, all of them focused on several men walking the perimeter at the top. All dressed in red robes.

"Those are the Prince's wizards," Delvin whispered near my ear. He didn't sound complimentary. I nodded. Where were they when we'd lost two of ours last night? We were issued two rifles each at the armory and Bel led us to the center wall. We climbed up narrow, stone steps and positioned ourselves at the top. The red robes were on either side of us, watching, just as we were. Sanded boards were beneath our feet—smoothed enough so we could kneel to get shots off while being protected behind metal guards spaced evenly apart. I wondered how the battlements and walls would hold up under attacks by wizards. A half-moon rose on the horizon, helping our troops see better. They'd be able to locate the enemy when they came to the walls. Of course, with this particular enemy, that might prove to be too late.

The military station covered the northern edge of Crown City; it was the edge facing the desert, from which the enemy would come.

Only a small space on the eastern end belonged to the city proper. "The east end has two of the Prince's wizards guarding it, leaving us short on power," Delvin explained quietly beside me. "They'll open a path if needed should the Prince be forced to flee." I nodded—we had a little time to talk as we scanned the desert for signs of the approaching enemy. I wasn't surprised, either, that an escape plan was in place for the Prince. It sounded as if he and his wives might be the only ones guarded if things went badly for us. Everybody else had to fend for themselves. Bel paced behind us on the narrow defender's ledge. He was working out his nervousness, I think. Delvin was keeping his at bay by talking quietly.

"Who taught you to cook?" he asked. His question surprised me.

"I learned from watching my brothers—the first thing I made successfully at age nine was pastry dough. My brother beat me because it was better than his."

"Re, don't tell me anything more," Delvin focused on scanning the desert for enemy. I shrugged at his words. I didn't know why I'd said that about Edan—it wasn't something I'd told anyone else.

"Delvin, there—do you see?" I'd caught the first pinpoints of light.

"Re—I don't see anything," he hissed. Bel was beside me in a tick, kneeling at my side and squinting into the night.

"Re, you must be mistaken, I don't see anything either," Bel whispered. I was seeing more than one set of lights, now. Many more, in fact.

"Bel, I see them," I insisted. Was I hallucinating, again? Imagining something because I was looking so hard for it?

"She's not wrong, Bel." Aris was behind Delvin, staring out at the desert where I'd seen the lights. "They're blocking them from your sight somehow. Re, I'm not sure how you're seeing this, but I'm grateful. Delvin, hand me your rifle. Re, when I say, we'll both start shooting. When the enemy falls, the rogue wizards will determine that we've found a way around their wizardry and drop the shields. On my mark." Aris lifted Delvin's rifle into his hands. I took careful aim, waiting for Aris to give the signal. It came all too soon. I fired as Aris did, and lights winked out. I fired again and again, as quickly as my weapon would shoot. Every wizard around me drew in a breath as the shield around the enemy dropped and lights appeared everywhere. Close, too—closer than we wanted.

The Prince's wizards were shouting down the lines of troops along the defender's ledge, commanding them to fire and pointing the way. Some hit their marks, most didn't. Only the wizards and I were accurate as we took down the enemy. The lights appeared as a sea of winking points as they heaved toward the walls of the station. I wanted to tell my friends—the few that I had there—that I was proud to serve with them. I was beginning to have no hope of survival—our enemies were greater in numbers than any of us had suspected.

*Steady, Reah.* Those words inserted themselves into my mind as I kept firing. My actions were automatic, now. The wizards and I made some inroads into the numbers where we were stationed along the wall, but elsewhere, things were not going so well. The enemy was within a few ticks of reaching the walls of the station.

Bel set his rifle aside and sent out power blasts. That cleared the walls for a few ticks until more of the enemy came. Two more blasts were sent out. Although Bel was killing the enemy in swaths, it didn't seem to matter. More came. I kept firing. The whistling noise came, indicating a wizard's attack. Section leaders shouted for their charges to get down. We all made ourselves as small a target as possible when an entire section of the wall was blasted open, raining stone blocks and dead troops upon the ones inside the walls. The enemy raced toward that section, causing the troops on either side of the breach to run, even as their commanders and section leaders were shouting at them to stay at their posts.

Aris had little time to react to this turn of events and employed the relocation spell on the Rangers and Reah, positioning them inside the blasted-out portion of the wall. They recovered quickly, firing their rifles at the advancing horde of spawn. Aris was firing as quickly as he could over Reah's head—she was still on one knee and killing the enemy as fast as her weapon would shoot. Another blast came from the outside and another section of the wall was blown out. This time, instead of running away, the troops on either side dropped to a knee and began firing into the breach, killing many of the spawn crowding inside. Aris would have to do something soon or the station would be overrun. The city would then fall quickly. He was considering desperate measures when the last thing he might have expected appeared in the newly created gap in the wall before him.

Little hope remained—even I knew that as we fired desperately at seemingly endless numbers of the enemy. Some still appeared as the men they'd once been, but many had the muddy, grayish brown skin and fangs of the older ones. I fired on the largest of those—some of them nearly twice as tall as a normal man might be. Sometimes it took two shots to bring one of those down.

Another man walked inside the wall with the latest wave, and nothing touched him. I fired and the shots were deflected. He kept walking toward us. Aris was now shouting something I didn't recognize. A purplish glow hovered about this one, and something about that aura disturbed me. Something instinctive, almost, was frantically trying to tell me something about this one. As if I recognized it somehow, and knew that it was wrong. More wrong than any of the others we'd killed already, even the larger monsters that had stomped inside, bent on destruction.

Slowly I rose from my kneeling position, no longer firing my rifle. A part of my mind told me to lift my weapon and shoot, but I failed to heed it. Something else was calling out to me—telling me that more forceful measures were called for on this one. Was he a wizard? My senses told me no. This was no hedge wizard from an outlying village. This had the stink of evil about it, and something needed to be done.

I was shouting at the creature as I tossed my rifle away. Bel reached out to haul me back, but I shook off his grip as easily as a cow's tail brushes away flies. I took a step. And then another, much larger step. I was looking over the heads of the Rangers who surrounded me now. How had I grown so tall? I had no time to be concerned with so trivial a matter.

The man knew I was coming for him. He also knew that I recognized him as something other than the man he appeared to be. The realization caused him to slough his humanoid disguise—it melted away from him and he grew. Somehow, smoke was blown away from my nostrils as my target lengthened and expanded into a coppery, serpent-like creature, longer than twenty men, lying end to end. The creature was thick through the middle, too—nearly two men thick, his coppery scales gleaming in the light of the moon shining overhead. He hissed at me, revealing lengthy, sharp teeth that I somehow knew were poisonous.

Rising higher over the heads of the ones around me, I screamed at the troops to get back—they would die if they came in contact with any part of this monster. My voice came out in a roar. Had I time to analyze my transformation and my subsequent actions, it might have frightened me. I didn't have time, and it didn't matter. My hands, when they reached toward the monster as he crawled in my direction were scaled in gold with sharp talons for fingernails.

Had I thought this creature slow? He wasn't. Had he thought I might be slow? I wasn't. He struck. I grasped. His throat was in my hands and I was squeezing, sinking my talons into his flesh, past nearly impenetrable scales and digging into the tender muscle underneath. The monster hissed in my grip and thrashed, attempting to get away from me. I laughed. That also came out as a roar, with more smoke pouring from my throat and nostrils.

Many of the smaller enemy now tried to help the one I gripped in strong, taloned hands, but when they touched any part of me, they shrieked and dusted. More came, not learning from their dying cousins. All tried to attack me. All died in agony, blasting out their particles in a storm of dust, as if that might have any effect on me. I squeezed my prey harder. His long, poison-scaled tail was killing some of his own as he whipped it about. He would have bitten me if he could. I held his throat too tightly and he had no opportunity.

Aris nearly dropped where he stood as he watched what Reah had become. She was squeezing the life from of the Ra'Ak—monster that it was. Aris—known as Aurelius to his associates, was sending out mindspeech swiftly. Only one thing might contain Reah after she finished off this monster, and that something was others of her kind. The message was curt that he sent—he was still working to contain the spread of spawn: they were flooding inside the walls, although most of them were now attempting to rescue their creator.

Aris was correct in calling them spawn—they were a Ra'Ak's spawn in every sense of the word. If left alone to grow and thrive, after twenty turns or so they would become Ra'Ak too—terrible monsters that could devour entire worlds if allowed to go unchallenged. Aurelius' duty was to fight spawn. He was not one of the elite Ra'Ak killers—Aurelius was but a soldier in their army. He was calling out to some of them now through mindspeech, but Reah was just about to finish this one off without help. The troops, seeing what they considered two monsters, had fled to hide. Aurelius, posing as Aris, had pulled his Rangers back and they continued to fire upon the spawn, even as Reah killed them by the dozens. They were blistering and dusting the moment they touched any part of her.

Reah stood at a height roughly equivalent to two very tall men, with scales of gold and jointed, membranous wings of iridescent gold. Only her hair was a different color—the white it had always been. Aris should have known. Should have taken the hint from the Larentii. He didn't. He knew better, now. "Get down!" Aris shouted. The Ra'Ak, when he died, would dust just as his spawn would, only his dusting would produce fist-sized chunks that would blast out at incredible speed. Just one of those chunks could easily kill a man.

The light was fading from the monster's eyes, leaving them a dull, slitted green before he died. The chunks of the creature blasted out when death came. Did he think to harm me with that last attempt at vengeance? He could have saved himself the trouble. I shouted out my victory, and my roar shook the walls and the ground beneath my feet. Turning, then, I went after the spawn running this way and that, completely leaderless, now. Rogue wizards, too, were rushing out of the holes in the walls. They didn't escape me, either, dying more easily than the spawn. Their power and spells had no effect on me when I jerked them up and crushed them in my hands. My fingers slippery with blood, I went after more of them.

❧

"We'll have to turn to capture him," Jaydevik Rath shouted at Aris. Aris blinked At Jaydevik and Jayd's brother, Gardevik, attempting to understand what they intended to do.

"What? Wait!" Aris shouted. He'd sent the message wrong. He'd left something out. Garde and Jayd were turning, their full Thifilathi dark and methodical as they unraveled a net between them, running after Reah, who was still killing spawn and rogue wizards. They were all running from her, now.

"Relax, father, we're here to help." Gavin was there with Winkler and several others.

"Child, no," Aris was desperate, now. "They can't net her. Get them back!"

"Aurelius, you can't stop a High Demon in full Thifilathi. What's wrong?" Kiarra was there, looking up into Aris' face in concern.

"That's Reah! They can't hurt her. I only wanted help bringing her back!"

"Oh, lord," Kiarra muttered. "Come on, we need to be there when they take her down."

❧

"Somehow, others had joined me in my fight. Others I didn't recognize. A very large wolf bounded past, snapping heads off spawn as he ran. Another man arrived, and he quickly had lengthy claws growing from his fingers. Heads were removed with casual swipes of his hands. Another wolf came. Where had these creatures come from? It didn't distract me from my goal, however. I was still killing spawn at a record pace. Two more creatures came. Tall creatures—taller than I, even. Their skin was dark and smoke poured from their nostrils as they came up on either side of me, a large net in their hands. They handled it carefully, as if it burned them, somehow. I gave it no thought, concentrating on my quarry instead. Would I have turned to fight them if I'd known what would happen? Perhaps. If I had, I have no idea how that fight would have ended.

"No!" Aris screamed as the net was tossed over Reah's head. She shrieked the moment the power web settled over her and began to burn her skin. Falling, she clawed and bit at the knotted strands, thrashing about on the ground in terrible pain. The nets had been designed and created to contain rogue High Demons. Reah was screaming—a high-pitched wail that hurt the ears. Her skin was smoking now from the burning, her wings scored and nearly burned through in places.

"Get it off, get it off!" Aris shouted as he flung himself toward Reah. Kiarra, powerful in her own right, folded space, lifted her hands and destroyed the net with a thought.

# CHAPTER 10

"Aurelius—father—you can't blame yourself. It was a miscommunication." Gavin rubbed his sire's shoulders. "Jayd and Garde have come back to themselves and are just as worried as the rest of us. They cannot understand how someone like Reah not only exists, but managed to escape notice until now."

"I didn't give them proper information. I only said I needed help getting a High Demon back to Le-Ath Veronis. I didn't tell them she was female and not rogue. Now she is in terrible pain."

"The Larentii and the healers are tending to her," Gavin attempted to soothe Aurelius.

"Karzac says the wings will heal, as will the burns. However, it will be painful for a few days before things get better." Lissa, Queen of Le-Ath Veronis walked into the kitchen to give Aurelius the news.

"Love, will she be in full Thifilatha the entire time?" Gavin was one of Lissa's mates and the father of her youngest child.

"Renegar says it's best—the wings might not heal properly otherwise."

Aurelius cursed softly. "Will she even understand what we're saying if we speak to her?"

"That is difficult to say—Garde says that he understands most of the time, but the closer it comes to the full moon, the less that happens." Lissa patted Aurelius' hand.

"How is she High Demon? She can't be full High Demon," Gavin said.

"She isn't," Lissa tapped her nose. "She's a quarter, but somehow received the full complement of High Demon gifts. The other thing I know and I'm waiting to talk to Glindarok about first, is that Reah belongs to Glinda's family. Somehow, one of Glinda's brothers fathered Reah's mother. Reah is Glinda's niece."

"I thought all her brothers were dead."

"So did we all. I've got a message out to Kifirin. If anybody can sort this out, he can."

"May I see her?" Aurelius sounded lost, and as a four-thousand-year-old modified vampire, that didn't happen often.

"She's sleeping now, so it shouldn't be a problem." Lissa pulled Aurelius off the barstool in the palace kitchen and folded space, taking Aurelius and Gavin to the dungeon beneath their feet in less than a blink.

"She's not in pain." Renegar assured Aurelius as he went to his knees at the sight of Reah. She lay in a golden-scaled heap in the floor of the largest cell in Lissa's dungeon.

"But she's lying on the cold floor," Aurelius buried his head in his hands.

"I will remedy that shortly, as soon as Karzac is done," Renegar assured the spawn hunter. Karzac, physician to the Saa Thalarr and the spawn hunters, was doing a last-minute inspection, making sure they'd missed no burns on Reah's naked flesh. The gold of her body and wings was scored with net burns, some overlapping others.

"The only other female High Demon that can turn is Glinda, and she's white when she's Thifilatha," Lissa murmured. "She keeps hoping her daughters will turn, but Jayd says that they haven't been angry or provoked enough to turn. Those husbands of theirs keep them happy and away from any stressful situations."

"Then I'm surprised that Reah didn't turn before now—she's had plenty of those things in her life," Aurelius sighed. Gavin pulled his vampire sire to his feet.

"Are you sure this cell will hold her?" Lissa looked up at Renegar. He towered over her at eight and a half feet. Lissa was only five feet tall.

"I have reinforced it with father's help. It will hold. I have also placed the command that she not turn back until given permission," Renegar nodded. Nodding was another human gesture he enjoyed using.

"How's the patient?" Garde, Jayd and Glinda all appeared, using the High Demon ability to skip from one place to another.

"Sleeping—I have numbed the pain," Renegar turned to look at the fifteen-foot creature inside the cell.

"Jayd, how could you not tell she was female?" Glinda glared at her mate. Jaydevik Rath was King of the High Demons, while Gardevik his brother was Prime Minister under his brother's rule. Garde was also one of Lissa's mates.

"We were under the impression that it was a rogue we were chasing. Gender didn't enter into this."

"Glinda, there's something else you should know," Lissa offered.

"What's that?" Glinda turned to Lissa, the question on her lips. Glinda was beautiful, with long, white-blonde hair falling down her back, blue eyes and short in stature. Anyone not taking Glinda seriously might find themselves on the wrong end of a very sharp knife. Glinda had worked as a bodyguard for a very long time before returning to her homeworld and taking her place as Queen of the High Demons.

"Reah is related to you," Lissa said, putting an arm around Glinda's shoulders. "One of your brothers fathered Reah's mother, I think."

"How did I miss this?" Aurelius moaned. "Reah looks very much like Glinda in her humanoid form."

"She's related to the royal family?" Jayd was blowing smoke. Tendrils of it curled from his nostrils. "How did one of Glinda's brothers escape?"

"Jayd, calm down," Glinda glared at him. Jayd made an effort to get himself in hand.

"You should not expect this one to pay for her father's sins." Kifirin appeared next to Lissa and pulled her into an embrace. "Avilepha, I have missed you. You should have called me before now."

"But which brother was it?" Glinda had reason to despise her brothers—they'd killed her parents before her oldest brother took the throne for himself, as shouldn't have been. Glinda had been named heir and betrothed to Jaydevik Rath barely a month after her birth. Her oldest brother wanted the throne for himself. Female High Demons were extremely rare and one born to the High Demon King was destined to have the throne instead of one of the males.

"Your youngest, Denevik," Kifirin replied. "And he left the others shortly after your parents were killed. He wanted no part of that and argued with your oldest brother before striking out on his own. Reah is his only remaining heir and grandchild."

"Denevik is still alive?" Glinda's voice was almost a whisper.

"Yes, little Queen. You are the youngest as you know, but Denevik is only five hundred turns older than you. I would have hunted him down if the crimes against your parents had been his responsibility. They were not. I have not prevented him from moving about freely. Should he commit any crimes, he will answer to me or one of mine. As it is, he feels he is outcast and does not attempt to return to my planet for that reason."

"You are sure he was not involved in the murder of my parents?"

"Little Queen, of course I am sure. Your eldest brother assured him it would be a peaceful takeover. As you know, it was not. Denevik was on the southern continent when the coup occurred." A bit of smoke curled from Kifirin's nostrils.

"Why did they lie to him?" Jayd muttered. He knew not to push Kifirin. The High Demon planet was named after the god who'd created not only that world, but all the dark realm. Sometimes they forgot who Kifirin was.

"Most likely so he wouldn't give them away," Lissa intervened. It was never wise to upset Kifirin too much.

"My mate is correct," Kifirin agreed. "What have you done to our youngest here?" He nodded toward the cell and Reah's body, still in full Thifilatha.

"We assumed she was rogue. We netted her." Gardevik offered, directing Kifirin's attention away from Jayd and Glinda. "If we had asked questions first, this would not have happened, High Lord." Gardevik bowed his head slightly toward Kifirin.

"How was the net removed?"

"Kiarra destroyed it." Aurelius also bowed his head slightly to Kifirin.

"She has enough power to do so," Kifirin agreed. "I will be watching how you treat our little one from now on. Be careful not to make too many mistakes." Kifirin disappeared swiftly.

"That's my great-niece." Glinda looked inside the enlarged cell at the winged, sleeping figure lying on thick mattresses upon the floor. Her scored and burned wings drooped about her, her short white hair spiked and tousled upon her head as if she'd sweated while she'd burned under the net.

"I know not what to do," Garde sighed.

"What would you do, if someone netted your mate?" Aurelius was now displaying his anger—something that seldom happened.

"Kill, most likely," Garde nodded and skipped away.

"Aurelius, you know not to start this," Lissa crossed arms over her chest. Gardevik was hers, just as Gavin, Aurelius' oldest living vampire child was.

"Yes, I know not to start this," Aurelius muttered. "Yet Garde just said he would kill for you. How do you think I feel?" Aurelius folded away, leaving Lissa, Gavin, Jayd and Glinda behind. Renegar had stood by, watching the entire exchange.

"The next three days will be difficult. Something must be brought for her to eat when she wakes, but I do not think she will eat. That will make things worse." Renegar folded away.

"What do High Demons eat while they're Thifilathi? Or in this case, Thifilatha?" Lissa asked.

"What wolves and the others eat when changed," Jaydevik replied, raking a hand through his hair. "Raw meat. We do not have to kill it, but if we eat at all, it must be raw. The prisoners we have held in the past have been offered live cattle or sheep. Failing that, freshly butchered meat was brought. They usually consumed that if not the other."

"And if she doesn't eat?"

"She will be emaciated when she wakes," Glinda said. "What are we to do, Lissa? That is my kin." Glinda's face looked drawn and weary as she stared at the creature inside the cell. "I thought all my brothers dead. I have only vague recollections of Denevik. I have hated my brothers—all of them—for a very long time." Glinda skipped away, leaving Jayd behind.

"You know that all her needs will be provided by the crown of Kifirin," Jayd offered stiffly.

"I think all her needs will be provided by my sire," Gavin replied almost as stiffly.

"Nevertheless, the offer stands." Jayd skipped after his mate.

"Gavin, this is the worst mess," Lissa looked up at her first mate.

"Yes, and I have never seen Aurelius this upset. We must attempt to smooth things over, somehow. Let us go find Norian. He holds the records on our High Demon there," Gavin nodded in Reah's direction.

"Yes. Let's go find Norian," Lissa sighed.

A noise woke me. It took several ticks for me to realize that it was my own moaning. My body felt as if it were still on fire. I remembered that much—I'd been burned by a net of some sort. Two tall, dark creatures had tossed it over me, causing intense and immediate pain. My screaming I also remembered and Aris' shouting. He'd been using a language I didn't recognize. Had he ordered this done? When I'd become whatever it was that I had become in order to fight off the monster, this had happened. Oh, they'd waited until most of the enemy was down, but they'd done it.

Blinking my eyes open, I worked to get them to focus. What I found had me rising off several thick mattresses placed upon a stone floor. I knew what surrounded me—a cell to hold prisoners. A large cell, but I was now quite large as well. My prison had me swallowing with difficulty—my throat was dry and the sobs when they came were also dry—I had no moisture within my body to produce tears. Rising with difficulty, I crept toward the thick metal bars that prevented me from escape—I tried them with my hands just to see.

Fear drove my sobbing now, and a loud keening came from my throat. All I could see was a bare white wall opposite my prison, with a washed stone floor extending from the back edge of my cell to the white wall. Nothing else lay down a long, brightly lit corridor. It did nothing to stay my fears—I'd been claustrophobic for as long as I could remember. Closed spaces had me worried if I wasn't sure I could escape my surroundings easily enough. My room at the military station had been windowless, but the door was near my bed and that led to a hallway and a simple escape if I needed it. The bars and walls of my prison kept me from escaping. My keening and my fright grew.

"What's that noise?" Lissa sat straight up in bed. Winkler, her werewolf mate had gone to bed with her and he sat up as well. "Oh, my gosh, it's coming from the dungeon." Lissa flipped covers aside and rose in a blink. Any vampire could move faster than sight and Lissa, as the Vampire Queen, could move faster than most. Winkler was right behind her, his sharp ears picking up the noise as well.

"Get Aurelius and call for a Larentii," Lissa shouted at Winkler as she took off at a run. Moments later Lissa was pressed as far against the white wall opposite Reah's cage as she could get—Reah, still in full Thifilatha, was beating her wings against the bars of her cage and when that failed to work, she hurled her body against the bars instead. Many of her burns had broken open and were bleeding now.

"Reah!" Aurelius shouted the moment he arrived. "Reah, stop! You're hurting yourself!" His words fell on temporarily deaf ears; Reah failed to notice anything or anyone.

"Little one." Renegar's father Pheligar appeared out of nothing, standing within arm's length of Reah as she continued to crash into the bars of her cage. He held out a hand while light formed around it. Reah blinked at this, stopping her assault against the bars for a moment—long enough for Pheligar to touch her forehead, sending her sliding to the floor, unconscious.

"I forgot to tell you, her records say she's slightly claustrophobic." Norian Keef appeared with Thurlow, another of Lissa's mates. Lissa had seventeen in all and occasionally had difficulty keeping them all sorted out.

"She's claustrophobic and we put her in a dungeon. That makes so much sense," Lissa muttered sarcastically and tossed up a hand.

"Your dungeon was one of the few places we could keep her confined," Gardevik appeared. Someone had called him—most likely Thurlow.

"I don't think she should wake up in a dungeon again," Aurelius moved to the bars and stared at Reah. Kneeling down, he stroked her face.

"Where can we move her? Any High Demon in full Thifilathi, or Thifilatha, in this case, is dangerous. You cannot depend on reasoning with them."

"Move her to my beach house. Surely Reemagar and Connegar can shield the entire place so she can't escape." Lissa named her two Larentii mates.

"And if she destroys the whole house?" Garde folded his arms.

"Then I'll build another," Lissa snapped. "If Reah hadn't been there, Aurelius would likely have become a snack for the Ra'Ak on Mandil. He's not Saa Thalarr and doesn't have enough power to fight off one of those things. He's only spawn hunter for them. The Ra'Ak were probably looking to kill him and a few other spawn hunters there, don't you think?" Lissa glared at her High Demon mate. "Reah recognized that piece of crap and killed him for us. Then she got netted—and by relatives on top of that."

"We're only in-laws," Gardevik huffed.

"We're only in-laws," Lissa mimicked, slapping Garde on the upper arm.

"Ow." Garde held his arm. Even a High Demon knew not to pick a fight with a vampire while in humanoid form. Garde knew not to pick a fight with Lissa, even while he was Full Thifilathi. Lissa had killed too many rogue High Demons. Garde knew better.

"We will move her." Reemagar and Connegar appeared. They knew when their mate mentioned their names. Nexus echo, a talent employed by the Larentii, enabled them to hear their names when spoken.

"Two more days." Aurelius buried his head in his arms on Gavin's desk. Gavin and all Lissa's mates were members of her Inner Circle and worked in some capacity or other to keep the palace and Le-Ath Veronis running smoothly. Gavin, along with Anthony, another of Lissa's vampire mates, oversaw the palace guards.

"Father, they meant to kill you on Mandil." Gavin observed. "They have gotten cocky after killing Rolfe. They saw that as their victory and not as his intended suicide. Had you not made use of the wizards already there, you might not have survived."

"If Reah hadn't been there, the wizards wouldn't have survived either," Aurelius muttered. "Child, this wait is killing me. How is she going to forgive this? How?"

"Father, what is there to forgive?"

"I used her. For my own purposes. Cut her hair and disguised her as a common soldier. Sent her into danger many times when I did not go myself. And then failed to get the proper message to the High Demons. She might have been killed."

"High Demons are difficult to kill, father."

"But Lissa says Reah isn't full High Demon. She has human traits. She must void as any other humanoid must."

"If you give her blood, that will cease."

"But will it have any effect upon someone of that race? Even a partial one?"

"I do not have the answer to that, father. Perhaps you should approach Kifirin when he is in a more charitable mood."

"Only Lissa can expect an answer when she calls out to him."

"He is her second mate."

"As Roff says, that is a technicality. Kifirin is her most powerful mate."

"All the dark races are his children. He created the vampires, the werewolves, the High Demons and the Ra'Ak. The shapeshifters and many others are also his. Had he not slept for a time, we would not be dealing with the Ra'Ak and their spawn now. As spawn hunters, perhaps he owes us answers, father."

"As one of Lissa's mates, you may not worry over approaching him," Aurelius sighed. "I am not so well-connected. He is not obligated to me in the least, I think."

"I'm not going to toss this meat in there like she's some wild animal." Lissa glared at Garde. Lissa and her vampire mates could stand on the bright side of Le-Ath Veronis. Any other vampire could not unless they were spawn hunters or Saa Thalarr. The planet rotated on its side, leaving half in constant darkness, the other half in perpetual light. Lissa's beach house was on the light half of the planet. Reah now slept in the large, well-lit foyer. The Larentii had shielded the house so Reah couldn't escape in her Thifilatha form.

"That's how we feed prisoners," Garde grumbled.

"She's not a prisoner. She's healing. There's a difference."

"Lay it on a tray beside her sleeping pad and I will wake her." Reemagar was listening to the verbal sparring between Lissa and Garde. As Larentii, he would not touch raw meat. Larentii fed on sunlight mostly, although any energy source would work. They preferred the light of a sun and often had lengthy discussions over red, yellow, green and blue-tinged sunlight. Most of those conversations occurred in mindspeech, so no humanoids had ever entered into that debate.

Garde seemed reluctant to approach the sleeping female, so Lissa took the tray that held the steak, turned both herself and the tray of meat to mist and left it beside Reah, reappearing beside Garde in seconds. Reemagar went to wake Reah.

My body almost refused to obey my command to move. I was stiff and still in some pain. I was no longer locked inside a cell, however. Sunlight shone around me as I sat up stiffly. Windows were all around, with light shining through the clear glass. Moaning as my head pounded after sitting up, I reached up and held it with both hands.

"Little one, you must eat." One of the Larentii stood before me. "We have done as much as we can for your pain—your body needs to heal itself. Except for this headache." Blue hands reached toward me and touched my temples. The throbbing pain went away quickly.

"Did you think I wouldn't be civil?" I looked up into his bright blue eyes as he drew his hands away.

"You speak in this form?"

"Was I not supposed to?"

"Most do not—they merely growl or roar."

"Well, I didn't know what I was. Therefore, I didn't know what I was or wasn't supposed to do."

"You need to eat." Two more people moved into my line of vision. The male had dark hair, dark eyes and was tall and handsome. The female was much shorter, had red-blonde hair and was very pretty.

"Who are you? And I'm not hungry, thank you." I wasn't—I felt as if I were about to heave, if truth be known.

"Reah, you must eat or you'll be weak when we allow you to turn back," the Larentii said.

"You're keeping me from turning back now? I thought I was going to be this from now on." I held a huge, clawed hand in front of me.

Scores and blisters remained on my skin and I was naked, I discovered. Most likely there wasn't clothing to be had off the rack to fit my enlarged frame.

"Clothing will merely burn off your body, were you to wear it. The net was a mistake—we thought you were a rogue High Demon," the handsome man coughed into his hand.

"You keep saying High Demon. What is that?" I blinked at him now.

"What you are," the woman spoke. "I am Lissa, Queen of Le-Ath Veronis. Although you're only a quarter. You've inherited all the High Demon gifts, though."

"They don't call us High Demon inside the Alliance—it's just what we call ourselves," the man spoke again. "The Alliance calls us Kiffs."

"From Kifirin? That's what that race is?" I'd done research in my dayschool classes—Kifirin hadn't belonged to the Alliance long. "So, who made the mistake and did this to me?" I held out my left arm—it was laced with burns down its length. Some of the burns looked more raw than others.

"Jayd and I did. Aurelius sent out the message that he needed help bringing a High Demon back in Full Thifilatha, and we mistakenly assumed you were rogue." The male backed up immediately when smoke curled from my nostrils.

"Who is Aurelius?" I hadn't heard that name before.

"Aris—that was the name he used," the Queen spoke again.

"He helped do this to me?" I looked at my other arm—it was just as bad as the first.

"Not intentionally, and he's been upset with us ever since." Those words brought a smoke-filled snort from me as I rose from my bed on the floor, my head nearly scraping the tall ceiling as I bent down to look out the windows. I'd never seen an ocean before, yet one stretched before me, the blue of the water something I'd only seen in vids until now.

"I can call him—he wants to see you—talk to you," Queen Lissa said.

"What if I don't want to talk to him?" I sat on the floor so I could have a better and more comfortable view through the windows.

"Reah, that will break his heart, I think," Lissa said softly.

"He wasn't worried about that before." Yes, my pain was probably talking for me right then and I felt light-headed and dizzy. "How long before sir Larentii here lets me become myself again? And since this is an Alliance world, is the military going to come calling and haul me back into service? I have to tell you I haven't gotten the best of treatment at their hands so far. And don't even suggest I contact my family. I want to separate myself from them—legally." I could—I was old enough and had reason enough. I just didn't have the courage to do it before now.

"Which family?" The High Demon male asked. He still hadn't introduced himself.

"What other family do I have? The one on Tulgalan, of course. And if Addah Desh wants his name back, he can have it. I'll keep the one they gave me on Mandil. At least there were people there who seemed to actually care about me."

"You could have your grandfather's name. It hasn't been used in nearly fifteen hundred years," the male said. "My name is Gardevik— Gardevik Rath. I am Prime Minister for Jaydevik Rath, King of Kifirin. His wife, Queen Glindarok, is your great-aunt. Her brother, Denevik, fathered your mother. We understand that she is dead. We are investigating her death, or at least Norian Keef is. There may have been nefarious intentions involved. Regardless, your grandfather's last name is Lith. You are only one of three members left alive who belong to that house."

"If my mother was killed, then I'd look at Marzi and Edan Desh first," I muttered sarcastically. Many things were coming clear for me now.

"I believe that's exactly who Norian is investigating," Lissa told me. She was holding something back, I could tell, but I didn't remark on it. I was here as her guest I figured and it wouldn't do to insult my hostess.

"Please talk to Aurelius," Lissa went on.

"How can he want to talk to me, when I look like this?" Holding my arms out hurt, so I dropped them after a few ticks.

"He knows what else you are and that you won't always look like this. Besides, there are things he needs to tell you," Lissa said. Perhaps if I'd met the Queen of Le-Ath Veronis under other circumstances, we might have been friends quickly. I didn't think that was possible. "Norian will come and speak with you soon. About your family on Tulgalan and your status as a member of the Alliance military. He'll sort that out for you. I think you have options, Reah Desh. Please consider all of them carefully. In the meantime, if you don't want that huge haunch of beef over there, we can probably find something else for you to eat."

"If you have a kitchen, I'll make it myself. I haven't gotten any good food since I cooked last time."

"That might be difficult with these hands." The Larentii gave me a beautiful smile. I hadn't realized they could or would smile.

"You are teasing me?" I watched his face. It was fascinating.

"Yes. Little one, you may cook again soon. I do not recommend it now, you are very weak and your body is healing. Your wings are most damaged and we want them to be healed and functional again. That is why you must wait to return to your normal size."

"I have wings?" I didn't know until then.

"I will not touch them—have someone else spread them for you when you are well and turn again. They are an iridescent gold, much like the rest of your scales and skin." The Larentii was giving me an encouraging look.

"I want a bath." I'd never been so forward before. Where had that come from?

"You have never been treated as a person in your own right before," the Larentii nodded at me. "You may have a bath if Lissa will consent to having her pool cleaned afterward."

"But the water may sting her skin," Lissa actually looked concerned.

"I will remove the chemicals and put in oatmeal—it will do her good," the Larentii replied. "I am Reemagar. Not to be confused with

Renegar. He and I are not related. We are named after our mothers, whose names were similar. Renegar's mother still lives. Mine died when I was born. Like yours, little one. We were both motherless when we came into the world."

"I hope your childhood was a good one," I said before thinking.

"My father was and still is very kind and loving. He watches over me still, as any Larentii parent will."

"Reah?" I stiffened when I heard his voice. What had they said his name was? I still thought of him as Aris.

"Aris, I was about to have a bath." I turned to look at him. Maybe he would take a look at me and walk away. As he should. He looked the same—dark-gold hair that swept his shoulders, making him lion-like in his appearance. Wide shoulders, tall, strong. Just the sight of him squeezed my heart.

"Reah, please talk to me. That's all I ask. I want to explain so many things to you."

"Aris, what can we have?" I turned away from him, looking out over the ocean again. "I still have five turns of service owed to the Alliance. I have no idea what they'll think about all this. I have family on Tulgalan from whom I wish to separate. They have nothing for me and never have had anything for me. If they want me back, it will be for my cooking skills only. I lost any hope of having their love when I was four."

"Reah, we are connected, you and I." Aris came to stand beside me. The Larentii and the others faded away. I still wondered how they did that. It made me desire that skill. "And my name is Aurelius. Most likely, you haven't studied old Earth. That is where I am from. I am more than four thousand years old and was a vampire before accepting a position as spawn hunter for the Saa Thalarr. That is how I walk in daylight and eat normal food. I still retain my vampire abilities." Lengthy claws slid from his fingers. I watched this in fascination, placing my much larger hand next to his. My talons were long, but his claws were longer.

"They are very sharp and will even cut through metal," Aris said. "I want you to call me Aurelius, or Auri. I still hold hope that you will say it with love in your voice someday." I watched as his claws slid back, leaving normal nails behind. "We are not so different, Reah," he coaxed. "Give us a chance. Come, Reemagar is sending mindspeech—the pool is ready for your bath. You let me bathe you once, when you were too exhausted to prevent it. Let me help you again. You have no idea how beautiful you are, love."

"I'm not." I didn't look at him. I ached. I felt as if I would be ill. Too many emotions warred with one another.

"Reah, come. Please." He would have helped me up if I hadn't been more than twice his height at the moment. Standing with difficulty, I wobbled toward the back of the massive home. It was lovely, as any home belonging to a Queen might be. Marble floors, plaster walls, sculpture, paintings—it put the Tulgalan Governor's home to shame. Aurelius led me; I followed unsteadily behind him until we found Reemagar standing beside a large pool in the back. Oatmeal powder had been mixed in the water, making it a cloudy color. Reemagar used power to lower me into the water; I was too weak to climb in on my own.

"My love, don't fall asleep in the water," Aurelius warned after a while. The warmth of the water lulled me and I closed my eyes.

"I will lift her out." Was that someone else's voice? I didn't care; I was nearly asleep. I was laid on a soft bed and covered carefully.

*Sleep my love* came into my head. Those words weren't needed; I was asleep already.

# CHAPTER 11

*I* woke in a normal size bed for the first time in days, still feeling weak and achy. "You'll feel that way for a few days still; you must eat and get your strength back to heal properly." Turning my head, I looked into the green-gold eyes of a man I hadn't seen before. "I have seen you," he gave a half-smile. "You have been unconscious while I have seen you. I am Karzac, healer for the Saa Thalarr and spawn hunters. I am one of Lissa's seventeen mates." He had light-brown hair, was nearly six blocks tall and seemed competent.

"I should be competent," he pulled the thoughts straight from my head. "I have been a physician for more than fifteen thousand years. Before that, I was a physician on Refizan."

"You're Refizani?" My eyebrows were lifting in surprise. "My father always bragged about his Refizani gardener."

"Many of my race make good gardeners. We have other talents," he was smiling again. "Someone will come and help you bathe. We are expecting you at the breakfast table this morning and Aurelius and I will be watching to make sure you eat. You don't have to eat much—we will be feeding you every two hours or so. Small meals so you won't become ill."

"I don't know if I can get up."

"I know." He reached out and placed his hands on me. I felt better after that. He took my hand and helped me off the bed. I discovered that someone had dressed me in a pretty nightdress. Aurelius walked into the room. I almost shrank away from him as he lifted me in his arms. Karzac left us, closing the bedroom door behind him.

"You're not afraid of me now, are you?" Aurelius kissed my forehead. I almost fell asleep again in the tub, he was so careful bathing me. "Love, stay with me," he murmured, kissing my palms. I was carried down long corridors later, after Aurelius dressed me in soft trousers and a matching tunic of deep green. I had no idea where he'd gotten the clothing. Socks were on my feet; "There is no need for shoes just yet," he'd told me.

Shocked best described how I reacted at the number of people sitting at the Queen's table. Nearly all of them male, I noticed. One other female was there, besides the Queen of Le-Ath Veronis. She had white hair like mine, only it was quite long, hanging past her waist. Her eyes were blue where mine were green. Gardevik was there—I recognized him from before. He sat next to another man who looked very much like him. The woman with the white hair drew my attention again when she hissed out a breath and stood.

"Jayd, she looks like my mother!"

I must have been staring at her—I didn't look like anyone except my mother; someone had let that slip when I was little.

"Reah, this is your great-aunt Glindarok, Queen of Kifirin." Lissa made the announcement as if she were used to telling people daily that they were related to royalty. It had been mentioned before, but it hadn't felt real. This was real. She'd said I looked like her mother.

"Does your lady mother still live?" I asked. Merely asking a question wearied me.

"No. My mother is dead. Nearly fifteen hundred years dead." Her words were a blow to both of us. I had hoped to meet someone who looked like me. Perhaps it was the hope of seeing my own mother, finally. I had never seen an image of her—those had been destroyed or hidden.

"Love, sit here." Aurelius lowered me beside a high-backed chair covered in gold-patterned fabric. After settling me in the chair, he sat beside me.

Karzac was there near the head of the table, watching me as promised. A plate of food was set in front of me—soft-cooked eggs with toast and fruit. The others were getting other things. I knew it was because I'd been ill that I was getting what I was—the meat dish might have been too spicy for a weak stomach.

I couldn't eat much and observed as a child sitting next to Lissa was eating properly under his father's watchful gaze. He looked to be twelve or thirteen, had dark hair and eyes and seemed to be tall for his age.

"That is Gavril, Gavin and Lissa's child," Aurelius whispered near my ear. I was doing my best to eat while feeling weary. This was my first meal since leaving Mandil.

"Aurelius, are Bel and the others all right?" I turned my gaze to his face. It was a good face—a handsome face—framed by the dark-gold hair that made me think of him as a lion of a man. Well, vampire, I suppose.

"Bel and the remaining wizards are well," Aurelius smiled at me. "You saved Mandil, my love, and the Rangers. I think they would be grateful, if they knew what they were truly seeing that night."

"I won't get to see them again, will I?" That upset me.

"Love, all of them saw you turn. They've had no dealings with High Demons—or vampires. Neither of us might be welcomed back to Mandil, though I think Bel and the Rangers might be happy to see us."

I stared at my plate. The first real friends I'd ever had and I'd never see them again.

"Reah, others will come." Aurelius rubbed my back gently.

"Aurelius, do you have the answer to everything?" I stood on shaky legs, intending to walk away. Where, exactly, I had no idea—I wasn't sure where I was in the first place.

"Reah, I do not mean to upset you like this." Aurelius was beside me suddenly—he had vampire speed and I had nothing at all at the moment, including a destination. I was at his mercy and it was best that I remember that.

"Our apologies," Aurelius turned to the others. "Reah is not feeling well." He was right about that at least—I didn't feel well at all. I wanted to curl in a ball and weep. I'd never see Bel, Delvin, Hish or any of the others. They'd counted me as one of their own and I'd felt as if I'd belonged with them there at the end. Here, I stood on unsteady ground. Slapped right back to the Alliance, whom I was sure would come calling soon to let me know how things stood between them and me. On Mandil, my family had become what they should be— ghosts that I wasn't forced to deal with any longer. Now, their specters were back and I'd have to deal with them, too. Aurelius? Where did he fit? He kept telling me we were connected; calling me his love. What was that supposed to mean? Nobody had ever loved me before. *Nobody.*

"Reah, I can't fix everything overnight," Aurelius lifted me up once we were outside the dining hall. "You must give me time. I wish to know you better, and you must know me better as well. Bring your troubles to me and we will work them out together. I promise." His golden-brown eyes looked into mine with concern.

"Aurelius, how can I tell you things like that? It's embarrassing," I muttered, burying my head against his shoulder.

"You can keep your head against my shoulder and tell me anything. You will learn that it is extremely difficult to embarrass, shame or surprise an old vampire." Was he smiling as he kissed the top of my head? It felt like it. Perhaps I was imagining things. "Come, love," he added, "I will take you to the light half of the planet where they grow the fruits and vegetables. You will see where much of the food comes from for Le-Ath Veronis."

"Jaydevik, I must return to Kifirin." Glinda's hands shook as she pushed her chair away from the table and stood.

"My love?" Jayd was beside her in seconds, taking her hands in his.

"It is too much. Like seeing my mother again, only this one will never be," Glinda couldn't finish, a sob escaped her. "Jayd, I know she's kin, but this is too hard."

"My apologies." Jayd said and skipped Glinda away.

~

Aurelius set me down in a grove of trees. Until then, I hadn't realized that Aurelius might take me anywhere on a whim, just by disappearing from one place and reappearing in another. "We call it folding space," he said softly as he settled me in the middle of an orchard. "Corent, how are you?" Aurelius said to the male who approached us. I stared in shock as the one called Corent walked toward us, his hair turning from a sea green to a deep blue in only a few ticks.

"Corent is of the Green Fae," Aurelius had an arm around my waist, helping to keep me upright without being obvious about it. "Corent can grow fruit trees in less than a third of the time it would normally take and his apples, peaches and pears are the best I've ever tasted," Aurelius held out his other hand to Corent, who smiled and took it.

"The ripening season will come soon," Corent was smiling at me, too. I could only stare as his hair turned yet another color—a medium blue this time.

"A storm is coming and the weather is somewhat unstable. My hair reflects this," Corent's smile was bigger. "I inherited this from my mother. She always knew what the weather would be. I know because of my hair."

"That must be most useful in growing crops," I said.

"It is. Would you like to see the berries? They are nearly ripe."

Spring must have arrived on Le-Ath Veronis—berries ripened in the spring and I always looked forward to seeing fresh berries come into the kitchen. They were a joy to work with and I loved to eat the fruit fresh from the vine, although Desh's customers preferred it in pastries or other concoctions.

"We will come," Aurelius was smiling down at me now. His eyes crinkled in a comforting way when he smiled. I decided I liked that. We walked behind Corent for a little way, Aurelius taking most of my weight with only an arm about me.

"These are the oxberry vines," Corent swept an arm out. "I have managed to grow them here when before, only Kifirin produced the best ones." I drew in a breath. *Oxberries.* They were next to impossible to get and the price if they were available was exorbitant. I'd only gotten to taste them once or twice while Edan wasn't looking. Mostly I made a special pastry with them, with a flavored cream and the berries nestled inside. The customers at Desh's number two had swooned and happily paid an exorbitant price for that pastry. I wondered if Edan had tried to reproduce it since I'd been gone. Just the thought of Edan made me frown.

"Reah, what troubles you?"

"Edan."

"Why did your thoughts turn to him?"

"I used to make an expensive dessert with oxberries—when we could get them," I mumbled. "Edan took the credit."

"As I understand, your brother took all the credit, when it should have been given to you," Aurelius brought me around to face him, his hand cupping my cheek. "You need never bow to your brother again, Reah. I will not allow him to harm you. If he wishes to die, he can raise his hand against you. I will make sure it does not fall."

"Aurelius, how can you say that?" He was talking of killing Edan Desh.

"We are allowed to protect our mates. I will protect my mate fiercely," Aurelius promised. "All you have to do is agree to become my mate and that protection will come."

"Aurelius," I sighed. He was moving too fast. I felt dizzy.

"My love, I will not push. Please know that. I will wait until you are comfortable with this. Know also that my kind can feel no jealousy. That is how the Queen of Le-Ath Veronis has so many mates. They cannot feel the bite of jealousy so many others might experience under the same circumstances. It is removed from us when we become what we are."

Why was he telling me that—that he couldn't be jealous? I had no other suitors and hadn't seen anyone that I wanted in that position. It was foolishness. "Reah, you never know what tomorrow may bring." His eyes were crinkling again. "I think I should take you back before the healer comes for my head."

"Thank you for showing me the oxberry vines," I turned to Corent. "I have only gotten to taste oxberries twice in my life, and they were worth the theft." Aurelius folded me away after my admission.

"Little thief, you need to rest." Aurelius was doing his best to settle me back into bed. We'd folded straight to the bedroom I'd wakened in earlier.

"I feel better now," I insisted, attempting to slide off the bed. "And I stole those oxberries when I was ten."

"Age does not mitigate the crime." Aurelius was smiling at me again and shoving me back in bed. "I once stole sweet cakes from a neighbor's cook. They'd been left to cool. I was twelve," Aurelius told me. "That is years uncounted ago, love. Still, I feel a twinge of guilt when I think about it."

"I'll make you sweet cakes as soon as I get out of this bed," I made one last halfhearted attempt to get away. Aurelius pushed me back gently with one hand. My head flopped onto the pillow. Wrestling with Aurelius had completely worn me out.

"I will watch you make cakes for me when you are better. Now, I only want to lie beside you and cover you as much as I can. Vampires protect the ones they love this way. My body over yours; my life given to protect yours."

"Aurelius, you can't mean that." I reached up to brush a stray lock of dark-gold hair off his forehead. "I thought you looked like a lion with this mane the first time I saw you," I said sleepily. My weariness had come calling suddenly.

"You saw through my disguise?" That surprised him, somehow.

"What disguise? What did you look like?" I blinked up at him. He lowered his head and took my lips for the first time. "The real Aris was dead—killed by spawn in the desert. I took his place. He had dark hair and wasn't nearly as tall as I. I can't believe you saw right through that."

I still tasted his kiss on my mouth. It had stirred something that hadn't wakened before that moment. I wanted him to do it again.

"No, Reah. If I kiss you again, I might be unwilling to stop. And tasting your lips is not the only taste of you I want. That part of the vampire is still alive within me. Do not tempt me, love. I have waited a very long time for you. I will wait longer, but it will be an agony. Go to sleep. Get well soon. We have unfinished business, you and I." Warm, golden-brown eyes smiled at me. I went to sleep with the vision of his face firmly placed in my mind.

"I know Aurelius has the M'Fiyah—the mate recognition, but surely he will not mind if we arrange something with one of ours. We have so few females, and even a quarter blood with a full complement of gifts can bring children to the race. Only three have been born in the last two centuries." Jayd paced before Lissa, Gavin and Norian Keef. "Garde and I have discussed this with Glinda. She doesn't like it, but she sees the reason in it."

"You want to use her to breed children? Jaydevik Rath, that child is only nineteen. Are you going to tell her that some High Demon that she doesn't love is going to sink his teeth into her neck?" Lissa was angry. It was a good thing her mate and Jayd's brother, Gardevik wasn't there at the moment. She wanted to tell him he might be going months without sharing her bed again.

"We can introduce her to likely candidates. Who knows, she might care for one of them and one of them might care for her. We do not know this, Lissa." Jayd settled on a guest chair in Lissa's private office.

"Well, I don't want her forced into anything. I realize that I don't hold much sway here, but Aurelius is hers. Do you want to do that to both of them?"

"Lissa, I don't want to mistreat her, but we have so few children. I have been hoping that my daughters will conceive, or that Glinda might get pregnant again and produce more daughters. The odds are against us in this—normally High Demon females only reproduce every seventy-five to one hundred years and nothing seems to work in making it sooner than that. Even so, it is likely that a son will come instead of a daughter. What would you do, Lissa, if the vampire race was dying?"

"Jaydevik, I would not go there with Lissa. You will lose that battle." Kifirin appeared without warning. "The vampire race was dying once before and the High Demons did nothing to prevent it, when that was their duty. Many of my dark races died because of High Demon indifference. Lissa is only trying to protect someone who deserves protection. I will tell you this: Reah will find her own way in this matter. Do not attempt to force the issue." Kifirin disappeared as quickly as he'd appeared, leaving Jayd to curse softly.

"The god has spoken," Gavin muttered.

I was bored. Well and truly. That was why I was sneaking down deserted corridors, attempting to locate the palace kitchen. I had to be careful—there were guards and they were watchful. I slipped past them, wearing warm trousers and a tunic I'd found inside my closet. Yes, I was beginning to think of it as my bedroom now. Those thoughts were likely a mistake. I had no possessions. Still, my conversation with Aurelius the day before about the theft of oxberries had given me the idea. The food at the palace was good— high quality, too, but I wanted something else. My appetite was coming back; I suppose that was a good thing. It meant I was recovering.

The kitchen, when I found it, made me stare in delight— everything was there that I could hope for, including a bank of cold-keepers, a pantry bigger than a two-bedroom house and any convenience and appliance I could wish for. I was digging through a cold keeper and almost hopping with joy at finding yaris fish when a voice spoke right behind me, frightening an unintentional squeal from my lips.

"Hungry? We are, too," The voice said. I was backed up against the cold keeper after I shrieked, staring at two males who were now staring at me. One was at least seven blocks tall. The other was more than half a block shorter and handsome didn't begin to describe him. He had dark hair and eyes with a lazy, beautiful smile, which was now pointed in my direction. The taller one had dark hair, blue eyes and a slight dimple that was showed as he also smiled at me.

"S-sorry," I stuttered. Was I in trouble? They weren't dressed as guards. They didn't wear the palace uniform of black and silver. Casual might describe best how they were clothed. Their clothing was also tailored; I knew that too. Were they mates to Queen Lissa? Mates I hadn't met before? What was I to do?

"I can cook something for you—I was about to cook some yaris fish for myself." I pulled the fish from the cold keeper.

"I love yaris fish if it's done right," the shorter one said. "I'm Ry, this is Tory," he smacked a hand against the taller one's chest.

"What are you two doing here? Does Lissa know?" Two more walked in and they looked exactly alike. I stared. These were Falchani, and twins. The Falchani were a warrior race and not members of the Alliance, but these two didn't seem to care about that. They were here, anyway. I'd studied Falchan and its many battles and Warlords in my history classes when I was younger.

"We got that project done for Uncle Norian, so we came home early," the one who called himself Ry answered smoothly. Those words made me blink. These were Lissa's children? They were grown men. Looked to be in their mid-twenties at least.

"That's Uncle Drake and Uncle Drew. I think they're hungry too," Tory said, offering me a wider grin. It transformed his face, making him just as handsome (in my opinion) as his brother.

"We could eat," one of the Falchani nodded, slipping onto a kitchen stool at the overly large kitchen island.

"Then I'll need more fish," I said, pulling more out of the cold keeper. They got yaris fish that night made with my own sauce, plus fresh vegetables and a good wine. I probably wasn't supposed to be drinking since the healer hadn't said I could, but it went with the meal.

"This is like a dream. Wake me up, Tory," Ry said while rubbing his stomach.

"Young woman, I hope you are the new cook," one of the twins said. "This is the best yaris fish I've ever eaten."

"Are you the new cook?" Tory had hope in his eyes as he blinked at me. I was tired now but determined to clean up the mess I'd made cooking. No sense in angering the actual cook more than necessary—I'd just cleaned out half his supply of yaris fish. I hoped it wasn't something he planned to prepare for lunch the next day. Aurelius might have to help me explain my way out of that.

"I'm not the new cook," I said, pulling Tory's empty plate away to wash.

"Then who are you? You can't have wandered in off the street—the guards would have had you in the dungeons answering questions if you were."

"I didn't wander in off the streets." Ry's plate was next. He was still sipping his wine so I left his glass alone.

"No, she did not wander off the streets. She wandered out of bed and Karzac will have something to say about *that*." Lissa now stood in the kitchen, her hands on her hips and a glare in her eyes. I was in trouble.

"Mom, you have to taste her yaris fish—it's the best ever," Ry slid off his stool and went to give Lissa a kiss on the cheek. Tory was right behind his brother.

"It really is the best," one of the twins offered his plate to Lissa. Only a bite or two of fish left remained on it. Lissa, after giving her sons a hug, picked up a fork and tasted the fish.

"Oh, my gosh," she chewed and swallowed. "Oh, my gosh. If you didn't need to get back in bed, I'd demand you make more of this for getting into the fish for tomorrow's lunch. As it is, I'll forgive you, since you cooked for this bunch," she nodded at the four males. "Drew, you could have sent mindspeech earlier before you ate it all." She made a face at one of the Falchani. At least I knew which was which now.

"We thought she was the new cook. She finally said she wasn't. That's when I sent the mindspeech." Drew glanced sheepishly at the Queen.

"Unbelievable," Lissa shook her head. "Reah, must I send for Aurelius, or do you want me to call Karzac instead? Believe me, Aurelius will be the lesser of those two evils when he finds you out of bed."

"I can find my way back," I muttered, hanging my head.

"We'll make sure she gets there," Ry was giving his mother the famous smile. It would make any female's heart melt, I think. I wondered what that smile had gotten him over the years.

"Tory, please make sure Reah gets back to her bedroom without mishap," Lissa frowned at Ry. Well, Ry wasn't fooling his mother, looked like. He didn't seem to mind; he just gave her another hug and motioned for his brother and me to follow him out of the kitchen. I went before Lissa changed her mind and called for Aurelius and Karzac anyway.

"Why are you supposed to be in bed, and why will Uncle Karzac be mad that you're not?'" Ry was full of questions the moment we left the kitchen.

"I'm still recovering," I admitted reluctantly. "I was hungry and I wanted to cook something," I added. Both those things were true.

"Recovering from what?" Tory asked.

"Somebody threw a net over me," I muttered. Sarcasm might have crept into my voice. If they'd left me alone, things might have turned out better. Aurelius assumed that I was uncontrollable after I turned; two High Demons had arrived, assumed I was rogue and I'd been netted. I got angry every time I thought about it. Netting was an agony I might remember for the rest of my life.

"They netted you? You're High Demon?" Tory's voice had a catch in it and he stopped in midstride to stare at me, a frown tugging at his mouth. Guards were nodding at us at every corner as we passed them by.

"They tell me I'm a quarter but I have the full complement of High Demon talents, whatever that means." I'd stopped when he did, causing Ry to stop as well. "They also tell me that Queen Glindarok is my great-aunt. I don't know what to do about that." I shrugged and started walking again. Ry and Tory caught up with me in a blink.

"Can you skip? Have they showed you that, yet?"

"Skip?" I was looking up—far up—at Tory. He towered over me, after all.

"Going from place to place, like skipping rocks on a pond."

"I've never skipped rocks on a pond. I've never seen a pond. I saw oxberry vines for the first time yesterday. I spent most of my life growing up working in a kitchen." I didn't say that those had been years filled with fear—fear of Edan Desh. The only pleasure I had was in creating new dishes to serve at the restaurant.

"We can take you to a pond tomorrow and we'll show you how to skip rocks." Ry was making a promise.

"When?" I said. "Karzac and Aurelius will try to stop me."

"We'll try to take you after breakfast. How's that?" Tory was smiling. I think he and his brother were used to getting into trouble over things like this.

"You wound us, lady," Ry gave me a courtly bow. The grin on his face when he straightened was competition for the sun, I think.

"So, you have that trick of mindreading, just like everyone else here," I said, turning away from his smile.

"It's not hard—we can teach you that, too. Just give us a little time," Tory said. "How old are you, anyway? You look young."

"Nineteen," I huffed. Who were they, telling me I looked young?

"We're twenty-eight," Ry pointed to himself and then his brother. "We've been working for the ASD—Uncle Norian sends us on special assignments occasionally."

"Ah—the ASD," I nodded, pretending knowledge I didn't have. I knew what ASD meant; I just had no idea what they actually did.

"Here we are." How Tory knew where my bedroom was I had no idea. "Now, go inside like a good girl, or mom will send for Aurelius.

She's sending mindspeech, saying she's saving Karzac in case you get out of bed again."

"Is he that terrible? He's been nice to me so far."

"You haven't disobeyed his orders before," Tory said, herding me inside the door. "And she says she's alerting all the guards. They'll be watching for you from now on. You don't want to be hauled off to Uncle Gavin or Uncle Tony. They get grumpy if they get pulled out of bed."

"Are you still offering to show me that skipping thing?" I looked up at Tory.

"Bro, she thinks like we do," Tory grinned at his brother. I went inside my bedroom and closed the door.

"I saw her first." Ry stopped in his tracks and stared up at his brother. Tory never said things like that. Ever.

"We both saw her," Ry hunched his shoulders.

"But what about Aurelius?"

"What about him?"

"Ry, I don't want to interfere."

"It won't be interfering."

"What will Dad say?"

"Your dad I don't know. *My* dad won't care."

"Come on, bro. Let's get in bed. If we don't get some sleep, we won't be awake to show Reah how to skip rocks."

"Fine," Ry grumped and followed his brother.

"Aurelius, I don't want you to be upset, but she was out of bed last night and cooking the best fish I've ever tasted." Lissa walked alongside Aurelius as he headed toward Reah's bedroom to wake her.

"My Queen, I would like very much for you to call me next time," Aurelius held his anger in check.

"I will. She was frightened when I mentioned calling you or Karzac. That's why I didn't," Lissa replied, not looking at Aurelius. He served as one of her advisors and often ran Council meetings with Aryn, another of her vampire mates, if Lissa wasn't available.

"I've spoken with Norian. That brother of hers has a lot to answer for," Aurelius snapped. Lissa was surprised—Aurelius never let his emotions show like this. Gavin, his only remaining vampire child, often said that Aurelius was more of a father to him than his natural father had been. Aurelius was doing his best to protect Reah, although they weren't mated yet. Lissa didn't want to bring up the conversation she'd had with Jayd either. Kifirin had put a stop to Jayd's idea anyway.

"Reah, if you are hungry again after bedtime, send for me. I will bring something for you." Aurelius was lecturing me before I was fully awake. Somebody had told him about my adventures in the palace kitchen.

"But it wouldn't be yaris fish and I won't have cooked it." I was pouting, I know. He'd once said to never show him that again.

"Yes, I listened to the cook rail over the fish he was planning to cook for lunch having disappeared overnight."

I turned over in bed, my back to Aurelius and curled into a ball. If he wanted to make me feel guilty and miserable, he was doing a fine job.

"Love, he would have butchered the fish. He is preparing a chicken dish instead. Lissa is searching for a new cook—this one does not like the constant darkness outside and wishes to move to the light half of the planet."

"I cooked for Ry and Tory. And Drake and Drew. That's why so much of the fish was used. I was only going to take a little. They were all really hungry."

"Reah." Covers rustled behind me as Aurelius slid into bed. An arm came around me, hugging me close. A kiss was pressed against the nape of my neck. My hair was still short. Much shorter than I ever wanted it to be. "Shhh," Aurelius said softly against my skin. I shivered.

$\sim$

"I saw you." Gavril came up beside me later as I walked next to Aurelius on our way to the dining hall.

"Really? Which time?" He seemed so serious for a child, his dark eyes examining my face as he looked at me. He was tall for his age—in fact he was as tall as I as we walked together, talking. I could look directly into his eyes as he spoke.

"I sneaked into the dungeon," he admitted with an uncomfortable shrug. "I saw you after Karzac and Renegar worked to heal you that first night."

"Then that must have been a terrible sight," I sighed. "I hope it didn't frighten you."

"I've seen Tory in Full Thifilathi. He growls and stomps through the palace. You were quiet and sleeping. Were the burns painful?"

My eyes widened when he mentioned Tory in Full Thifilathi. Tory was High Demon. He must be Lissa's child with her High Demon mate, Gardevik. It took a moment for me to come back to Gavril's question. "As much as the burns hurt, I was more scared about being in prison when I woke," I admitted. "I am terrified of being in tight places if I can't get out. I don't remember much—just screaming at first." My face felt hot—my weakness embarrassed me. Aurelius walked beside me while I spoke with Gavril. He remained silent.

"I don't think I'd like waking up in a cell either," Gavril said, seriously considering the prospect.

"But you wouldn't be throwing yourself against the bars because you couldn't control yourself. You seem like an intelligent and brave young man. I think you'd be working out a way to escape instead," I told him.

"I was thinking of ways to get you out," he admitted.

"Then you just went to the top of my friends list," I smiled at him.

"Really?" He seemed pleased with that.

"I'm sorry to say it's a short list—I don't have any friends," I said. "Except you."

"Then I am an exclusive," he was smiling, now.

"Most definitely one of a kind," I agreed.

"Grandfather Auri, may I sit beside Reah at breakfast?" Gavril now looked up at Aurelius.

"If your lady mother agrees. And Gavin of course."

"Father will allow it if you give permission, Grandfather."

Gavril did sit next to me at breakfast—Lissa said there was no harm in it. Gavril ate and we talked during the entire meal. "Ry and Tory were nearly grown when I was born," he said, spreading butter on his hotcakes. "I tried to follow them around when I was five, but they left me behind." I knew that wistful look he wore. I'd wanted to follow behind some of my older siblings. I was never allowed. I turned toward him in my seat and used the Alliance finger-speech—all Alliance troops knew it. I wanted to see if Gavril had been curious enough to learn on his own. He had.

*Be in my room after breakfast. Don't let anyone see you,* I worked out on my fingers quickly. He nodded. He had no idea what was in store, but he was up for an adventure anyway. I figured he was lonely; I hadn't seen any other children around the palace. Tory and Ry were about to have another guest to take when they showed me how to skip rocks.

# CHAPTER 12

"Here, squirt, hold the rock like this." Tory was showing Gavril how to hold the flat stone in his hands. "Now, flip it out, like this." He made the motion with his hand. Gavril flicked his wrist, flinging the rock toward the smooth water of the pond we'd found on the light half of the planet. It bounced three times on the water before sinking.

"See, you're getting the hang of it now," Tory tousled Gavril's hair. Ry was trying to teach me the same thing, but I was watching Gavril, instead. He was so pleased to find he was included on our secret excursion that he'd almost vibrated with excitement in the beginning. Gavril picked up another flat stone, determined to make it go farther this time. He did—it skipped five times. He was bouncing on his feet as he watched the stone make five quick hops across the surface of the water before sinking.

"Reah, are you paying attention to me?" Ry's face appeared in front of mine.

"I was watching how Gavril did his so I could do it too," I said. That caused Gavril to turn to me, his face beaming with pleasure. The bright sunlight of the new day brought mist up from the water on the far side of the pond, where cattails grew and willow trees on the bank beyond. Lush grasses surrounded us—it was the ideal place to learn to skip rocks. I'd only seen things such as this in vids before now. Winged insects also abounded, but they left us alone. I wondered about that. Gavril skipped another rock. It went farther this time. He was a quick study and soaking up his older brother's praise like a sponge.

"Gavril needed this, didn't he?" Ry now stood next to me, his lips near my ear. I nodded.

"Come on, squirt—we have to get you back for your lessons," Tory hugged Gavril to him after he tossed one last rock.

"Maybe we can sneak away again so I can practice more," I told Gavril before Ry folded us back to the palace. We landed inside my bedroom where we'd met in the beginning. Gavril grabbed his comp-vid off my bed and took off at a near-run to make it to his tutor's suite on time.

"Now, how about some time spent with just us?" Ry grinned. Time spent with "just us" turned out to mean time in the pool and spa inside the palace. I hadn't even known there was a huge room devoted to those two things.

"Most vampires don't come here," Tory floated lazily on his back in the pool. I could see why—sunlamps were scattered throughout the space.

"What happens if they come in and the lamps are on?" I asked.

"Their skin fries," Ry replied. "Only the ones who are modified can stand to be in here. Uncle Tony loves it."

I knew how to swim—it had been included in my dayschool lessons. Otherwise, Edan would never have allowed me to go swimming. I certainly had never been allowed to play with any friends. Not that I'd had many, growing up. They'd deserted me quickly after learning I could never see them outside lessons.

"Reah, come out to dinner with us. Tory and I want to go to Casino City to eat tonight." Ry was asking me something I was too afraid to say yes to.

"Reah, tell Aurelius. He can come too, if he wants." Tory lowered his legs into the water and now stood beside Ry and me.

"Tell Aurelius what? I handle a council meeting and what do I find when I am done?" Aurelius stood on the slate tile floor at the edge of the pool.

"Uncle Auri, we took Gavril to a pond on the light side to teach him how to skip rocks this morning, before he had to go for his lessons. And then we convinced Reah to get in the pool. We also want to go to Casino City for dinner tonight." I stared at Tory—he was telling Aurelius everything.

"He'll know anyway—Uncle Auri can smell a lie," Tory laughed. "Mom can, too. It's better to tell the truth around here," he added. "And you never ever want to lie to Uncle Jayd. He's a guli."

"A guli is a High Demon truth-speaker," Ry offered at my blank stare. "They can see through any lie. Nobody gets past them."

"Reah, will you come out of the pool or are you going to force me to come in after you?" Aurelius stared down at me. I looked down, afraid to meet the accusation in his eyes. He'd caught me with two other males. I wondered what he would do to me.

"Come, Reah." Aurelius had a towel in his hands suddenly.

*Uncle Auri, you're scaring her.* Ry sent the mindspeech to Aurelius.

*She should be resting and you two are hauling her about,* Aurelius returned.

*We didn't tire her out, we promise.* Tory joined the mental conversation.

*Young ones, if you wish to spend time with Reah, then check with Karzac or me. We will let you know how much time is wise. You have had her out for five hours.* Aurelius sent the mental chastisement. Reah climbed out of the pool as Tory and Ry watched. Aurelius wrapped her in the towel and folded her away.

"He didn't say she couldn't come to dinner with us," Ry floated away from his brother.

"Reah, I do not mind if you spend time with them. Gavril certainly needs someone young with whom to spend time. Those other two miscreants know better. They know you are recovering, yet they haul you from one end of the planet to the other," Aurelius huffed as he dried me with the towel. Ry had scrounged a swimsuit for me earlier, although he'd suggested we climb into the pool naked. I certainly wasn't ready for that and even more glad I'd insisted on swimsuits when Aurelius showed up.

"I wasn't tired," I ventured as Aurelius rubbed the towel over my exposed skin.

"Reah, do you wish to remove the swimsuit or do you want me to do it?" Aurelius bumped his forehead against mine, his golden-brown eyes staring into mine from close quarters.

I was afraid to let him do it. There was something in his eyes begging me to allow it. That frightened me. I wasn't prepared for that. Not yet.

~

"Your daughter was rescued from Mandil, but was wounded in the attempt. She is recovering now on an Alliance planet." Lendill Schaff sat at a table in Desh's restaurant in Targis, watching Addah Desh's reaction to the news. Addah had little emotion on his face as Lendill gave him what should have been very good news.

"Does the Alliance expect her to finish out her remaining time as a recruit?" Addah asked instead.

"Yes. In fact, she will be transferred to the ASD as soon as she is healthy enough to report for duty. She not only managed to remain undercover while on a non-Alliance world, but was successful in taking down an enemy that could threaten the Alliance. The Director and I are quite pleased with her work, therefore she will be doing her remaining years of service with us."

"Very well," Addah Desh said stiffly and rose. "Since I cannot have an important member of my family back to assist with the family business, then I will leave you. Today is a busy day, Vice-Director

Schaff. I hope you'll excuse me—I have work to do." Addah Desh gave Lendill a curt nod and walked toward the kitchen.

"Do you wish to send a message to her?" Lendill called out. Addah Desh turned to level a scowl at the Vice-Director. "She is no good to me at the moment. I have no message to send." Addah stalked away. Lendill watched him go through the door before rising to leave. He pulled out his communicator and had Norian Keef on vidscreen as he walked out of the restaurant.

"Nothing, Director. No emotion, no questions, didn't even ask which planet she was on or how badly she was wounded. Didn't offer to send a message, either. He's only interested in what she might do for his restaurants."

"Sounds like a such a good parent," Norian muttered sarcastically.

"I found the doctor who tended her mother and he's so frightened he's handing everything to us," Lendill continued. "Reah isn't Addah Desh's daughter—she's Edan Desh's. I get the idea that the pregnancy was definitely unplanned. The drugs administered to her mother after the birth could cause unusual bleeding, and the mother died of hemorrhage. I know it's just my opinion at the moment, but I think Marzi Desh had a hand in this to keep her son away from prison for rape. Too bad; he could end up there anyway. With his mother to keep him company."

"Keep your men on this—I want to get to the rot of this," Norian Keef terminated the call. Lendill pocketed his communicator and turned up the collar on his heavy coat—it was winter in Targis and very cold.

"Reah, Norian wants to talk to you now." Gavril and I were sitting side by side on a large chaise near the pool. We were doing research for a report that he'd been assigned. It excited him that we could do this and he was bouncing ideas off me, which led us down many paths as far as the research went. Lissa had appeared right next to us to give me the news.

"Mom—we were doing research," Gavril moaned.

"Honey, Reah needs to talk to your Uncle Nori. She'll come back later." Lissa sat next to Gavril and brushed dark hair off his forehead.

"Where should I go? Where is he?" I asked, standing and stretching to hide my sudden nervousness.

"Norian is in my office. Do you know where it is?" Lissa had beautiful blue eyes. I could see why she had so many mates.

"I think I can find it," I nodded and walked out of the huge room that held the spa and the pool. The water, combined with shining sunlamps, caused the ceiling to reflect as I walked away from Gavril and his mother.

I stood outside the office door for several ticks before knocking, trying to get my heart to slow. Why would the Director of the ASD want to see me? Why? I knocked and a voice called out for me to enter.

"Director Keef." I nodded respectfully to him. He didn't stand when I entered. He sat behind Lissa's beautifully carved wooden desk, his fingertips together, watching me as I walked in. He had brown hair and green eyes, wasn't nearly as tall as Lissa's other mates and felt dangerous, somehow, even if his looks said otherwise.

"Sit down, recruit Desh," he nodded toward the two chairs placed before the desk. I chose the nearest one and sat down. "Now," he said as I settled into my seat, "you have more than five years' service left in the Alliance Military."

"Yes, Director Keef." I'd been wondering about that. Not once had Aurelius brought it up, and the small amount of time I'd spent with Ry and Tory hadn't brought the subject up either.

"I have already had your assignment transferred," Director Keef informed me. That statement forced me to raise my head and stare into his eyes. I wanted to ask him where I'd been transferred. Was it far away? What would I be doing? Did Aurelius know? I knew not to ask—I was a recruit again and any freedom I'd had was now gone. One didn't blurt out their questions to a ranking officer. As Director of the ASD, Norian Keef outranked just about everyone in the Alliance Military.

"You will be working for the ASD from now on. We can make use of, well, your unusual abilities. Aurelius says that when you aim a rifle at something, you don't miss. I have reviewed all your training records and questioned Aurelius thoroughly. Your rank has also changed—you are now one of my more unusual special agents. Torevik Rath and Rylend Morphis also hold this rank, in an unofficial capacity. I would like you to work with them, I think. Our enemies will not be expecting you to be as strong or as talented as you are. They will underestimate you. That will work to our advantage. They will be looking to Ry and Tory to take them down, when you can be the one to get them, special agent Desh." Norian tapped fingertips on Lissa's desk.

"By the way," he went on, "I've learned from Lissa that you may wish to separate from your family legally. I can expedite the paperwork for you and you may choose another name. In fact, I can change that this afternoon. Karzac says that you will be released from his care tomorrow, and can report for duty the day after that. You will be stationed here as Le-Ath Veronis is now permanent ASD headquarters. If you do not wish to stay at the palace or somewhere else of your choosing, you may live in the barracks with my other special agents. Bear in mind that you will frighten most of them if you make your High Demon status known. That information will only be given to those who can be trusted with the information. Feel free to talk with me or my Vice-Director, Lendill Schaff. He has been updated on your records."

His words swam inside my head and I had trouble sorting them for a moment. "Yes, I do wish to separate from my family and I would prefer to be known as Re Nilvas, if possible. That was the name I was given on Mandil."

"I ask you not to give up the Reah," Director Keef sighed. "I think it will upset Aurelius greatly."

"Then leave my first name as Reah," I looked down at my hands. What had I gotten into? What would I be doing? Working with Ry and Tory didn't sound bad, but I had no idea what they really did for the ASD.

"Your name will be changed by tomorrow and I imagine that the legal separation will be completed within the week. Your former family will be notified, agent Reah Nilvas. Vice-Director Schaff will contact you with your first assignment. Meanwhile, feel free to let Lissa or Aurelius know of your housing preferences."

I'd been dismissed, so I dipped my head respectfully to Director Keef and scurried out the door. My heart was pounding triple time as I made my way down the long hall toward my bedroom. Well, it might not be my bedroom for much longer. What should I do? I didn't want to live in the barracks with the other agents. I'd gotten enough of that during my military training. I felt cold as I opened the door to my bedroom and curled up on the bed, hugging myself tightly.

"Reah?" Ry popped into my bedroom. Well, perhaps not popped, but close enough. Everybody appeared and disappeared at will. Except me.

"Ry, what do you want?" I was huddled against the headboard of the bed, an extra blanket wrapped around me. I was shivering.

"Reah, we're not so bad to work with," Ry sat on the edge of my bed.

"That's not what concerns me."

"Then what is it?"

"Where am I supposed to go? Where will I live? I don't want to live in the barracks—there's probably no privacy there—and too many people." I pulled my blanket tighter around me. I'd been cast out on a wild ocean that carried me farther and farther away from anything familiar. Silently I cursed Master Vyn. And Edan. And my father. I wanted to weep, too, for the mother I'd never known, as well as the great-aunt I had who hadn't bothered to visit or talk with me. Is this the way it was with any family I ever had? They just left me to fend for myself unless they wanted something? They'd never said anything about my grandfather, either—only that one of Glinda's brothers had fathered my mother.

I had no way to contact Aurelius, and didn't know if I wanted to anyway. What would he do? The Alliance would send me off somewhere to work with Ry, Tory or others perhaps, and we'd only see each other once in a while. Too many worries crowded my mind and there was no relief for any of them.

"Reah, it's not that bad. We're usually gone two or three weeks at a stretch, then we're back home."

"Ry, this is your home. It's not mine."

"I heard you were a woman without a country now." Ry scooted up in the bed until he was sitting next to me.

"What are you talking about?" I turned to look at him.

"It's just a strange phrase my mother uses. She's from old Earth, you know."

"Is she as old as Aurelius?"

That question caused Ry to laugh. "No," he shook his head after the laughter died down. "Only a few vampires might be older than Aurelius. Jeral and Aryn. A couple of others. That's it. Gavril wants to know what happened to you, Reah. And it's nearly time for dinner. Why don't you get dressed and I'll take you in."

I wasn't hungry and I wanted to talk to Aurelius. Just to find out how things were going to be. Was he just going to let me go without a word? And I was back to where I was going to live for the next five years or so.

"Reah, why are you not dressed for dinner?" Aurelius came through the door without knocking. "Young one, I will take over now," Aurelius gave Ry a pointed stare. Ry grinned and waved a hand before disappearing. "Reah, why are you wrapped in a blanket?" Aurelius came to stand beside the bed.

"I'm cold." I huddled farther into the soft coverlet.

"Reah, are you ill? It isn't particularly cold at the moment. We had a fine spring day, today."

"For you, maybe. You didn't have the Director of the ASD telling you that he's conscripting you for the next five years and you can live in the barracks if you want."

"Reah, he did not say you had to live in the barracks. He listed that as one of your choices. There are others."

"Living on someone's charity." I was pouting again.

"Reah, you have back pay coming for your stay on Mandil and you can move your account from Tulgalan. Several good banks are located here in Lissia, and any one of them will be happy to make the transfers for you."

"I didn't have an account on Tulgalan. I kept my money on a credit chip bracelet, and it was left behind when Master Vyn decided to play his joke. Edan never let me have much money and refused to let me open an account. His way of controlling me, I'm sure. I have nothing, Aurelius. I asked Director Keef to submit the paperwork to separate me from my family and give me another name. If they cared, they would have contacted me while I've been here. They haven't. I'm sure Edan was dancing with joy when I was shipped to the military, and he'll be dancing again when he learns I've cut my ties to him and the rest of the family. Family." I huffed out the word. "I have no family."

"Reah, you are related to the Queen of Kifirin." Aurelius' golden-brown eyes searched my face.

"Really? How can you tell?" I tossed off my blanket, slid off the bed before Aurelius could put his hands on me and walked into the spacious bathroom and its adjoining closet.

"Things are not that desperate, love. You are blowing this out of proportion." Aurelius came up behind me as I sorted through my meager wardrobe hanging in the closet. The clothes were quite fine, but I still hadn't learned where they'd come from and there weren't many outfits. I blew out a breath and selected a black tunic and trousers. Black to match my mood. Closing the door to the bathroom and shutting Aurelius out at the same time, I dressed, slipped on soft-soled shoes and walked out running a comb through my short hair. It didn't matter with my hair—there wasn't enough length there to do anything with it.

Saying nothing to Aurelius, we walked out the bedroom door only to find Gavril waiting. "Reah, I waited for you." He was doing some pouting of his own.

"I'm sorry, Chash." Chash was a nickname—an endearment on Tulgalan. Mostly it was reserved for young males—it was a common name for a very tall, curious bird. I was explaining the nickname to Gavril as we walked down the hall toward our dinner. Gavril was quite happy with having a nickname, once he learned what it meant. He and I had an arm around each other as we walked into the dining hall.

That night I learned that Lissa had a daughter who was working as a Master Wizard at Grey House, along with her first husband named Toff, who was also a Master Wizard. Lissa had a foster son named Trik at Grey House, too. Trik, Nissa's second husband, was classified as a First-Level Wizard. I saw Toff's father—he came to dinner for the first time. His name was Roff and I was shocked when I saw he was a Winged Vampire. No, he was not ugly or ill-formed—quite the opposite, in fact. He was beautiful to see and moved gracefully to take his chair. I envied him a little, I think. I always felt out of place and awkward when I came to the Queen's table.

"I have to report for duty tomorrow," I said unhappily when Gavril asked if we could do more research. "I don't know what I'll be doing or if I'll be sent out right away. If I have free time, I'll let you know."

"Grandfather, will you let me know if Reah is all right when she is away?" Gavril looked around me at Aurelius.

"I will do what I can, young one." Aurelius gave Gavril a warm smile.

⌁

"Norian, if you didn't have her conscripted, I'd ask her to stay and keep Gavril company," Lissa poked Norian in the chest with a finger.

"Breah-mul, we need her. More and more drakus seed is making its way into the Alliance. Those fools who crush it and drink it like tea are killing themselves in droves. They keep using more and more of it for the visions it brings, until it is too much and they are dead. We have to stop it and your sons and Reah will help us in this."

"Because they are young and look the part of the ones who use it?" Lissa didn't know whether she liked this or not.

"Lissa, you gave permission for them to work with me, as did their fathers. Reah is a recruit and will go where she's sent. That is the rule of Alliance conscription. I know Aurelius doesn't like it—he's already made his feelings known."

"Then I don't want to be anywhere near you if that girl gets hurt again, Norian Keef."

"Funny, Aurelius said almost the same thing," Norian grinned.

"Reah, there are many things I want and many things that I cannot ask," Aurelius stopped outside the bedroom door. "If I come inside with you, I will not leave. Therefore, I will stay outside. We will find a place for you to live. A place where you will feel comfortable while you are here. You needn't fret over this, my love." Aurelius held my face in his hands and placed his forehead against mine. When he kissed me, it was a deeper kiss—a more sensuous kiss that left me breathless. A sharpness had nipped my lower lip, too—that was something I hadn't experienced before. My body tightened when he did that, and I almost asked him to come inside anyway. A shiver of fear held me back. I'd never done anything like that before and wasn't sure I'd be prepared for it, now.

"The house next to Bryan's is empty." Lissa told Aurelius. He'd come directly to her after leaving Reah. He was afraid he'd turn right around otherwise and work his way into Reah's bed.

"Bryan Riley?"

"Yes. He can help keep an eye on her when she's not on assignment."

"Will he have time? He's always buried in those news programs he produces."

"Bryan is hyperactive and can do fifteen things at once. Stop worrying, Aurelius. I know you don't want to push her, but maybe you need to make your feelings known a little better."

"Lissa, she's only nineteen. I'm over four thousand. If my heart didn't squeeze in my chest every time I see her, I might be questioning this relationship. I don't think I can live without her. Sometimes I have to force myself to stay away so I won't crowd her and frighten her more than she is already."

"Well, if Gavin got his possessiveness from you, then I feel sorry for her," Lissa sniffed.

"I am a little possessive," Aurelius sighed and raked a hand through his mane of dark-gold hair.

"Did you tell her how nice she looked tonight?"

"I didn't."

"Aurelius, what are you doing? Cheedas was at the table tonight and he didn't take his eyes off her."

"I hope I don't have to compete with every vampire on Le-Ath Veronis for her affections." Aurelius covered his face with both hands.

"We'll be sending you in two days to Tulgalan." Just the one word had me cringing. I'd hoped not to go back—at least for a very long time. Ry, Tory and I sat in front of Vice-Director Lendill Schaff in his office at ASD headquarters. We weren't far from the palace, actually—a quarter click's walk got me there. Ry and Tory showed up in their usual fashion. "Drakus seed is finding its way there," Lendill Schaff continued, "and we want to learn how that's happening and shut the sources down. It's easy enough to find the dealers—we need to find their suppliers. Hundreds of deaths have occurred in the past three moon-turns."

Drakus seed—Drakus meant dragon in the old Alliance languages. An old myth said that dragons brought dreams. Drakus seed reportedly brought dreams and visions to life. I'd heard tales that the experiences felt real and brought the user's most desired fantasies to life. That's why it was so popular among those who sought any kind of drug—and the most expensive as well. It might be a competition with the young and wealthy—to see who could afford it most often. This held no allure to me at all, and merely the thought of being immersed in the drug culture on Tulgalan made me want to shake.

"Reah, here is your back pay—I understand you don't have an account anywhere." The Vice-Director pushed a credit chip across his desk toward me. "I suggest you spend the afternoon getting a bank account set up; your new name and information are all contained on the chip." I watched Vice-Director Schaff—he was quite good looking. Perhaps not as handsome as Ry, but then few were. "You have the next day and a half to pack—transport will be waiting at the space station at six bells on fifth-day. Don't be late."

It wasn't Ry or Tory I took with me to the bank—I invited Gavril. He was excited to go with me, already had an account and walked me through it. The Vice-Director had been correct—everything I needed was on the credit chip. I only had to give my thumbprints and an eyescan and we were done. My pay had been increased, too—I saw that when the amounts were deposited from the credit chip. I suppose being a special agent for the ASD had its advantages. Lissa had given Gavril permission to go to Casino City with me afterward—it was one of the two very large gambling cities on Le-Ath Veronis and the reason that tourists flocked to the planet.

"Every application to visit has to be checked and approved—mom doesn't want anybody here who has a criminal background." We were eating ice cream inside Niff's. I'd only heard of the sweet shops before; I'd never had an opportunity to visit any of them. Niff's franchises were scattered across the Alliance, but those owners had also been carefully vetted. Niff's was quite particular about the product they served, much like Desh's. The difference was that Addah would never allow a restaurant to open under the Desh name that wasn't in the hands of family. I sighed. I was no longer a member of the Desh family, by my own choice.

"This is exceptional," I licked my spoon.

"Mom owns Niff's, with her assistants Grant and Heathe. They make a ship load of money off it." Gavril was also enjoying his ice cream, scraping up the last of it from the bottom of his dish.

"Your mother owns Niff's." It was as if he'd said his mother owned Desh's to someone from Tulgalan.

"Yeah. The cookie recipes are all hers. You'll have to try those sometime."

"I will. I love cookies. I just don't get them very often." I wanted to ask Gavril how it came to be that his vampire mother and father ate like anybody else, and if they ever consumed blood or blood substitute. I'd seen bottles of the substitute stocked in a cold keeper inside the kitchen the night I'd sneaked in to cook.

"Ask Mom when she's not busy sometime. She'll make you some."

"If she makes dessert, I'll make dinner," I promised, smiling at Gavril. He was my friend—perhaps the first real one I'd ever had. I didn't know what to call Aurelius. Or Tory and Ry, although I liked both of them. I found myself staring at Tory sometimes. He was so tall he towered over everyone else, although he didn't seem self-conscious about it.

"Re," Gavril looked at me seriously for a moment.

"Chash?" I blinked at him just as seriously.

"Re, you have to promise you'll always be my friend. I've never had a friend that I could just talk to about anything. Nobody's ever helped with my homework before. Not like you. Dad will go over my math homework and tell me where I went wrong, but that's not the same."

"Well, do you have free time before dinner?" I asked, giving him a grin. "I have some homework to do now."

"Really? For the ASD?" Gavril was excited.

"Yes. For the ASD. But you can't tell anybody, all right?"

"My lips are permanently closed on the matter," he placed a finger over his mouth.

"Good enough," I said. "Where do we catch the bus to get back to Lissia? And did they name the whole city after your mother?"

"Yeah." Gavril used a slang term at times that I hadn't heard before, but then Ry and Tory used it too. It was one of their mother's terms and meant yes. The term, I learned, came from old Earth. I didn't ask any other questions about that.

❧

"Here—it says that the plants need plenty of water to grow." Gavril handed his comp-vid to me—there was an image of Drakus seed plants growing in a field. The plant had compound leaves—seven on a stem—which were rounded on the ends. The leaves were a grayish green and the seedpods were small nodules about the size of my thumb. One nodule would produce enough seed for five doses, according to the information Gavril and I found, so the seeds were potent. Our information indicated that five seedpods, called a hand, could sell for a quarter of a million Alliance credits. That sounded high to me—who could afford that? That would be ten thousand Alliance credits per hit.

Granted, one hit made a good pot of tea that might serve ten or more, but it was still expensive. I had nearly eight thousand Alliance credits in my account, which was four months' pay minus taxes. The drakus seeds were tiny—we found pictures of those, too. They looked to be the same size as the seeds used to make seedcakes, but the drakus seeds were red where the others were black.

"I heard there was a problem with this stuff and it was getting bigger," Gavril lay on his stomach atop his bed—we'd gone to his bedroom to do our research. "It's all over the news vids now. People taking too much and dying."

"Promise me you'll never touch this *stuff*." I used his slang term as I leaned down and bumped my forehead against his.

"That's a promise," he agreed, his dark eyes looking right into mine.

My head was full of information as we walked down the halls to dinner that night. "You look like your father," I whispered to Gavril as we made our way into the dining hall. Gavin was there already with Lissa. I noticed that Gavin seldom smiled and wondered about that.

Of course, Aurelius didn't smile that often, either. Vampires must be serious most of the time.

"Mom says he's handsome." Gavril looked up at me, the unasked question on his lips.

"So are you, Chash." I gave him a hug before he went to sit between his parents.

"We've been hoping you'd sneak into the kitchen again," Drake and Drew walked past me, headed toward seats on the opposite side of the table. Drake was the one who spoke. I could tell the difference between them, although I couldn't explain it.

"I was told the guards were watching out for me, so I didn't try," I said, smiling back at Drake when he grinned.

"Those guards. Maybe we ought to have a word with them," Drew grinned, too. They had the traditional fold in their eyes that most Falchani had. Their eyes were dark and both had very long, very black hair they wore in a thick braid down their backs. It made me miss my hair.

"It will grow back." Aurelius was at my elbow and steering me toward a chair.

"Why does everybody around here read minds?" I grumbled as I sat.

"Because we can." A new male appeared and I knew immediately who he was. This was Ry's father. Ry looked so much like him it was frightening. Both of them were so handsome they might cause people to faint wherever they went.

"What do you do when someone mentally insults you?"

"If we don't know them well, we keep it to ourselves until the opportunity for payback comes." Ry had come in right behind his father. "Hi, Dad. How's Em-pah?" Ry gave his father a hug.

"Your great-grandfather is as irascible as usual. Three rogue warlocks are giving him grief and he is so angry he is about to burn the palace down."

Those words had my eyebrows lifting. Palace? Warlocks? Only one place fit the criteria. "You're Karathian?" I gasped before I thought.

"Rylend Morphis, have you not been forthcoming with your new friend and coworker?" Ry's father admonished. "I am Erland Morphis, Special Attachment to Wylend Arden, King of Karathia, who is my forgetful son's great-grandfather." Erland gave me the same smile that Ry was capable of giving. It was like the sun breaking through dark clouds.

"I didn't want to scare her, Dad." Ry was grinning right back at his father.

"Well, there's that," Erland agreed. "What's for dinner? I'm starved."

# CHAPTER 13

"This fish isn't anything like what Reah can do." Ry was grumbling the moment he took his first bite.

"Not many can come near what Reah can do," Aurelius spoke up for the first time. "She made military rations taste like a night at an expensive restaurant."

"When we got the fresh fruit and vegetables from the desert villages," I said. "And if you have enough eggs. That always helps."

"If we get a place with a kitchen on Tulgalan, will you make yaris fish again?" Tory came in late, followed by his father—Gardevik Rath.

"If you want," I said. "Who's paying for the groceries?"

"The Alliance will give us an allowance for that, plus we'll be throwing a little money around. Mom spent the day getting extra clothes for you—you ran off to the bank and then holed up with the Squirt the rest of the day."

"Gavril and I had fun," I said, feeling huffy at his accusation.

"Don't be mad—we didn't want to disturb you or cut into your time with Gav. That's why Mom had the dress shops bring stuff in your size. She got Aunt Grace and Aunt Devin to help."

"Karzac has other mates," Aurelius said quietly beside me when I'd blinked stupidly at Tory, who sat on Aurelius' other side, next to his father.

"We have an extended family; you should meet Great-Uncle Dragon and Great-Uncle Crane. Great-Uncle Dragon is Drake and Drew's dad. Get them to show you the tattoos, sometime," Tory was smiling.

I knew Falchani had their chests, backs and arms tattooed whenever they proved themselves in battle. A full set meant all those places had been tattooed. Yes—that race had fascinated me since I was in dayschool. I now looked up at Aurelius. "I want to go to Falchan," I breathed.

"No time now, but we'd be happy to take you when you have a couple of days off," Drake was grinning again.

"Maybe you should teach her bladework," Ry suggested, picking at his fish.

"Ry, it's not that bad," I said, nodding at his fish.

"It is after tasting yours," he muttered.

"Reah killed spawn with a skillet and a knife—I'm not sure teaching her bladework is a good idea," Aurelius was smiling for the first time in days.

"No kidding?" Drew was laughing. "How did you do that?"

"And she was naked at the time," Aurelius was suddenly enjoying himself.

"You didn't have to tell them that." My face felt hot. "I was in the baths when the attack came. I was wrapped in a towel inside the kitchen when two of the enemy came in. The first was humanoid so I cracked his skull with an iron skillet. He dropped like a sack of flour. The next one was spawn. He fell when I hit him with the skillet but he wasn't unconscious. When he got up it took me two passes with my best carving knife to take his head."

"Reah moves pretty fast," Aurelius was still chuckling.

"She'd have to; otherwise that spawn would have had her from that distance." Drew agreed. "You had the skillet in one hand and the knife in the other?"

"Yes," I nodded, pushing some of my own fish around. "I wish they'd called me, I would have made the fish for you," I said.

"See," Ry pointed his fork at me.

"It's not the worst I've tasted," I said.

"What was the worst?" Tory asked.

"Master Cook Vyn's," I was hiding a grin while ducking my head.

"He is in prison now for his little mistake." Norian Keef walked in with his second-in-command, Vice-Director Schaff. "As are those two glorified vegetable slicers."

"They couldn't even do that right," I said. "Vyn kept them around for what they gave him in bed."

"Well, they managed to get him convicted for a lengthy sentence," Norian took a chair farther down the table. "Are we having fish again?" he grumped.

"Is there more fish in the cold keepers?" I asked. "I can make fish in no time."

"We just got a fresh batch of yaris fish," Another male I didn't know spoke up.

"That's Cheedas. He's vampire now but he used to be head cook," Drew told me.

"Give me a click, you'll have good fish," I said, rising from the table.

They did have good fish—even Addah Desh had loved it and he was the worst critic anyone might have as far as food went.

"Reah, this is so good," Gavril was having more. I was thankful the kitchen island was as large as it was—everybody was either sitting or standing around it, eating fresh yaris fish with sauce and vegetables.

"Chash, it was a pleasure to get to cook for you," I gave him a hard squeeze.

"Reah, you could cook for anyone in the Alliance," Norian Keef rolled his eyes in ecstasy.

"Director Keef, I have cooked for just about everyone important in the Alliance," I told him. "When Desh's number two started getting the top awards, they all came. If I had more time, I'd make my special ox-roast for you."

"You'll like that," Aurelius was nodding his head. "I thought the officers on Mandil were going to fight each other over who got whatever was left."

"We have a house for you, Reah, and clothing and traveling bags and toiletries have already been taken there. Aurelius will show it to you after dinner." Lissa came to stand beside me. I was perched on a tall stool at the end of the island while Aurelius stood beside me. Unconsciously I reached out with my left hand and rubbed his back while I blinked at Lissa.

"I have a house?" My voice sounded squeaky.

"Every vampire who relocates to Le-Ath Veronis gets a basic house, free of charge. If they want something nicer, they can pay for the upgrade. This house is located next to a good friend of mine, and it was vacated recently. You're welcome to use it as long as you want. If you want it decorated, you can do that yourself. The fish is wonderful, Reah. I think Gavin is in ecstasy. If Norian and the Alliance didn't have a stranglehold on you, I'd pay you top dollar to run my kitchen," Lissa offered a genuine smile.

"We'll try not to strangle her, breah-mul. We need her. You can wrangle over the head cook's job when she's finished her tour of duty." Norian Keef put an arm around Lissa and grinned.

"Does he always get the better of you?" I asked before I thought.

"Oooh, Norian, you are in trouble now," Lissa poked him in the ribs.

"I think Lissa will get the better of me in the next few days," Norian's smile was on the wry side as Lissa ducked from beneath his arm and walked away.

"My love," Aurelius whispered next to my ear, "if you do not stop touching me, I will have you out of here so fast you will not know how it happened, and I cannot be held accountable for my actions after that."

My hand stopped making circles on Aurelius' back—I'd wandered down to the small of his back to do that and only then noticed that Aurelius' breathing had gone ragged.

"Sorry," I mumbled, taking my hand away. I think that may have been the first time I'd ever voluntarily touched a male with affection.

"My love, I will ask you to do that again when we are alone," Aurelius nuzzled my ear and then my neck before pulling away. "Someone else will clean up. Let us see this house of yours."

Aurelius must not have been expecting the crowd that came with us—Ry, Tory, Gavril, Lissa, Norian, Lendill Schaff, Erland and Gardevik all came, as did a few others. The house was very nice—three bedrooms and a basement that locked and looked strong enough to withstand a bomb blast.

"Vampires are very wary—this is a holdover from our days of living on planets with bright sunlight every day. If we wanted to live, we protected ourselves in such ways," Aurelius explained as I looked around the spacious underground room that held a bed, a cold keeper and a vid screen. The house was furnished and thankfully it had a kitchen in it. The kitchen looked as if it hadn't been used, except for the cold keeper. That suited me just fine; the stone on the countertops and the island was more than acceptable.

"I like it very much," I said, causing Lissa to smile. I'd never hoped to have this much space to call my own before. The only thing it lacked was dishes and cookware. I was going to shop for those things the moment I got back from Tulgalan. Somehow, my clothing and things—some of it I hadn't seen before—had made their way into a large, walk-in closet inside the spacious master bedroom.

"Reah, you need to pack." Ry and Tory were examining my closet with a critical eye. I think Aurelius just wanted them to disappear.

"I will help her pack." Aurelius gave the obvious hint. I felt nervous suddenly. Tory and Ry looked at each other, eyebrows lifted perceptibly. Both said hasty farewells and disappeared. Everyone else had already gone. "Reah, there is no need to be frightened, love." Aurelius' hands were tilting my face up, his thumbs under my chin. Bending down, he gave me a kiss that took my breath and quickened my pusle. He began to nip his way down my neck.

*My fangs will not harm you, sweet girl,* Aurelius' voice was in my mind, causing me to draw in a breath. His arms pulled me hard against him and I felt the piercing of my neck, just before the waves of pleasure came. They became so intense, I fainted.

"Love, that was only the smallest part of what we can do together," Aurelius was stroking hair back from my forehead. How had we gotten into bed? And the smallest part? That had caused me to lose consciousness, it was so intense. I'd never felt anything like that before. Was that why people were so anxious to have sex? I blinked up at Aurelius' face as a small smile played about his lips. He watched me carefully, no doubt reading my thoughts. Again. A hand reached up and touched a nipple. My nipple. When had he undressed me?

"Shhh," Aurelius bent his head to the same nipple and put his mouth on it. How did he do what he did with those teeth of his? I nearly came off the bed. I think he was holding back, too; somehow I got the idea that if I'd not been virgin he would have been more urgent in his demands and would have taken what he wanted more quickly. As it is, he was gentle. Careful. And when the pain came from the initial coupling, he understood and made it all worthwhile.

"Reah, drink this." Aurelius woke me after our second time, offering a glass of juice.

"What is it?" I asked as he offered it to me.

"Red citrus," he said, placing the glass in my hands. "With protein mixed in. Drink it. It will be good for you."

I drank it. It tasted strange but I finished it as he asked. Feeling extremely sleepy afterward, Aurelius tucked me against him, curved his body around and over mine and lulled me to sleep.

# CHAPTER 14

Two trunks and two wheeled cases. That's what Aurelius helped me pack. I didn't understand why I might need so much in the way of clothing, toiletries and such, but he wouldn't consider sending me to Tulgalan with less. I found I had some jewelry, too, when I woke. I'd slept a full eight hours, though I'd planned to get up earlier than that to see Gavril and do other things before taking the shuttle to the space station orbiting Le-Ath Veronis.

"Are you ready yet?" Ry's voice teased me as he and Tory showed up from nowhere inside my new living room. Aurelius had kept me so busy the night before that I hadn't had time to fully explore my new home.

"She is nearly so," Aurelius crossed arms over his chest and glared at our visitors.

"I wanted to say good-bye to Chash before I left," I said, slipping into a chocolate-colored jacket that someone had purchased for me. A heavier coat lay draped over one of my bags—it was winter on Tulgalan and I'd need the coat the moment I stepped off the shuttle onto my home planet.

"I'll go get him—he can go to the station with us," Tory grinned and disappeared.

"Our bags have already been sent up," Ry examined what Aurelius had piled in my floor. "Is this all you're taking?"

"All? I have enough to clothe a small continent," I sighed, looking at the pile of luggage.

"Love, there is barely enough there to last three weeks," Aurelius informed me. "I will take you shopping as soon as you return. The jewelry, too I was guessing at, so we will buy more later."

"You bought jewelry?" My voice squeaked annoyingly on the question.

"And this, but you cannot take it with you on assignment." Aurelius sounded sad about that fact as he lifted a small box from his pocket. Inside was the most beautiful ring, with a large, clear stone that winked brightly in the light.

"But what does this mean?" I could barely draw breath to finish the question.

"It is a token of my love. We are mated, you and I," Aurelius slipped the ring on my finger. "See, it fits. Unfortunately, Director Keef does not want you to have it with you on your mission. I will keep it safe until you return." Aurelius pulled it off my finger and returned it to the small box. I chewed my lip. Even though it seemed presumptuous of Aurelius to buy the thing, I wanted it.

"Come, we should go. If I look at you much longer, I will not be able to let you go," Aurelius whispered. Tory was back with Gavril, who came to slip an arm around my waist. That is how we were folded to the shuttle station.

"Reah, be careful." Gavril sounded just as concerned as Aurelius.

"Bro, she's with us," Ry pointed to Tory and then himself.

"Ry, if she doesn't come back, I'll hold you responsible." Gavril had arms crossed angrily over his chest. He looked like a smaller version of Aurelius at the moment.

"Chash, you shouldn't worry so," I pulled his head next to mine and gave him a kiss on the cheek. I'd never had anyone so concerned about me before. Aurelius, too. Perhaps he'd been worried on Mandil. More than he'd shown, anyway.

"Re, just come back, okay?" I wasn't sure what okay meant—another unfamiliar slang term.

*It means all right*, Aurelius supplied mentally. "Okay," I nodded to Gavril and let him go.

"Reah, I will be working away at Director Keef to get us time together when you return," Aurelius informed me. He kissed me before taking Gavril by the arm and disappearing.

"Wow," Ry said, herding me toward the shuttle. Our bags had already been taken aboard—we were getting a private shuttle to the space station.

I didn't realize that Vice-Director Schaff would be traveling with us. "I'll get off first, so we won't be seen together," he told me as he settled into his seat. A private compartment, large enough for six, had been booked for us—we were traveling first class. "Reah, you'll be using your new name—there's no need for an alias just yet," the Vice-Director informed me. "Rylend and Torevik will be using different last names."

"Yeah—we're the Garell brothers now," Ry grinned. "You're our poor cousin from Shirves." Ry patted my head and sat next to Lendill. Tory took the chair beside me and buckled in.

"He means poor as in unfortunate, being related to us and all," Tory chuckled. "At least your hair is growing out." He touched the hair in question.

"This haircut wasn't my idea," I grumbled. "Aris—Aurelius—cut it so I could pass as a male recruit."

"How much did he cut off?" Lendill Schaff was interested, for some reason.

"My hair was nearly to my waist," I said. "I kept it braided while I was doing my Alliance training, otherwise they would have made me cut it then. I worked so hard to keep it, but Aurelius had a barber whack it off with barely a thought." It still upset me—I'd kept my hair long by choice, only having it trimmed occasionally if I could afford it. Only once before had it been whacked off when I was younger, and that certainly hadn't been my choice.

"Your images in your Alliance records must have shown you with it braided, then," Lendill sighed.

"My hair was as long as my great-aunt's," I ducked my head and stared at my hands.

"And the same color." Tory stroked my hair before removing his hand. If he wanted to confuse me, he was doing a fine job—his hand on my head sent tingles through me. What was I supposed to do about that?

"Child, she is so young." Gavin watched his vampire sire closely—Aurelius had never been this forthcoming with his emotions. Now he was obsessing over the age and safety of his mate.

"I thought Lissa young—and she was nearly fifty when I found her. I have no words of advice, Father."

"Did it cause friction—the difference in your ages?" Aurelius was worried.

"At times. But I feel I am more rigid than you in that respect," Gavin admitted.

"It is difficult relinquishing that control, is it not?" Aurelius' smile was wry.

"And Lissa was headstrong—still is." Gavin gave a small smile of his own. "I find myself wishing that Reah could have stayed—not just for you, father, but for Gavril. She pulled him along when Ry and Tory took her out. He doesn't get to spend time with his older brothers, and I am so old I no longer remember the things a boy might like to do. I didn't remember skipping rocks until Reah took him with her and his brothers."

"And Gavril was the one she chose to go to the bank with her, and she helped him do research. I don't think any of us were aware of how lonely Gavril was until now."

"He's back to his usual silence," Gavin sighed.

"I have an idea," Aurelius gave Gavin a pointed look.

~

"Lissa, I like this idea. I was wondering how to make them appear more normal—I mean if anyone was looking to find who might be ASD, it would be the newcomers. Having Gavril and a tutor there with them would put that idea to rest immediately." Norian was doing his best to convince Lissa to allow Gavril to go. Lissa didn't know what to think—Gavin and Aurelius had come up with the original idea, since Gavril had sunk into a silence unnatural even for him. Reah had only been gone two days.

"But he won't be safe," Lissa muttered.

"He will. Morwin isn't anyone to trifle with and Rylend has had an offer from your grandfather. King Wylend thinks that Wyatt needs more experience in defensive spells. This would provide a good learning experience for him."

Lissa stared hard at Norian. Wyatt was her half-brother and she seldom saw him. She also seldom saw her and Wyatt's father, Griffin. "Wylend thinks he needs the experience?"

"And Tory and Ry can help him get it. Wylend thinks that having someone under his care—such as Gavril—will be good for him. Plus, you can fold to the housing we've got for them anytime, love." Norian sat on the edge of Lissa's desk, attempting to convince her that the idea was a sound one. He merely wanted Ry, Tory and Reah to provide the ASD with information gathered from the young people with whom they would associate. The ASD would be making the investigations and arrests. Norian didn't add that Aurelius had offered to go as a bodyguard. That would be too much in his opinion. Aurelius had been disappointed at Norian's refusal.

"Gavin, what do you really think?" Lissa turned to her first mate and Gavril's father.

"I think our son would enjoy this," his dark eyes watched Lissa's face carefully. "You and I know he is a modified vampire—only the second known to be born that way. He has strength and agility that no other twelve-year-old has. I think he will be fine. He has already done his lessons with the Falchani—he can wield two blades with ease."

"But these people may have laser tazers," Lissa grumped.

"Then allow Wyatt to shield him." Norian added to Gavin's argument.

"Fine—I see I'm outvoted on this," Lissa muttered. "Let's go tell him."

"You're letting me go?" Gavril could barely contain his excitement. The bonus was that this was a treat he hadn't even asked for.

"It will only be for a few weeks at the most," Norian pointed out. "And you have to obey Master Morwin and your older brothers. If you do not, you may never be allowed outside the palace again." Norian cut his eyes toward Lissa who was standing nearby, a frown plastered across her face.

"I get to go," Gavril stood and whispered in disbelief.

"Pack your things, son. Your mother and I will fold you to your brothers in an hour." Gavin ruffled Gavril's dark hair affectionately.

"We have to do this now and I have to skip you. It isn't becoming for one of our supposed status to be out grocery shopping," Tory dumped the armload of fiber bags filled with groceries on the expansive kitchen island. We'd gone to the market extremely early in the morning—none of our neighbors would be awake. Tory had volunteered to go with me—Ry had been out late the night before making new friends. I translated that to drinking heavily in a nearby tavern with other locals, but didn't say anything. We'd been placed in Taritha Village—a high-end collection of condominiums and apartments that catered to the young among the wealthy and aristocratic.

"Since you got up and helped, what do you want for breakfast?" I was unloading food and putting it away. He ended up with coddled eggs and my special sauce. He ate four I think, before Ry wandered into the kitchen. He got two.

"I thought you'd have a hangover and would sleep until noon," I teased Ry as I slid his breakfast in front of him.

"I have a spell that neutralizes alcohol," Ry yawned widely. Apparently, the spell didn't make up for lack of sleep. "Food's good." He accepted the cup of tea I gave him with half a dawn-inducing smile. That's where Director Keef, Lissa, Gavin and Gavril found us later, sipping tea at the kitchen island after we'd eaten. Someone else was with them that I didn't recognize, and I was introduced to Master Morwin, Gavril's Amterean Dwarf tutor.

"I'm here to make things look more normal," Gavril grinned at me and came to give me a hard hug. "I'm supposed to be your little brother, Gavril Nilvas."

"Oh, yeah?" I was picking up slang from Ry, Tory and Gavril without intending to.

"Yeah." Gavril was still grinning.

"Wyatt's here." Ry stood up and bowed—yes, bowed—to two people who'd suddenly appeared in our huge apartment. I was beginning to be glad that it had six bedrooms. At first, I thought it was wasted space.

"Reah, this is Wyatt, heir to the Karathian throne," Ry straightened and offered polite introductions. "And this is his grandfather—my great-grandfather—Wylend Arden, King of Karathia." Wylend looked only a few years older than the one introduced as Wyatt. I dipped my head respectfully to both of them. Little doubt existed that they were related—both had medium brown hair, hazel eyes with noticeable gold flecks and were taller than Ry but not as tall as Tory. They weren't as handsome as Ry, but then few people were.

"Would you like breakfast?" I asked. It was the polite thing to do.

"It smells wonderful—I think I would like breakfast." That's how I ended up cooking for the King of Karathia, his heir, Prince Wyatt, the Queen of Le-Ath Veronis, three of her four children and her mates Gavin and Norian Keef. Master Morwin, Gavril's Amterean Dwarf tutor, was shorter than I was but not by much, had thick red hair, bushy red eyebrows and could eat more than two ordinary people. Since I was now serving royalty, I added sliced fruit, a hastily put-together pastry and the eggs with sauce.

"I can't get anything this good from my own kitchens," Wylend Arden declared, having more fresh-squeezed juice. I was going to have to return to the market—I'd just used up the last of the eggs we'd purchased.

"Reah has five more years with the Alliance," Lissa grumbled. "And we saw her first." She gave a pointed look to King Wylend.

"She can do that, she's his granddaughter," Morwin whispered next to me. "And the food is exceptional. I was worried about being uprooted from Le-Ath Veronis, but this, it seems, will have its compensations." He smiled at me.

"Then I may have to engage in a bidding war with my granddaughter," Wylend was smiling at me. It wasn't as spectacular as Ry's smile, but it was sincere. I think that's what impressed me about King Wylend Arden—his sincerity. I might have imagined that the King of the Karathian Warlocks and Witches might have been a bit less genuine. Wyatt, his heir, ate at Wylend's elbow and barely said four words past the initial introductions. He seemed uncomfortable, somehow. Everyone else was ignoring his discomfort, or didn't see it.

"Wyatt, would you like more juice or some tea?" I asked.

"Tea would be wonderful, Reah." He hadn't expected anyone to notice him, I think. I made him tea and passed along honey to go with it.

"I will return to check on my heir," Wylend said later as he prepared to leave. "I think I can arrange to be here two days from now, in time for dinner." He nodded to me and disappeared.

"Well, I suppose we need to go back to the grocery store," I muttered.

"I have to get out of bed again before dawn," Tory moaned.

"I'll go with her," Wyatt volunteered.

"I want to go—I've never been to a grocery store," Gavril spoke up. Therefore, the following morning Wyatt, Gavril, Master Morwin and I all went to the market very early and laid in enough supplies for a siege. I was going to prepare my special ox-roast for the King of Karathia—I thought he might like it. All of us were laden with bags when Wyatt folded us back to our apartment.

"Chash, it's icy outside—are you sure you want to go walking?" I asked him the next morning after we'd pulled heavy coats from closets.

"Yeah—it never gets this cold on Le-Ath Veronis. And it hardly ever snows."

"Well, you might get enough snow here—it's supposed to come tonight," I pointed out as we bundled up. Master Morwin was content to let us go out without his supervision—he wanted to stay inside with his books and a cup of hot tea. Wyatt was the one who came with us.

Gavril was looking over the railing at the streets below us later—there was an entire park built above pedestrian level in Taritha Village. Of course, Gavril wanted to see the people and not the scenery.

"I wish I were twelve again," Wyatt sighed next to me. That made me turn to him in surprise.

"Whatever for?" I asked. I never wanted to be twelve again. Edan had broken my wrist and given me more bruises than I could count at age twelve.

"I didn't have all this looming over my head," he muttered. "Em-pah keeps telling me what I need to do to take his place one day." A light came on for me as I stared at him.

"You don't want that, do you?" I said without thinking.

"No," he admitted, ducking his head. "I want to be a healer, like my mother. But Em-pah won't listen to me. He just keeps pushing me in the direction he thinks I should go."

"Have you told him what you want?"

"He doesn't ever give me the chance."

"Wyatt, maybe you should be more forceful about this. I know your grandfather is a powerful man, but he doesn't seem to be the type who might mistreat his grandchild."

"But I'm his named heir."

"Doesn't he have other heirs?"

"Yes."

"Wyatt, if you don't tell him soon, you may regret that decision. He's not going to hit you."

"How do you know that?"

"I don't—he just doesn't seem the type."

"How would you know if somebody is the hitting type or not?" Wyatt huffed.

"My brother Edan broke my left leg by kicking me when I was eight," I said. "Then he broke my right ankle the next year. Crushed my right foot when I was eleven, broke my wrist when I was twelve, knocked me into a heavy chair and cracked three ribs when I was fourteen, fractured my skull when I was fifteen, cracked two vertebrae when I was sixteen." I stopped when Wyatt stared at me, openmouthed. "Has your grandfather even given you a swat before?" I asked.

"Maybe a light swat on the backside when I was little—I don't remember," he muttered, turning away from me.

"I don't think he'll harm you now if you tell him how you feel," I said. "Besides, maybe he has his reasons, too. You should listen to one another. If Edan had been a reasonable person, I might have tried talking to him. He wasn't. He angered easily and took all his anger out on me."

"Reah, I only hear about children getting abused; I've never met one before. I might be able to help them, if I become a healer. I want to help them. My mother is a healer. I want to do what she's done. She's still working with children at hospitals and things. I just want that chance." Wyatt was truly passionate about this, I could tell.

"Lissa's your sister, isn't she?"

"Half-sister, yes."

"How well do you know her?"

"Not that well—she and our father don't get along."

"But I'll bet she'd listen to you. She looks as if she might have some clout with your grandfather."

"Dad's the other problem."

"He wants you to be King of Karathia someday?"

"Well, he keeps saying that."

"Talk to your sister."

"I'll talk to my sister." Wyatt sounded defeated as he hunched inside his heavy wool jacket. Gavril was done watching the street below and walked toward us.

"Had enough of watching Tulgalan go past?" I hugged him as he came up beside me.

"I want to ride on one of those long buses," Gavril said.

"They're very crowded this time of year," I said. "Everybody wants out of the cold."

"Come on, squirt, let's go home," Wyatt jerked his head toward our apartment. We were nearly there when three people walked past about twenty hands away from us. They were talking and not paying attention to us. I was grateful for that fact. Two I didn't recognize. The third one—not only did I recognize him, but my fear warred with my curiosity over how he'd come to be where he was.

"Reah, people look the same much of the time." Vice-Director Lendill Schaff paced in front of me later. Erland, Ry's father had folded Lendill in after I'd contacted him on my comp-vid. I'd been upset when we'd gone back to the apartment, and had to get myself under control before convincing myself that I hadn't been hallucinating, just as Lendill thought I was.

"Vice-Director, I'd know that face anywhere," I mumbled. Lendill Schaff was telling me I was wrong. He was likely correct. The more I thought about it, the less likely it seemed that Nods Whitlin would ever make it off Mandil to begin with. There were even greater odds that he would never have any reason to make his way onto Tulgalan or any other Alliance world.

"What about the others he was with?" Lendill asked, raking a hand through his hair.

"I didn't recognize them," I said.

"Reah, even if that one is here, he likely has nothing to do with your assignment. And I'll be honest—we have much more urgent business to attend to than one illegal immigrant. If you see him again and determine that he's the one you know from Mandil, then keep an eye on him and pay attention to where he goes. I'll have someone investigate it as soon as we have time."

"Of course, Vice-Director." I hung my head—I shouldn't have called him. I knew that, now.

"Reah, I know it's important to you—it's just not important to the ASD right now."

"I understand."

Ry's father had folded the Vice-Director in, so they both left. "You should have talked to us first," Tory said as I prepared dinner later. I just wanted to go curl up in a corner somewhere. I should have talked to Tory and Ry, but it had shocked me so much, seeing Nods— or someone I thought was Nods, that I'd gone ahead and contacted the Vice-Director right away. He'd be slower to answer my call the next time. I felt embarrassed and ashamed—I'd pulled the Vice-Director of the ASD and Ry's father away from important business, I was sure.

"Re, don't feel bad." Gavril was there after finishing his lessons with Master Morwin. Even the Amterean Dwarf had come out of his bedroom when the smell of dinner cooking wafted in his direction. Tonight was the night Wyatt's grandfather and Ry's great-grandfather (one and the same person) was supposed to arrive for dinner to check on his heir. I was making the ox-roast as planned. Right then, cooking was my only solace. At least I could do that tolerably well.

I served cuts of the roast with tiny roasted potatoes, pearl onions and longbeans, with a salad that had a special dressing. I'd also asked Tory if there was any way to get oxberries. He'd skipped away and returned with a small basket. I made the dessert that Desh's number two had been famous for—oxberries in a puff pastry with cream. King Wylend showed up just as the meal was about to go onto plates.

"Reah, I will pay whatever you want to come to Karathia," King Wylend said after the first bite. If I could have gotten out of the ASD and the Alliance, I'd have gone right then. My experience from earlier in the day still stung.

"I'm glad you only made enough of this for one serving each," Master Morwin sighed after finishing his oxberry dessert. I turned to him in surprise. "I would have eaten myself sick," Morwin raised a hand.

~

"Come on, shortness, we have work to do," Ry informed me after I'd gotten the kitchen cleaned. His grandfather had left earlier.

"Re, what will you be doing?" Gavril was standing in my doorway as I added jewelry after dressing in a nice outfit. I wasn't about to wear a dress or skirt—it was much too cold for that. I found an emerald-green tunic and trousers in a rich, raw silk with embroidery around the neck and cuffs. Nice shoes with a short heel went with the outfit—they weren't warm, but the boots I had didn't go with the outfit. I had a long coat that went over the whole ensemble. I was just going to have to deal with cold feet until we arrived at the tavern.

"We're meeting some people Ry has made friends with. He hopes we'll be invited to their apartment after we have a few drinks."

"You look wonderful."

"I'd rather be comfortable and not going," I answered truthfully. "Are you going to be all right? You, Wyatt and Master Morwin?"

"I brought my blades with me," Gavril gave me a sly grin.

"You have blades?" That had me worried.

"Yeah—Drake and Drew gave them to me when they taught me how to fight," Gavril nodded.

"They taught you bladework?"

"Yeah. They usually make me spar with them two or three times a week, just to stay in practice."

"Chash, you worry me at times." I pulled his head forward until we bumped foreheads.

"Don't worry, Master Morwin can take care of himself and Wyatt's pretty good with his spells," Gavril was still grinning when I let him go. "Next year, Dad and Uncle Tony are going to teach me how to hand fight."

"Really?" I must have sounded skeptical.

"Re, don't worry about me. I'm all right. Plus, Mom temporarily lifted the ban on my mindspeech. I can call out for anybody who can hear me. Okay?"

"You have mindspeech?" That raised at least one of my eyebrows.

"I do. Mom just blocked it before so I wouldn't abuse the privilege."

"Everybody else has mindspeech." I just tossed up a hand in disbelief and walked past Gavril and out of my bedroom.

The music was too loud for my taste, but I couldn't just walk out. Ry and Tory got me seated at a small table. Eventually three others came to join us. Tory ordered drinks for us—he knew what Ry wanted but didn't ask me. I got something with fruit juice in it. The thumping from the music was pounding in my chest as I was introduced to Jeno, Silvastra and Inis. Jeno and Inis, the two young men, were as different as they could possibly be. Inis was short and heavy, growing a half-attempt at a moustache. He would have done better just to shave it off. His hair was dark, too, whereas Jeno's was a light brown. Jeno was clean-shaven, tall and very thin. Silvastra, who asked to be called Silva, came to Ry's shoulder and was doing her best to rub against him. Of course she would—he'd turned every woman's head inside the tavern, in addition to several of the men. Silva was very pretty, with red hair that was not natural, although she looked very good in the color. She also wore a short skirt, a low-cut top and heels much higher than mine. She'd obviously spent many Alliance credits on enhancing her eyelashes and lips, too. She'd certainly gotten her money's worth.

"What's your name?" Inis sat next to me and placed an arm around my shoulders. He'd been drinking before coming to the tavern. I wanted to shudder and gag at his nearness.

*Just play along,* Ry sent. I almost jerked at the mindspeech. I was hoping he didn't expect me to prostitute myself for the Alliance. "I'm Reah," I said, trying not to shudder under Inis' touch.

"Reah, I think you and I could have some fun," Inis ran a finger down my cheek.

"That depends on what kind of fun you're talking about." I wasn't about to let this one put his hands or his mouth all over me.

"Inis, you're drunk," Jeno snapped. "And she doesn't need your money." Inis let his hand fall.

"Sorry," he mumbled. The tavern was popular with the crowd from Taritha Village. More people came in while we sat there; none of whom looked older than thirty. Some were students—Taritha Village was close to the University in Targis. Residents had to be wealthy to live in the area, but that didn't mean their parents weren't expecting them to finish school. I'd never had that chance. Addah Desh wouldn't have paid for it, though he had the money. The Alliance would have given me an exemption if I'd been at one of the universities littered across Tulgalan. I wasn't, so I'd been conscripted by the Alliance. Perhaps some of these wealthy students had avoided their Alliance conscription by attending school. I didn't know them, so I couldn't say for sure.

The tavern was decorated in an appropriate manner—intentionally shabby to give the wealthy youth of the area the idea that they were stepping down a little, visiting it. The prices catered to the clientele, though. I saw that right away. They served some food—not much—and it was something that could be prepared quickly, most of it prepackaged.

"I have reservations at Desh's for next eight-day," Silva announced, placing a kiss on Ry's cheek. "It's my birthday." She'd been drinking before she'd come to the tavern, just as Inis had. The mention of Desh's had me in a cold sweat, almost. I needed to stay far away from there.

"Come on, let's go back to our place; my older brother has some of his friends coming in," Inis announced after two drinks. I wondered if he would be able to stand and walk to his condo, but Ry and Tory were already saying we'd come.

Inis used me as a crutch to walk along—his arm around my shoulders. I really didn't want to help him, but I did. Their condo was huge and much larger than ours, although their kitchen wasn't nearly as nice. It had an indoor pool and Inis' brother and his friends were already lounging around the pool and spa—some of them naked or nearly so—both male and female.

"Inis, who have you brought?" His brother, whom Inis had introduced as Danthus, asked suspiciously.

"They're all right," Jeno said. "Ry and Tory here are watching Reah and her younger brother while their parents are off-planet."

"Reah is scheduled to attend University next quad," Ry was smiling and holding out his hand. "Gav has his tutor with him tonight; that's how we sneaked away."

"I understand babysitting." Danthus handed Inis a less than friendly look as he shook Ry's hand. Inis was perhaps twenty—Danthus looked to be five turns older, at least. You had to be eighteen to drink legally on Tulgalan. I figured Inis had been drinking for a lot longer than two turns.

Someone turned the music up as more people undressed and hopped into the pool. The water was warm—I got splashed as we followed Danthus toward a bar on the far side. Inis still had an arm draped around me. I was hoping to unload him as soon as we reached the padded chairs scattered around the bar.

"What will you have?" A bored woman stood behind the bar. It made me wonder if she were a paid employee. She didn't look as if she fit in with the others. Tory ordered for us again and Inis got another of the drinks he'd had at the tavern. Gratefully I dropped Inis into a chair so I could take my drink from Tory. At least three couples had sex in the pool before the party was over. I just turned my head and began to chat with Danthus, who'd come to sit with us.

"So, University, is that right?" he asked, sipping his drink. He wasn't heavy like Inis was, and hadn't opted for the moustache.

"Yes. I took a year off after my dayclasses before coming."

"Good idea—I hear the Alliance is conscripting everyone who doesn't have an exemption," Danthus finished off his drink and held up his glass, silently asking for a refill. The bartender made another and brought it to him, taking away the empty.

"I heard that, too," I agreed.

"I think they'd probably send you home, though, since you're so small." He grinned. Well, they'd tried. I hadn't wanted to go home.

"So, no conscription for you?" I was smiling back at him. At least he wasn't obnoxious, like his brother.

"Absolutely not. My father is a High Council member. I have a chronic condition," Danthus said, pretending to cough.

"I can see that," I agreed amiably. Mentally, though, I was cringing. A High Council member. The Governor of the Realm presided over the High Council. I'd worked in his kitchen, after all. The High Council had a lot of influence. Of course, so did the ASD. I didn't think any of the High Council on Tulgalan wanted to go against Norian Keef. Word had it that he had the twenty founding members behind him. That was a lot of influence.

"Our family owns a large percentage of the stock in Niff's," Ry came to sit beside me. Well, he was telling the truth on that one. His mother owned the controlling share in that, if Gavril was correct. He'd had no reason to lie about it.

"I love Niff's—is there a way to get a cake from there for my birthday? We can have it after we go to Desh's." Silva scooted Ry over and sat on the same chair with him. She draped an arm around him, too.

"I think we can get you something really good—we're thinking about selling specialty cakes, aren't we, Reah?" Ry swatted my arm.

"Absolutely," I said, failing to understand where he was going with this.

"We'll get you one of the prototypes. You'll be the first to have it—just for your birthday," Ry was grinning.

*He means for you to make it*, Tory sent. He'd been trying to fend off a nearly naked girl who was still wet from swimming.

"Oh, you know—we could probably get one of those made for her with the berry and chocolate swirls, and the frosting decorated with fresh berries," I said.

"That sounds great. I like everything that Niff's makes," Silva said. "Those chocolate ice-cream cookies are wonderful."

"Maybe we could talk to the dragon after cake?" Silva was looking hopefully at Danthus.

"We'll see," Danthus said.

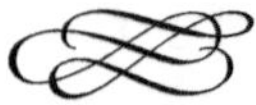

# CHAPTER 15

"Reah, what does this cake taste like?" Ry was fretting after we got home and discussed what we'd seen and heard with the Vice-Director.

"Ry, calm down—it has chocolate, redberry sauce and cream baked into it. Then it's frosted with a white frosting and covered in the center with fresh berries, mint sprigs and chocolate curls," I said. "If Tory can get me more oxberries, it'll be even better."

"That sounds good and I'm not even hungry," Tory declared.

"Your mother's reputation will be safe," I said. "Although a little ice cream to go with it will help your family business, I'm sure."

"But does Desh's serve the same thing?" Ry was still worried.

"No, Ry. They never got this recipe from me—I made it for the Governor of the Realm but he and his family are the only ones who did get it. So, unless you intend to invite them over, you're safe."

"All right," Ry breathed a relieved sigh.

"Bro, I don't know why you're worried all of a sudden—you're the one who offered," Tory smacked his brother on the chest. "Don't upset Reah—she's the one who had stinky Inis draped all over her tonight."

I had a difficult time getting out of bed the following day, and was having hot tea in the kitchen when Gavril came in on his midmorning break. "How about something quick to eat, and then we'll go out in the snow?" He looked so hopeful I couldn't turn him down.

"Sure, Chash," I gave him a hug as I slid off my stool. Wyatt came in and shared the late breakfast. Gavril complained that they'd only gotten toast for breakfast.

"It's all Master Morwin knows how to make," he teased.

"Chash, aren't you cold?" I was wrapped in my thick coat with a hat, gloves and a scarf on and still shivered. Gavril was trying to coax Wyatt into a snowball fight. Wyatt eventually capitulated and they went after each other. I hoped Wyatt had a spell for keeping warm and making his clothing dry.

"Wait." I held Gavril back and hid behind him—I was seeing the one who looked so much like Nods it was uncanny. *Again.* He failed to notice me—he was with four others this time, none of whom were the ones I'd seen him with before. It made me think of something I hadn't remembered in a while.

"Tory, I know you'll think I'm crazy, just as the Vice-Director does, but when I told the Wizards on Mandil who my father was, one of the Wizards recognized Addah Desh and knew he owned restaurants here," I was trying to convince Tory of something. What that something was, even I couldn't put a finger on at the moment. "Aurelius was there—he heard it too."

Tory was the only one inside the apartment at the moment who would willingly listen to me—Gavril was at his lessons with Master Morwin, Wyatt was watching a vid in his bedroom and Ry had gone out to meet with more of the people we'd seen at the party three nights before. Ry certainly had a way of gaining the confidence of others.

"Reah," Tory sighed, "that information could have come from anywhere. You've said yourself that Mandil is a mix of technology and archaic skills. They could have a handful of comp-vids available. Your father has been interviewed so many times for the newsfeeds—they could have seen that."

"Tory, you're giving me a headache." I covered my ears with my hands and bumped my head against the kitchen island. I'd been sitting on a stool there, trying to get my point across.

"Reah." Tory's hand was now on my neck and he was massaging it gently. "Reah, Reah, Reah." Somehow, his hand moved and a kiss was planted on the back of my neck. "Reah," his breath was warm against my neck. "My Thifilathi wants you, Reah. Do you know what that means?" I didn't. Tory had been staying at least an arm's length away from me, too, ever since we'd landed on Tulgalan.

"Reah, when the Thifilathi wants someone, well," Tory didn't get to finish—Wyatt chose that moment to walk into the kitchen for a drink. Tory moved his mouth and his hands away and I sat up. Tory wasn't willing to listen to me and I had no idea what he'd meant when he'd said what he did. Anytime he touched me, though, he made my skin tingle and my breaths shallow and fast. What would Aurelius say? He was waiting for me to come back. Tory and I didn't have a future, Thifilathi or not.

"I'm going to talk to Chash." I slid off the stool and went looking for Gavril.

~

"You think that guy looks like somebody from Mandil?" Gavril was working his way through the facts.

"Yes. And not a nice somebody. If that's Nods—he gave me a black eye once. He seemed to enjoy making others miserable."

"Well, lots of people look alike," Gavril was giving me Vice-Director Schaff's argument.

"Lots of people look similar," I gave my argument.

"But what is he doing here?"

"I don't know, but I've seen him with two different sets of people now. Two the first day, four this morning."

"Were any of them at the party the other night?" Gavril asked.

"One of them maybe," I nodded. One of the men was a possibility, but I hadn't gotten a good look at his face during the party—he'd been naked and I had turned my eyes away as much as possible.

"Do you think he might have anything to do with the drakus seed?" Gavril asked.

"I don't see how he could," I said without thinking. "He was just a nasty sophomore recruit—one step out of the new recruits."

"Let's table this for now and think on it," Gavril suggested. "We can talk more in the next few days. If we see him again, maybe we can follow and see where he's staying."

"That sounds good," I agreed. "I'm glad you came along. Nobody else is listening to me," I grumped.

"Re, I'll always listen to you," Gavril promised.

After that, Gavril and I made a point to go out every morning for a walk or to wade through the snow. Wyatt came with us—he was protecting Gavril as much as anyone else. We saw the one who looked like Nods again on the third day.

"Stay behind me," Gavril hissed. I did my best to hide behind him as we walked slowly along, pretending we weren't watching. The one we followed now had three people with him, two of whom I recognized from Danthus' party. They talked as they strolled along; we stopped occasionally, pretending we were looking at this or that. The three broke off after a while and went inside an apartment on the opposite side of the park. The Nods look-alike trotted down the steps leading toward street level, and we watched from above as he headed toward the bus stop, waited for a short while and then climbed aboard the bus when it came.

"Damn, we should have followed him down and I could have ridden the bus," Gavril cursed.

"Gav, are you supposed to be using that language?" Wyatt teased.

Wyatt had played along with our little game, pretending not to be bored.

"You should hear Mom, sometimes," Gavril grinned. I realized then that Wyatt was Gavril's uncle. It made my head swim for a moment.

"I think I'll go talk to your mother, sometime soon. Maybe she'll pull some of those words out for me," Wyatt smiled. Well, he might be going to Lissa to see if she would speak with his grandfather.

~

"I don't think your look-alike could be dealing drakus seed—remember, that stuff needs a lot of water to grow," Gavril pointed out the following day as we took our walk. Wyatt was ranging ahead of us—our culprit was nowhere in sight. "Mandil is mostly desert," Gavril added. "Not an ideal place to grow the stuff. So, if it is the one you're thinking of—he's just an illegal, I think."

I was only half-listening to Gavril. Earlier that morning, Tory had come up behind me as I sat at the island, having a cup of tea. Ry was sleeping late after a night out with new friends. The back of my neck held some fascination for Tory—he was stroking it and then planting another kiss there before moving away. Merely his touch was making my body tighten, just as it did when Aurelius kissed and nipped. I wasn't sure what to do. I should have told him not to touch me, but I liked it. I was trying to sort out my emotions afterward when I'd gotten a secure message from Aurelius on my comp-vid.

"I miss you, Reah, are you well?" he'd asked.

"I am," I'd replied. "And you?" Our conversation sounded awkward, as if neither of us could say what we felt or wanted.

"Love, come home to me soon," Aurelius had ended the call after only a little while. I'd sighed and closed my comp-vid to save the charge.

"Chash, we'll work on this later," I put an arm around his waist as we walked along.

"I noticed you were someplace else," he said, draping an arm over my shoulders.

I'd thought of something, but Ry was out again and Tory—well, I was afraid to go talk to him. Afraid that I'd invite his touch, and that felt like betraying Aurelius. Honestly, I was trying to puzzle this out in my mind. I went over everything that Gavril had told me—even though my mind had been elsewhere earlier, I could still remember most of his words, including his opinion that our quarry was only an illegal. I wished that we had followed him the day we'd seen him climb onto the bus. If he weren't Nods, then he looked enough like him to be a twin. An identical twin.

"King Wylend, Ry was so worried about the cake that I wanted to bake one ahead of time, just to get his approval," I handed a slice of cake to the King of Karathia, who'd shown up for dinner and to check on his heir again. The slice of cake had a little extra redberry sauce and chocolate drizzled over it, in addition to the fresh berries and chocolate curls on top. I'd cooked a lamb dish for them, and now they were having dessert.

"Reah, slap me the next time I have doubts about your cooking," Ry talked around a mouthful of cake.

"Reah, darling, this is magnificent," King Wylend announced, cutting another bite with his fork. Tory ate without talking. I think he was enjoying his dessert—he was smiling as he ate. Gavril wanted a second slice and Master Morwin had three.

"Reah, if I gain weight, it will most certainly be your fault," Morwin said, sliding his dessert plate toward me and patting his belly.

"Should I cook plain chicken tomorrow?" I asked, teasing him lightly.

"Absolutely not," Morwin huffed and slid off his stool.

Aurelius sat before Lissa's desk. Lissa, Gavin, Erland and Norian had also come—Kifirin had commanded it. They all waited to see what the Lord of the Dark Realm had to say.

~

"Chash, there's a hole in your theory." We sat on his bed the following afternoon—Master Morwin had assigned a report and Gavril had asked me to help him do research.

"No—see—the Alliance didn't really lose any money after Trell was destroyed—Grey House took up the slack in tax payments all by itself," Gavril insisted.

"Chash, that's not the theory I was thinking about," I said, gazing into his dark eyes. We both sat cross-legged, staring at our comp-vids. "I know you did your research, and all of it says that Mandil is mostly desert. But it's not an Alliance world."

"Meaning?" Gavril asked.

"Meaning that they don't have all the facts. When I landed there, the information that they sold some of their women into slavery was swimming in my head. That turned out to be false."

"It's not true?" Gavril was now pulling up information on Mandil on his comp-vid.

"No. If it were true—I might have been sold. I got paid for cooking instead. They don't allow females in their army, though, so that's why Aurelius disguised me as a male recruit and cut my hair." I mimed whacking through my braid for Gavril.

"What else is wrong with the information we have?" Gavril asked.

"The fact that most of it's desert. Only the uninhabited northern continent is covered in trees and gets a lot of rainfall. Mandil is desert —to the outside observer. The Alliance has more than likely gotten that information from their satellites, right?"

"More than likely," Gavril nodded.

"Well, what they don't know is there's underground water there. There was never a shortage of water and there should have been— Aurelius and I were stationed at a post in the middle of the desert.

There was plenty of water there. They even had a large pool for the hot baths. If water had been scarce—that shouldn't have been. And out on the grounds there was an iron fence around a large well—there were stones set in the ground to mark it and plants grew all around it. One of the soldiers there told me that the fence had been put up to prevent drunken recruits from falling into the well. That sounded like it was deep and had water in it—he never said it was dry. The other thing I know is we were getting shipments of produce from the outlying villages, and they were sending us citrus. It takes a lot of water to grow citrus, Chash. They have a lot of water on Mandil—it's coming from below ground."

"Holy crap," Gavril stared at me. I wasn't sure what the epithet meant—I'd never heard of excrement being sacred.

"Now," I said, "the Prince Royal put up three posts, trying to keep those spawn out of the desert. Why would he do that? It would have been more prudent to order the outlying villages to come to Crown City until the troops could deal with the situation. But he didn't. He didn't try to get the people in until they were already getting killed or turned. The only post that survived was the one that had wizard Rangers. He probably knew, or his High Commander did, that the posts that didn't have wizards would likely fall. They were left out there anyway." Just thinking about the High Commander had me wondering. Aurelius had said something about his withholding information from the Prince. And the High Commander would have access to the recruits, making Nods a very good recruit to other purposes. I was saying that aloud, I think.

"They could be growing drakus seed out there in the desert, in the middle of the citrus trees and vegetables. The spawn may have thrown things off schedule, but the Mandili may have had enough seed stored that it didn't interrupt the shipments," I mused.

"But how are they getting it here? Their wizards don't have folding capabilities and never have. Not to our knowledge," Gavril started tapping on his comp-vid again.

"What does Mandil have that someone else might want?" I asked.

"They have ranos technology," Gavril gasped. I'd known that

already—those ranos rifles had allowed us to kill spawn when they attacked. "Mandil is off-limits to all Alliance worlds, but do you know how many non-Alliance worlds have space travel?"

"Or, what if it's somebody who doesn't need space travel? I mean, just about everybody I've met from Le-Ath Veronis can appear and disappear whenever they want," I huffed. I'd wanted to learn how to skip, like the other High Demons. Tory had mentioned it once to me —that had been the purpose of going to skip rocks. He'd never brought it up again, though.

"I know the reason why," Gavril drew designs into his coverlet with a finger. He'd read my mind, just as the others could.

"Why?" I was staring at him, now.

"Aurelius asked them not to," Gavril admitted reluctantly. "He was afraid you'd skip away and he might not be able to get you back."

"Holy crap," I repeated Gavril's statement from before.

"Exactly," Gavril muttered.

❧

"Don't you think he ought to ask her at least?" Lissa had her hands on her hips, glaring at Jayd and Garde.

"If he explains it in detail, she may object," Garde pointed out.

"Karzac and the Larentii have already volunteered to do for her what was done for your nieces, Gardevik Rath," Lissa shook a finger at her High Demon mate. "They don't remember any part of this. Their mates still feel guilty, but then you all should."

"A High Demon should always feel guilt over that," Kifirin said.

"You should feel guilt for making them that way," Lissa turned on Kifirin.

"Yes, but the deed is done and I cannot go back and unmake it," Kifirin huffed.

"Uh-huh. You and those High Demons of yours can kiss my ass."

"Love, you cannot mean that, but I think I can get most of them to volunteer." Kifirin was smiling.

"Aurelius wants time with her first—the full moon comes in three weeks, you know. Norian is hopeful that we can bring them home, soon. Rylend has made some contacts—he knows who is buying now, but hasn't gotten the supplier's name yet. We hope to have that soon," Garde said. Aurelius didn't object to Garde's son being the High Demon who claimed Reah—he just wanted Reah to be comfortable with it. Jayd and Garde wanted to keep the information from her until after the deed was done—they were afraid she'd balk if it were explained to her.

"Have you talked with our son?" Lissa hadn't talked to Tory since he'd admitted to both his parents that his Thifilathi wanted Reah.

"I talked with him yesterday," Garde admitted. "He's worried that he'll scare her so badly she'll not want anything to do with him."

"I didn't want anything to do with you afterward, and I knew what was coming," Lissa snapped.

"But I apologized and you still love me," Garde grinned.

"Don't remind me—it's one of my failings," Lissa said.

"Avilepha, don't say that," Garde breathed smoke on Lissa's neck after he pulled her against him.

"I will try to keep our youngest from suffering," Kifirin said.

"Are you going to tell Ry and Tory?" Gavril asked as he watched me pour the cream, chocolate sauce and redberry sauce into the cake batter.

"And let them poke holes in my theory? They'll just laugh at me, like the Vice Director did." I wasn't up to dealing with that kind of rejection right then.

"I don't think the Vice-Director laughed—he doesn't laugh very often," Gavril observed.

"Well, restrained ridicule, then," I said, lifting the large cake pan and sliding it into the oven.

"Restrained ridicule—I think I like that phrase. Maybe I can use it in one of my reports," Gavril beamed.

"Want some tea or something else to drink?" I asked my helper. He was done with his lessons for the day. Ry, Tory and I had been invited to the birthday party at Desh's. I'd said to send my apologies, telling them I had a headache. Truthfully, just the thought of going to Desh's number one made my head hurt.

"We'll tell you what they served," Tory had grinned at me and rubbed my neck. Ry and Tory had then gone out to buy something to wear for the occasion while Gavril and I baked the cake.

❲

"Dad doesn't want to tell her, Mom does," Tory's breath blew out in front of him as he walked beside his brother.

"But that sucks—just letting her wake up with your claiming marks on her neck?" Ry glanced up at his taller sibling.

"Don't remind me. Oh, I want them there, don't get me wrong," Tory hunched his shoulders against the Tulgalan winter. "But I want to talk to her first—explain things a little. Dad doesn't want to give her any opportunity to refuse. Aurelius doesn't mind—he just said he doesn't want her to suffer. They've already made arrangements to do the anesthetic and the aftercare. I did find out from Uncle Jayd that they wanted to offer her to one of the others—from Weth or Foth, I think. Kifirin said no. He said something else was coming. It turned out to be me."

"Well, if anybody would know, it would be Kifirin."

"Yeah."

❲

"That looks good enough to eat." Ry examined the cake after I'd frosted it. It was going into the keeper—I'd put the berries and drizzle on just before it would be cut. Ry and Tory had brought the ice cream —they'd had to go back to Le-Ath Veronis to get what they called *the real thing,* but it was stowed inside the freezer, waiting to be served with the cake.

"It better be good enough to eat," I sighed. "And Gavril and Master Morwin want a piece, so try to save some, all right?" I was going to finish the cake when Tory sent the message that they were on their way from Desh's, then hide in my room. I was supposed to have the headache, after all. Ry was going to try to get the name of the seller for the drakus seed—rumor had it that someone would bring the drug with them. Morwin was going to stay inside Gavril's room, just to make sure he was kept safe. I'd suggested that he be sent home but Ry, Tory and Gavril had all protested.

"If we have to bring the squirt out to make us seem harmless, then we'll do it,"

Ry had sighed. Gavril had been bouncing on his toes when his older brothers said he could stay.

～

*We're on our way,* Tory sent the message later. Gavril was in the kitchen with me, watching as I placed fresh berries, mint sprigs and the chocolate and berry drizzle over the cake before sliding it back into the keeper.

"Come on, Chash—they could be here any minute." I hooked my arm with his and pulled him toward the bedrooms.

"Come and stay with me and Master Morwin," Gavril begged. That's how I ended up in his bedroom. Morwin was reading something on a comp-vid in the corner, so Gavril and I sat on Gavril's bed to play a vid-game. We'd been at it for nearly a click when the knock came on the door. Gavril gave me a hopeful look before hopping off the bed to go answer it. What I wasn't expecting was to see Inis with Tory at the door.

"So, pleading a headache so you wouldn't have to come out with us?" Inis was already drunk. I was surprised that he was able to stand, he was so inebriated.

"I did have one earlier," I made the excuse. I wasn't lying—I had felt a twinge of a headache over all this—worrying that Gavril shouldn't have stayed.

"What's going on?" Wyatt was there suddenly behind Inis and Tory —he'd been inside his bedroom until now.

"We wanted Gavril to come out and have some cake," Tory said. Well, somebody had gotten suspicious, I figured.

"And Reah should come, too," Inis announced. "She can have cake with me." He hiccupped rudely.

"Reah, come on," Tory said. "Since you don't have a headache now." I blinked at him. Yes—I was coming—if only to make sure Gavril didn't see anything he shouldn't, or be exposed to any drugs, especially something as dangerous as drakus seed.

"Come on, Chash, let's go have cake." I slid off the bed and draped an arm on Gavril's shoulder. Inis tried to take my hand when we walked out the door, but Wyatt managed to get in his way. Inis grumbled all the way to the kitchen.

"Here are the cousins," Tory announced when we walked into the kitchen. I stopped dead still when I recognized four people I shouldn't have. Nods was there—there was no mistaking him—and he stared at me, his mouth working silently for a few ticks before he could get the words out. When they did come, he was screaming them.

"Treachery!" He shouted, before raising his ranos pistol and firing.

el, Max and Hish were there and disguised, but I could see right through that. Bel had leapt toward Nods to keep him from firing, but the pistol had already discharged, straight toward Gavril and me. I barely had time to flip Gavril aside as the ranos blast tore through my right shoulder. I think I screamed as I was hit. Chaos came right behind that shot as Ry and Wyatt engaged in a battle with the former Ranger wizards. Tory had turned somehow, into a shorter version of his Thifilathi. I barely had time to register that fact as I whimpered in pain and tried to shove Gavril toward the back of the kitchen. Inis, Silva, Danthus and ten others were shouting and attempting to rush from the kitchen. Nods, the fool, began shooting recklessly. I saw Jeno go down, a huge hole in his chest. Two more died as Nods kept shooting and shouting.

"Get down," I shouted to Gavril, who was struggling in my grip. Master Morwin was there suddenly and helping me push Gavril beneath the stone-topped kitchen island. Nods was still shooting. Wizard blasts were shooting around us, too, although they didn't touch either Gavril or me—they bounced off the shield I had, ricocheting and knocking large holes in the ceiling and the walls. I shoved Gavril beneath the island again so he'd be protected from falling debris; he'd attempted to escape. The ceiling and one of the walls was now on fire and the fire sprinklers had activated, quickly drenching everything and everyone inside the kitchen. I heard Nods scream, so I poked my head up to see if he'd been hit.

Tory, in his small Thifilathi, had Nods by the throat and was squeezing. "No, Tory," I shouted, "Don't kill him—we need to question him!" I started running toward Tory, although my shoulder felt as if it were on fire. "Tory, no!" I shouted again at him as smoke poured out of his nostrils. Tory, in his smaller Thifilathi, was dark-skinned, with a broad face. He had short horns, too, that curved around, like a ram's might. He was terrifying like that. Ry and Wyatt were shouting at the Ranger wizards to give up. Of course they sent more blasts—Bel's talent, I knew. Ry sent one of his own back, blowing an entire wall out of the kitchen.

Cold air from the outside came pouring through the gaping hole and people nearby were screaming, now. I heard constabulary sirens off in the distance while Tory was still trying to kill Nods. I didn't think the average citizens who might now see into our apartment needed to see a High Demon like this.

"Tory!" I shouted again. I couldn't move my right arm—the ranos pistol had hit me high in the right shoulder. That part of my body was now pain-filled and useless. I had to pound Tory on the back with my left hand—he was just about to squeeze the life from Nods. He turned his head after a tick or two, blowing smoke and looking down at me. "Let him go," I shouted over the din of the wizard's battle going on around us. Tory had the same shield I did—the spells and blasts were bouncing off both of us.

Tory blew more smoke as he stared at me for a few moments, then dropped Nods as if he suddenly held no interest. I wasn't expecting what came next. Tory snatched me up instead, and if I'd ever wondered if he could skip while Thifilathi, well, that answer turned out to be yes.

"Tory," I whimpered; he'd crushed my body against his and my right arm and shoulder hurt horribly. "Tory, put me down." I didn't know where we were—somewhere in the middle of a field. Tall grasses surrounded us and mountains in the distance shone brightly on a moonlit night. I had to start beating on Tory's chest, although I didn't think he even felt it—the scales of his Thifilathi were thick and hard. He thundered through the grass, running swiftly until he reached a spot—I have no idea why he chose that particular one. I was dropped there.

"Tory, I need a physician, I begged." I looked up at him from my spot on the ground. He'd dumped me on my backside and I cradled my right arm against me, trying not to cry, it hurt so badly. He blew more smoke, then leaned down and casually ripped my shirt away.

I must have screamed again—I nearly blacked out with the pain it caused—having the right arm jerked like that when he tore off my shirt. I didn't have enough sense to get up and try to run, though it wouldn't have done any good, I'm sure. He'd told me once that his Thifilathi wanted me. When he reached for me and flipped me onto my belly, I discovered the reality of that statement.

"Where's Reah?" Gavril was shouting at Ry, Wyatt, Vice-Director Schaff and half a dozen ASD operatives. Bodies of the dead that Nods had shot with his ranos pistol littered what was left of the apartment —Ry and Wyatt had gotten the better of Bel and the others, who were now subdued and held inside a spelled cage.

"Where is Reah? Where's Tory?" Lendill Schaff finally had the sense to ask—caging the wizards and getting medical attention for the one with the ranos pistol had come first—he had questions to ask of that captive.

"Reah got shot," Gavril shouted. "She needs help—where is she?"

"I think Tory took her—he, uh, changed," Ry admitted, only now realizing just how dangerous a thing that might turn out to be. "Get Mom, and ask her to bring Uncle Garde," Ry sat down and rubbed his forehead. He was in complete exhaustion—he hadn't wanted to deliver any killing blows—Lendill and Norian wanted live bodies to question. The wizards he and Wyatt had fought turned out to be more powerful than he might have guessed.

There comes a time when pain can be so intense and debilitating that you cannot form words or even whimper. That was my condition—Tory's lengthened canines were in the back of my neck and I was now in the worst imaginable agony. Only my left hand worked and I was clawing at the soft soil beneath me. I know—the strangest things can register on your mind in a sort of detachment—the grass had been pulled up by the handfuls as I endured the attack—the long blades slick with dew and sliding through my fingers at first, before I looped my hand in them and pulled. Tory was grunting behind me, his teeth still in my neck, his smoky breath curling past my cheek. Somewhere, amid the pain, I was afraid I might die. And then, as the searing pain continued, came the hope that death would actually come.

Torevik Rath, in his smaller Thifilathi, carefully pulled his canines from his mate's neck. She was motionless beneath him. Even in his primal state, he realized it shouldn't be that way. He lifted one of her hands; it dropped bonelessly as he released it. He turned her over—her eyes were closed. A gaping hole was in her shoulder; how had that happened? Tory knelt and sniffed the wound—it smelled raw—burned. He hadn't done that—it smelled nothing like him. He breathed on her face—surely that would wake her. It didn't. His demon heart began to pump fearfully faster—what had happened? He had claimed his mate—she bore his marks—but now she was unresponsive. He lifted his head and howled in misery.

The End